G000149895

Mr B. Prophecy

A Clara Fitzgerald Mystery
Book 16

by
Evelyn James

Red Raven Publications
2021

Mr Lynch's Prophecy is the sixteenth book in the
Clara Fitzgerald series

Other titles in the Series:

Chapter One

Private Peterson stared helplessly at his bloodied hands. He stumbled forward, a sharp pain jabbing into his lower back and making each step agonising.

Where was he?

It was dark and very late. Flashes of memory came back to him fitfully. There had been the picture house; a couple of the men had talked about going to see a screening of the latest silent flick, Nosferatu. Peterson had overheard them and, although not invited, had thought he might make his separate way to the movie theatre to watch the film. He had read about it in the papers. It was all about a vampire. Reviews said it was appropriately horrifying and warned that those of a nervous disposition should not attempt to watch it. The film had been out a few months but, when it was first screened, Peterson had not wanted to go – he was having nightmares and didn't think watching a flick about a murderous vampire would help.

However, he had been feeling much better lately, almost like his old self, and he had thought he would find out why

1

everyone was calling this the scariest picture ever. Thus, when the other men left the house, he followed them at a distance, waited for them to get inside the picture house and then bought his own ticket and sat in the back row.

That was about the last thing he could remember clearly. After that things became... complicated. He was pretty certain he had left before the end of the picture. He hadn't liked it; the vampire was terrible in appearance and he had started to feel uneasy. He had always been a little worried about the supernatural – his mother was a firm believer in ghosts, fairies and witchcraft. She made little charms to hang around people's necks; one's for easing teething pains in babies; ones for bringing luck; ones for soothing headaches. She had made a very special one for Peterson just before he left to go to the war. He had been made to promise to wear it at all times. It would keep him safe, his mother said, it would bring him home again.

Seemingly, it had worked, it had certainly brought him home. There were occasions when he wished it hadn't, when he wished he had ripped the charm from his neck and let some German bullet find its target. But he had made a promise to his mum and he wasn't going to let her down. Peterson might be messed up, his mind might be broken into pieces, but he never forgot his loyalty to his family.

Peterson's foot caught on a raised slab in the road as he shuffled forward. He stubbed his toe, but it was the pain the shot through his back that nearly downed him. He reached out a hand to the nearby wall and leaned heavily against the brickwork, panting through the pain, tears pricking his eyes.

What had happened after he left the picture house?

He had slipped out a side door, not wanting the other men to notice him. They had never been unkind to him, or anything like that, but they were of a different class and he found it hard to mix with them. He also didn't want them to see he was leaving, in case they thought he was unsettled by the movie – which was the truth, but he didn't want them to know that. He supposed it was his pride that made him want to avoid letting anyone know he was finding the vampire on the screen upsetting.

After that things became hazy. He had started walking, heading for home. There was a slight nip in the air, now that September was slowly drawing in. Peterson had shoved his hands in his pockets and walked quickly. He was uneasy, his mind playing tricks on him and conjuring up long-fanged vampires around every corner. He should never have watched that film. His mind was not nearly as 'fixed' as he had hoped. He jumped at shadows, and when people appeared from side roads or out of doors, they made him startle. He could feel he was breathing hard, beginning to panic and that was when he had ducked down an alley and headed for the quieter back streets. He didn't want anyone to see him in the middle of a panic attack. It was humiliating.

The attacks had started at the Front. Never when he was on duty or in the middle of fighting; somehow he always held himself together then. It was usually afterwards, or when he was on respite, when everything was quiet and peaceful. Then this crippling fear would engulf him; he would start to tremble and quake. His hands would flick and twitch, he would need to get up and move, to pace about or sometimes to just run. Eventually the panic would catch him no matter what he did. It would grab him about the throat like a savage dog, it would narrow his vision to a pinprick, the world around him would become meaningless as he fought himself. He would gasp, cry out, shake from head to foot and often end up curled in a ball just rocking back and forth. Tears would stream down his face and he could not bear for anyone to touch him, then it would pass, like a dreadful pain in the gut that suddenly eased. He would relax, he would go icy cold and slowly the crippling fear would lift.

All that was left afterwards was a sensation of being utterly drained and then the shame of how he had behaved during the episode. It didn't matter if people were sympathetic to him or not, he still felt embarrassed at himself. And even if he told himself not to let the panic take him over like that again, he still let it do so the next time. It was like he had no control, and that was the worst of it.

That night he had been in the alleyways of Brighton, trying to navigate towards home, while also losing his mind to panic. He wanted to run, to bolt – the sensation was terrible. Fighting himself all the way he had bumbled about in the dark, knocking into metal bins, spooking a cat that hissed at him. Then there had been something else, something that his panicked mind had caught a glimpse of just before everything evaporated from his memory.

Peterson felt as though his strength was being sapped from him. He was using the wall as a prop now, moving his hand along with each tentative step. He wasn't sure how much longer he could keep conscious and he was lost. The roads looked unfamiliar and he had no idea if he was heading towards home or away from it. There was just this lingering sense in the back of his brain that he had to keep moving, that he had to get away from whatever was behind him. That could be a fictional vampire from his imagination, or it could be something real. There was a gulf in his thoughts that meant he could not explain to himself why he must keep walking, only that he would use all his remaining strength to keep going. It was like some primitive instinct was driving him on and no rational contemplation of the situation was going to change that.

He had left a bloody handprint on the wall, he wondered whose blood it was, some strangely calm part of his mind contemplating this issue, which, right then, was really irrelevant. It might be his blood, it might be someone else's, whatever the case, he had to get help. But that pain in his back was getting worse and his left leg was starting to drag. He was having trouble feeling his foot.

Had he been in a fight? Peterson looked at his right hand, the one not helping him to balance against the wall. It was covered in blood but, aside from his back, he did not feel as if he had been in a brawl. He wrapped his right arm around his middle, pressing it into his stomach to try to counteract the sharp thudding that was now shifting up his spine. His world was becoming absorbed by that pain.

"Help! Can anyone help me?" He called out.

He had not done so before because he had been so desperate to get away with no one seeing him like this. Now he knew that without help he was not going to make it. His strength was fading, each step was a test of will.

"Anyone? I need help! Please…" his voice tailed off to a choking gasp that made the agony in his back a thousand times worse. He clenched his teeth until his jaw ached and tears crept from his eyes.

"I'm going to die."

Peterson came to a halt, the astonishment of this realisation overcoming that instinct to drive on. He had survived a war, escaped shrapnel that had killed his comrades, miraculously avoided the bullets that had mown down his mates, been in just the right place to avoid being blown to smithereens by a shell or buried alive by the earth it threw up, and it would be here, in Brighton, that he died.

Peterson sank to his knees. It wasn't just the irony of the situation that had finally stopped his momentum, it was the peace the sudden understanding had brought him. Finally, to be released from the horror which had tracked him for so long – it felt like a mercy. Whatever had happened to him, it appeared to be a blessing in disguise. He could stop fighting, he could stop the unhappy battle for survival. He could give up and no one would blame him, because you can't fight death, not in the end.

Peterson cast his eyes up to the sky. There was a crescent moon creeping through the clouds. He shut his eyes and his body started to sag. He hadn't expected to die that night, but he was at peace with himself, and with death. He was glad of it.

The pain surged in his back again and he dipped his head, clenched his jaw against a scream. He clutched his right arm as tightly around himself as he could, his fingers reaching around his waist and to the spot on his back where all this trouble seemed to stem from. He could feel wet blood beneath his fingers and then, his groping hand trying to compress the wound and quell the hurt, touched something else, something cold and hard.

There was a knife in Peterson's back.

Suddenly a new spark dragged Peterson from the brink of oblivion. He had been stabbed! His fingers probed the knife, what little he could feel of it and instead of release, Peterson now felt fury. Someone had stabbed him! He tried to get to his feet, but his legs were completely numb. The panic started to return – could his attacker still be nearby? No, surely not. He had been stumbling along for a while, had they wanted to finish him off they could have done so by now.

Peterson tried to get to his feet again, without success. He wasn't going to die here, of that he was determined. He might have been willing to embrace death a moment ago, but now he was just as eager to survive and find out who did this to him.

"Help me! Someone help me!" He called out again.

If he could not get to his feet, then there was nothing else for it but to crawl. He started to drag himself forward, inch by perilous inch, knees scraping the ground, the pain in his back almost too much to bear.

"I need help!" He cried. "Anyone, please, can you hear me?"

So many of his comrades had endured similar fates in the muddy battlefields of Belgium and France, calling out for help as they lay dying, not knowing if anyone could hear or whether they would be reached in time. Peterson had heard those cries and, when he had been able, he gone to them. Now he hoped someone would return that kindness to him.

"I am hurt! Please! Someone…" a fresh groan cut off his words, the pain in his back was too much.

He was now having to drag his entire body by the strength of his arms, he could not even move his legs to crawl on his knees. He could feel nothing below his hips, though that pain in his back was as vivid as ever, a burning blot on his mindscape. He managed to scrape himself forward a few more inches by using his forearms to pull himself along.

"If anyone can hear me, I am injured!" He cried out, starting to feel hopeless.

He didn't think he could remain conscious for much longer and he was scared of what might come after he closed his eyes. He no longer wanted to die. His fight had returned, just when it was too late.

Peterson looked around him, trying to see somewhere to go and get assistance. He was in a narrow alley with yards either side. There were gates into the yards, but all were shut. All he could do was crawl to the nearest and try to open it. He put his last strength into moving the two feet to a gate. Every inch was torture and he didn't seem to get any closer. He had to stop, barely able to breath. It was over. His body was spent.

This was not the way Peterson had thought his last moments would come and he was baffled as to why he had ended up this way. He could not think why he had been stabbed; he had no memory of the attack, and it seemed that whoever had done the deed was going to get away with it. All there was left to do was to lay his head down on his hands and let his last energy slip away.

The pain, at least, was easing in his back. He managed to take a long breath and expel it without being crippled by agony. As he lay still, letting his life sap away, he saw one of the yard gates open and a pair of feet emerged. He could see no higher than the lower legs of the owner of the feet as they came towards him.

"Good God!" A voice above him cried out. "Are you alive?"

A hand touched his shoulder, the warmth of the touch was like a drop of water to a man dying of thirst, it flooded through Peterson's system, rousing him. He took a raspy breath.

"He's alive!" The person above him called over his shoulder to someone else. "Go fetch the doctor, hurry!

There's a knife in the fellow's back!"

The person knelt nearer to Peterson.

"Can you hear me, son?"

Peterson wanted to nod his head, he could not. All he could do was whisper a last word before he slipped away.

"Nosferatu."

Chapter Two

Clara Fitzgerald had been a private detective for nearly three years. And in all that time, she had never been summoned to the opening of a magic box. She had never even considered it a possibility. But that morning, upon the arrival of the first post, there was a letter among all the usual bills and correspondence that was decidedly different. The envelope, for a start, was printed with an image of an owl perching in the lower right corner and staring out at the recipient. When Clara opened the curious piece of mail, she discovered it had been sent to her by the Director of the Brighton Institute for Astronomy, a man named Professor Hugo Montgomery. He had a lot of initials after his name which meant nothing to Clara, but she assumed they were impressive to other astronomers.

Professor Hugo Montgomery had a problem. Twenty years earlier, his predecessor had passed away leaving a number of his books to the institute's library. Nothing odd about that, and there were several rare editions in the collection that were very welcome. However, unbeknown to the current director, his predecessor had also left a box to the institute, to be kept in the safe hands of the librarian until a given date when it could be revealed. The librarian had kept the box a secret, as had been requested of him, until twenty years to the day of the man's death. That day had been Monday last, and the librarian had dramatically produced the box, as he had been instructed to do.

So far, not a great deal to cause a stir. Except, the last director had been somewhat peculiar and in his final days had taken to making prophecies. He based them on the star alignments in the skies and some of his students felt there was more to them than just clever talk. They had begun to believe them.

It had been rumoured that the director had been working on an important prophecy shortly before his death, one that could change the course of history. It was thought he had died before completing his work, there had been no sign of this prophecy among his papers. That is, until the librarian revealed the box, given to him just days before the director's death and with strict instructions he had not dared to ignore. The box contained this last great prophecy, along with something that would save Britain from catastrophe in the near future – or so the orders the librarian had been given stated.

Now, the current director considered this all poppycock and would have gladly thrown the box out, never even opening it. Unfortunately, some of the other fellows at the institute were less sceptical and were insistent the box should be opened. This created another complication, as the past director had commanded that the box should only be opened in the presence of four bishops and the king. There were members of the institute in the process of writing letters to the Crown to arrange this, much to the director's horror.

In short, the horrid box was driving him mad and had everyone in a dither. The people who believed that the last director was onto something would not allow it to be opened without the appropriate arrangements. While others, like the director, just wanted to rip off the lid and demonstrate it was all nonsense. The whole pickle had divided the institute's faculty and students and was leading to such turmoil that Montgomery had decided the only thing to do was to get an outsider involved – someone who was impartial, who could look into the whole affair and suggest a course of action. He had settled on Clara as the best candidate for the job.

Clara was certainly amused by the matter. She had heard about similar prophecy boxes before; they had become quite a fad in the eighteenth and nineteenth century. She had never actually seen one before, however. She was intrigued enough by the situation to accept the case and head over to the Institute just after breakfast. Professor Montgomery had mentioned in his letter that he was to be found at the Institute between 9am and 5pm during the week, and that he would make time for her whenever she turned up.

Clara could read between the lines of his hastily written letter that he was desperate.

Brighton's Institute for Astronomy had been built in 1842 on the outskirts of town and close to the coast. It consisted of a sprawling red-brick building behind imposing gates, where various courses were taught on astronomy and related areas of science. There was also an observatory in the grounds, with one of the best telescopes in the country. Astronomers would often visit from other areas to use the telescope and there was always a range of research projects ongoing at the place at any given time. Clara noted as she entered the gates that this was a heavily male-dominated discipline. She noticed the odd girl among the students and researchers wandering about – the Institute did not exclude women – but they were by far in the minority.

Clara walked along a circular gravel drive and came to the main doors. They were open and students were spilling out at speed, apparently heading for lectures in various parts of the building. Clara had to wait until they had cleared before she could enter. A porter was sitting in a tiny office near the doors. He had a window into the corridor so he could see who was coming and going. He saw Clara.

"Good morning, I am here to see Professor Montgomery. He is expecting me," Clara explained to the porter.

The porter asked for her name and then pulled out an old-fashioned speaking tube that was located next to his desk. There were several, in fact, and they resembled the tubes that connected decks on ships. Clara assumed they went to various departments in the building to enable communication. As the porter tapped three times on the cap of the speaking tube to announce he was about to communicate, Clara wondered that the institute had not installed an internal telephone system, as were appearing in so many public buildings. As a place of modern science, it seemed strange they were using such an old-fashioned means of communication.

The porter stopped talking and rose from his chair.

"Professor Montgomery wishes me to escort you upstairs to his office," he said before exiting his tiny box of a room into the corridor and leading Clara to a large staircase that spiralled away into the ceiling.

"The professor informed me you were coming," the porter continued conversationally. "He is very worried about this business with old Professor Lynch's box."

"He told you about that?" Clara asked.

"Everyone in the Institute knows about it. It's the only thing anyone talks about. Professor Lynch was a peculiar sort, doesn't surprise me he left this strange box. He had very odd ideas towards the end."

The porter said this last statement with the dramatic declaration of a stage performer. Clara was curious and would have asked him to elaborate, but they were already nearing Montgomery's office. The porter knocked on a door with a brass label bearing the director's name and Clara was invited inside. She found herself in an enormous room with a ceiling that seemed to disappear into the heavens. Her eye was caught by the decoration on the ceiling plaster – a complete astronomical diagram of the night sky with all the relevant constellations picked out and named in ornate script. It quite distracted her, and Professor Montgomery had to cough to regain her attention.

"It catches a lot of people like that," he remarked, as she looked back.

He was stood behind a large Victorian desk, at his back was a vast arched window that let in a great deal of light and a telescope sat just to one side. Professor Montgomery motioned to the seat before his desk.

"Thank you for coming, Miss Fitzgerald."

"I was intrigued," Clara replied. "I've never investigated a box of prophecies before."

"I am calling it Pandora's box," Professor Montgomery snorted bitterly, "for all the troubles it is causing. I even have the Dean telling me I should just open the damn thing and get it over with, but you see why I cannot? For a start, there is all this nonsense about involving the king, which would draw vast amounts of publicity, and then the whole scientific community would know that we had this box and were taken in by its supposed prophecies and magic. The Institute would be a laughing stock, we would lose all credibility for endorsing such nonsense. How would our students go on to find respectable positions after that? They would be turned away the second people saw where they had studied.

"We cannot risk our academic reputation over such a thing. Honestly, I am very concerned about the wider world learning that the late Professor Lynch was dabbling in fortune telling. He was indulged, you see, due to his age and the length of time he had been at the Institute and he was very respected. He was a very good astronomer, no one cannot deny that, but his external hobbies caused a little embarrassment. We liked to keep them quiet. I don't care to think what people will say if they discover our former director was trying to predict the future.

"We have rivals who would use it as an excuse to deride us. The discipline of astronomy is a cut-throat business, we don't get the same level of interest as other popular sciences that are seen to be more... useful. Chemistry and biology, for instance, attract all sorts of funding because they are the means for producing new industrial processes and medicines, and all manner of other things that everyday folk find important. No one appreciates that the study of the solar system is also important. The Institute must fight against other similar bodies for financial support, I won't lie about that. We rely on generous donations from wealthy sponsors not just to keep running, but to continuously upgrade our equipment.

"This box could ruin all that. We might lose sponsors who think we have lost our heads. Then where will we be? I have tried to make this point to those among my colleagues who are obsessed by the box, to no avail. They seem blinded."

Professor Montgomery paused, somewhat breathless from his long speech. His face had a desperate look to it.

"I feel under attack, Miss Fitzgerald, I feel there are brutes and thugs on every side waiting for me to misstep so they can assault me," Montgomery clenched his hands together. "Our yearly financial reports just arrived, the Bursar was sitting with me for two hours yesterday as we went through them. The Institute is in serious debt, we need to raise extra funds to secure our future. I fear that if the story of this box becomes public, we shall lose any chance of that."

Professor Montgomery grimaced.

"Unfortunately, the Bursar is one of those enamoured with Lynch's box and is pushing the idea of having it opened as a way of attracting attention to us. He seems to think we can use it for fundraising, rather like a novelty act. He does not appreciate the long-term damage such a stunt could do to our academic standing. We would lose more than we would gain, I am sure of it."

Clara understood the difficulties Montgomery was under and the anxiety he was suffering as a consequence. He had dark shadows under his eyes and a nervous twitch in his fingers.

"You are under a lot of pressure," Clara said sympathetically. "But, I do have to mention that my services are not free. If you are already in debt…"

"Miss Fitzgerald, say no more, I intend to pay you out of my own purse. For the sake of the Institute, I am happy to go to the expense."

Clara now saw that to Montgomery the Institute was more than just a job, it was his passion, his home, his life. That was why he was so upset and desperate, he feared how much he could lose not just from a financial position, but from an emotional one. Clara suspected the professor was the sort of man whose world revolved around his work, who let that work define him and could not imagine a life without it.

"I shall do everything I can to help. I assume you want me to find something to convince your colleagues that this box is just an old man's fancy?"

"Broadly speaking, yes," Professor Montgomery nodded. "If you could determine the contents of the box without opening it, all the better. We have retained all of Professor Lynch's notes and papers from his time here, it was another of the stipulations of his will. You may be able to find something among them.

"I hate to say this, because I was fond of Lynch too, but if you could find evidence that the man was… losing his mind a little towards the end, then that would probably go a long way to ending this talk about a grand opening of the box. Ultimately, I don't know how to resolve this, and I am hoping that an outside perspective will see things I do not and offer me hope."

Professor Montgomery pulled a tight smile.

"I am sure my predecessor never meant for this to happen. He loved this Institute as much as I do. He was tireless in seeking funds to improve our observatory and get more powerful lens for our telescope. Once, he was a great man, who pursued the stars with a passion few have today. He wanted to promote astronomy not as a hobby science, but something important, something vital. I don't know what went wrong and why that changed."

Professor Montgomery became quiet and Clara saw there was more to this than just his fears about the Institute. He was genuinely upset at the thought that such a great man, a man he admired, had slipped into superstition and pseudo-science. Clara didn't think she would be able to help him with that, but she might be able to help with this box.

"Can I see the box?" She asked.

Professor Montgomery roused himself.

"Of course, it is in the library, where it has always been," Montgomery pulled a face. "Had I known of its existence, I might have seen to it that it discreetly vanished."

He sighed.

"Too late for that now."

Chapter Three

The library proved to be on the third floor of the Institute, an area that many would think of as an attic, but which had been transformed into a functional space for the purpose of storing the thousands of books and papers the Institute possessed. The panelled walls were lined with shelves and over them rose an arched roof, divided into rectangular spaces by thin beams of wood. The space within these rectangles was painted white and contained the section name for that particular part of the library's collection. One rectangle proclaimed the section it expanded over was 'Ancient Greek Astronomers' while another informed you that the shelves beneath it contained books by or about Isaac Newton. Clara could not see any rectangles that talked about books on prophecies or sealed boxes.

The middle space of the library contained a number of reading tables and a handful of students were seated at them working their way through heavy-duty volumes on stargazing. In the corner opposite the entrance door, was a circular desk ornamented very grandly with carved images of the zodiac. Whoever had built the Institute had certainly spared no expense on the fittings and fixtures. The librarian was behind the desk; a little old man, with brilliantly white hair and a pair of gold half-moon spectacles that clung perilously to the very tip of his nose. He was remarkably short, not quite the height of Clara and she was only around five foot three. This meant he constantly had to peer up at everyone and the position of his glasses forced him to squint. There was something extremely comical about the man's appearance, though it was far from intentional.

"Mr McGhie," Professor Montgomery approached the librarian. "I have a visitor who I would like to show Professor Lynch's box."

Mr McGhie's previously open and merry face became sullen at the mention of this. He scowled at Clara with surprising ferocity and had she been of a shyer nature she might have felt intimidated. As it was, she was merely amused and curious at his demeanour.

"I don't know about that Professor Montgomery. I don't know if Professor Lynch would like it being shown to random people, especially a woman. Professor Lynch was very sceptical about women astronomers," despite his short stature, Mr McGhie did an impressive job of looking down his nose at Clara.

She smiled back at him, refusing to take offence.

"Professor Lynch has been dead these last twenty years and I doubt he cares anymore who looks at his box," Professor Montgomery said, trying his hardest to keep his temper. "And I happen to be the director of this institute and I can show the box to whoever I please."

Mr McGhie looked duly chastened and fussed with his glasses.

"I don't know, I don't know," he muttered to himself as he went through a small door just behind him and into what Clara presumed was his office. They could still hear him talking to himself. "What would poor Professor Lynch say? It was his box and he put it in my hands for special keeping. I don't know, doesn't seem right. He'll be turning in his grave."

His words were accompanied by the sound of keys

rattling in a lock. He finally reappeared with a small metal box in his hands. It looked rather like a biscuit box, the sort you buy great grandma at Christmas, only this did not have the usual cute decorations of scampering Scottie dogs or a quaint cottage on it. It was a dull colour and you could see where the edges of the metal had been folded over each other to make the sides. It was wrapped in parcel string; two strands going from front to back across the lid and two strands going across the lid from the sides. Where the strings crossed over, they had been heavily covered in sealing wax and impressed by a stamp that appeared to be an intertwined P and L.

"Thank you," Professor Montgomery said to the librarian, taking the box from his reluctant hands. "We shall bring it back shortly."

Mr McGhie twitched the corner of his mouth; the horror of the box being removed from his care almost too much for him. Then he recovered himself and went back to his work.

"You see the spell it has over some people?" Montgomery whispered in Clara's ear. "These are men of science! Yet they act as if they are no better than medieval peasants viewing a magician's tricks. Their gullibility is shocking!"

Clara had no comment, she did not think a passion for science excluded people from being somewhat superstitious. Sometimes the black and white of academic studies made people crave the unexplainable.

Professor Montgomery placed the tin box on a table well away from the students in the room and waved his hands at it.

"There you go."

Clara took a seat and examined the box closely.

"It appears handmade. I was expecting a box from a factory, something a machine pressed, but this is really rather crude," Clara ran a finger over a side seam. "Someone has created the shape of a box out of metal, then folded it up – rather like making a cardboard box – and finally overlapped the edges and very roughly soldered them together. I would hazard a guess that Professor Lynch made this himself."

Professor Montgomery did not seem pleased with the revelation.

"I would rather he had used a biscuit tin. It would have made the thing all the more laughable. You can't take a prophecy seriously when it is in a tin that formerly contained shortbread."

"I imagine that is the reason he made his own box," Clara said gently. "He went to a lot of trouble. I am afraid this means that Professor Lynch was probably very serious about his prophecies. I had wondered if this was a ort of joke, Professor Lynch seeing how long he could have people fawning over this box. Now, I think he believed in it. This is too much trouble to go to for a very insular prank."

"Towards the end, Professor Lynch was very obsessed with astrology," Professor Montgomery explained. "Many people confuse the two disciplines, I have been accused of being an astrologer before now. As astronomers, we watch and study the motions of the stars and other celestial bodies to understand our universe better. It is a science, pure and simple. Astrology attempts to link those movements of stars and planets to world events or to things that occur in people's lives. Astrology is about discovering if the motion of the planet Venus can influence whether you are going to be an optimist or a pessimist, whether you will be lucky in love or have vast wealth. It is pure nonsense. Planets and stars have no concern about us.

"Yet there are those that firmly believe in these things and draw up astrological charts – horoscopes – to predict the future. They might create charts for themselves, for family or even for politicians and monarchs. They might attempt to use astrology to predict the future of our nation. Before the scientific revolution, astrology was deemed as much a science as alchemy. Queen Elizabeth I had charts drawn up for her, and many people dabbled harmlessly in the subject. But it was never real, never quantifiable. Astrology is guesswork and sometimes the astrologer gets lucky and by chance predicts an event, or at least seems to, as most astrological predictions are wholly vague and easy to interpret as you please.

"These odd triumphs give hope to people who believe in this stuff. They ignore all the times the astrologers were wrong and instead fixate on this one dubious claim of success. Astronomers should never be astrologers, it is like a doctor dabbling in magic charms to heal his patients. You cannot find a person credible when they do something like that."

Clara looked at the seals on the box.

"P.L.?" She asked.

"Percival Lynch. He had a signet ring with the initials on, he was rather fond of sealing wax on letters," Professor Montgomery raised a sentimental smile. "There was no harm in Percival, he was the sort of man you could not help but like. I really don't want to see his name sullied by all this business, he does not deserve that. He is in Who's Who, you know, had an entry since 1888. Let me find a copy."

Professor Montgomery rose and disappeared to study the stacks around him. Clara turned the box around on the table, looking at it from all angles. It was a labour of love, she was sure of that. Professor Lynch had taken the time to cut out the metal and bend it to shape and then solder it together. It had probably taken him hours, considering he did not appear a natural metalworker. And all for some strange prophecy and secret magic he believed in. Just what was driving this man when he created this thing?

Montgomery returned with the 1902 edition of Who's Who.

"This was published just after he died," he said.

He spread the book before Clara and pointed out Professor Lynch's entry. It was a typical Who's Who rendition of someone's life; rather bland and boring, talking about academic credentials and not a lot else. Clara was far more interested in the people behind such entries, the personal details – who they married, who they didn't, what they believed, what they were like. However, the review of Professor Lynch's public life in the book was certainly glowing and he was clearly a well-respected astronomer, even if he had done nothing truly remarkable, other than identify a previously unknown (and rather unimportant) star.

"I hate to think of his reputation being cut to pieces by talk that he turned to fortune telling in his later years," Montgomery dropped his voice as he spoke.

Clara was peering at the seams of the box, trying to see if there was a gap that she might be able to pull the papers through, but Professor Lynch had been very thorough with his solder.

"Tell me about Professor Lynch's obsession with astrology," Clara asked Montgomery.

"I don't think there is a lot to say. It started perhaps five or six years before he died. We noticed he was not quite himself. Little things, memory slips, forgetting meetings, sometimes calling people by the wrong name. Around the same time, he began visiting the observatory on a nightly basis, some thought he was on to the discovery of another star," Montgomery smiled wistfully at the memory. "If only that had been true. He was clearly looking at the stars to make his charts. He had been doing it all in secret, I guess he knew what we would all think, but in the last eighteen months of his life he began to talk about his new hobby openly. He was very unwell by then, the doctors had told him there was no hope, which is the cruellest thing of all. He was often bedridden for days and that depressed him. It was terrible to see.

"I don't recall it all in detail now, but I remember one of my colleagues mentioning to me that Professor Lynch had been speaking some wild ideas. It was already known I would take his place as director, and I felt an overwhelming duty of care towards the old man. After I heard this talk, I went to see Lynch. I found him surrounded by all these papers, they were astrological charts. I was flabbergasted, but Lynch merely smiled. Told me he had been writing his own horoscope and it looked promising. He was certain the stars had revealed he would get better soon.

"How can you deny a man his delusions when he is plainly dying? I never questioned him on the matter, I just kept it as quiet as possible."

"I completely agree with your actions, Professor Montgomery," Clara reassured him. "There is no point upsetting a man on his death bed. If it gave him comfort to think the stars predicted he would recover, then who are we to judge him?"

"Oh, but I did judge him," Montgomery said sadly. "Not aloud, you see, but in my head. I judged him a silly old fool and I was angry to see him playing with such nonsense. I regret that so much now. I was a lot younger then, I thought I understood everything, I thought there was only science and any man who looked to something other than that for his answers had to be insane. As you grow older, you begin to question your opinions. You perhaps mellow a bit."

Clara smiled at him politely.

"You do not need to explain yourself to me," she said. "We are all allowed our private opinions."

"And now we have this box," Professor Montgomery sighed. "Maybe if I had not been so… dismissive of old Lynch's views back then, we might have talked about this and I could have… I don't know, maybe persuaded him it was a bad idea?"

"We cannot second guess ourselves, we have to go with what is here, before us. Now we have a problem to attempt to resolve," Clara paused. "I need to know, Professor Montgomery, how honest do you expect me to be in this matter?"

"I do not follow?" Montgomery looked confused.

"One of the ways to discredit this box and to put off your colleagues from going through this complicated opening ritual, is to produce evidence that Professor Lynch had lost his mind in his final days. If it could be medically proven he was imbalanced mentally by his sickness, then it would be hard for your colleagues to continue to place faith in the contents of this box."

Montgomery paused, understanding what she was saying and also faced by a dilemma. He frowned, then he dropped his head a little.

"Miss Fitzgerald, as much as I would prefer to mask my predecessor's madness in his final months, I also see that this would be a necessary evil to, as much as anything, save his reputation as an astronomer. Better that he be proved to have been insane in his last days, and that all this astrology nonsense was a product of that madness, than for him to be held up as a leading example of a worthy astronomer giving room to astrology."

Professor Montgomery looked miserable, but his options were limited.

"I believe it would be for the best if you could prove Professor Lynch was insane when he began this astrology mischief."

"I shall see what I can find out," Clara said gently.

"Thank you," Professor Montgomery managed a weak smile. "Now, I'll show you were the Lynch papers are kept. They will hopefully prove useful to you, though I regret to say they have never been catalogued and are in the same order as when they were deposited here twenty years ago."

"I'm sure I'll manage," Clara promised.

Chapter Four

Someone was hammering on the Fitzgeralds' front door. Tommy Fitzgerald had been in the morning room, which overlooked the garden at the back of the house, reading a newspaper. He rose to see who was trying to get their attention so urgently. He met with Annie in the hallway, also summoned by the knocking.

"Somebody sounds upset," she remarked to Tommy as she stepped ahead of him and opened the door.

Captain O'Harris was stood on the doorstep. The former RFC pilot was looking extremely frantic, his eyes were a little wild as he stepped over the threshold.

"Is Clara in?"

"Sorry, old chap," Tommy said, concerned at his friend's appearance. "She is out on a case."

"By Jove, man, I need to see her!" O'Harris ran a hand across his face, from forehead to chin, as if he was trying to pull off the anxiety that was engulfing him. "But I can't stop and wait, I'll have to call on her later."

"What on earth has happened?" Tommy asked him. "Do you think you should sit down?"

"I can't hang about," O'Harris refused the offer. "I have to get to the hospital. It's a terrible mess, Tommy. Look, why don't you come with me? You might not be Clara, but you aren't too shabby."

O'Harris managed a half-hearted grin at his joke. Tommy could see the man was desperate for someone to confide in and did not want to face whatever emergency was worrying him alone.

"Of course I'll come," Tommy agreed. "We'll leave a message for Clara, so if she returns before we do, she will know to come to the hospital."

"Yes, that is a grand idea!" O'Harris nodded.

He watched Tommy with impatience as he fetched his coat.

"Don't worry, Captain," Annie patted his arm. "I'll make sure Clara knows where you are."

O'Harris pulled a tight smile, it looked rather pained.

"Thanks Annie."

Tommy was finally ready and hurried out the door with O'Harris. The captain had come to the house in his car and the great, shiny green beast was parked just outside on the road attracting curious glances from the neighbours. Jones, O'Harris' driver, was waiting patiently inside.

"This has to be the worst day I have had in a long while," O'Harris muttered to Tommy as they climbed in the car. "Jones, straight to the hospital please."

The car pulled from the curb and Tommy settled back in the leather seat.

"You better explain," he said.

"Last night we realised that one of the guests at the home was missing," Captain O'Harris ran a convalescence home for servicemen who were suffering mental health problems caused by their war experiences. He admitted what he was doing was a drop in the ocean when it came to the true extent of the problem – so many men were still reliving the traumas of war, years after their service. But it was a start. O'Harris never called his clients 'patients', they were always his guests. The very word 'patient' could make the men feel judged. "We were very concerned about his absence, and I had some of the staff check about the grounds for him. The men are free to come and go from the home, however, we do insist they are back by ten o'clock at night. That is when we lock up and we like to know where everyone is. Honestly, Tommy, I thought the fellow might have done himself in when he was nowhere in the house. In some regards, as horrid as that would have been, it would have been easier to deal with than what had actually occurred."

"This sounds very serious," Tommy had his full attention on O'Harris now.

"We had no success searching the grounds, so we expanded the search into the town, with little result. We were trying to avoid drawing too much attention to what we were doing. You know that some people have been critical of the presence of the Home in Brighton?"

Tommy admitted that he had heard this. Some people thought the men who were coming to O'Harris' Home were dangerous lunatics, criminally insane and trained to fight from their time at the Front. They had resented the project; there had been outcry that they would be murdered in their beds. The protests had been unable to stop O'Harris' scheme, but it had left a strain on him. He constantly felt the need to prove that his guests were not going to cause anyone any harm, in fact, the only person who was usually at risk from them, was themselves.

"The search was fruitless, and I hoped that when morning came we could discover the fellow. With any luck he had just been out drinking too late. I kept myself awake all night wondering if he might have jumped off the pier or walked into the sea. I envisioned all the ways he might have killed himself. I never contemplated another option."

"You are worrying me now," Tommy said, dropping his voice even though they were in the car. "What has occurred?"

"Inspector Park-Coombs appeared on my doorstep this morning," O'Harris continued. "As you might imagine, I thought he had come to tell me they had recovered a body. As it happened, the police had found our lost guest alive, but he was in hospital."

"He had tried to kill himself?" Tommy asked.

"Not unless he had found a way to stab himself in the back," O'Harris replied, his tone bleak. "He was found in an alley, the blade still in him. He had crawled there. He had lost a lot of blood."

"Crikey!" Tommy gasped. "Who would do such a thing?"

"I don't know, but there is more," O'Harris said glumly. "They traced his route back to where the incident had occurred, it was quite easy to follow the trail of blood. They found the body of a woman. She had been stabbed too, in the stomach. She had not managed to crawl away and had died where she was attacked. She was partially hidden by some dustbins. The police are working on the theory that she was stabbed by my fellow and then managed to grab the knife and stab him in the back."

"They have no proof of that?" Tommy asked quickly.

"Well, my chap had blood all over his hands. The police say because the knife was still in his back, he had not bled enough to have gotten all that blood over him from his own wound. His shirt was sodden with blood. Tommy, this does not look good, as much as I want to believe the fellow innocent, he does, literally, have blood on his hands."

Tommy groaned. It did sound damning, and if the scenario the police envisioned was true, it would not just be the end of the man, but probably the end of O'Harris' Home. The doomsayers would be proven right that the 'guests' were dangerous. Captain O'Harris would not be able to carry on under such an atmosphere of fear and suspicion.

"Who is the fellow?" Tommy asked.

"That's the worst of it, Tommy, it's Private Peterson."

Tommy closed his eyes for a minute. Private Peterson was one of O'Harris' subsidised patients. Most of the men at the Home paid for their care, it was a private venture, after all; but the captain had made provision for one or two 'charity' cases, men who desperately needed the help he could offer, but who lacked the money to afford it. Private Peterson had been the first such patient, and O'Harris had offered him the place because he was an extreme case. He suffered hallucinations and chronic depression. He had been in and out of his local lunatic asylum, every occasion he seemed to have recovered, it was only a matter of time before he succumbed to his demons again. He was suicidal and barely clinging onto life.

O'Harris had been warned that he was too tough a case, but he wanted such a challenge, he wanted to prove that his methods, his Home, could transform even a man so woefully lost to his mental nightmares. Maybe it had been arrogant, maybe it had been a foolish act of pride, to prove himself to all those who criticised what he was doing, but O'Harris had made up his mind.

"I thought Peterson was doing better," he explained. "He seemed so much happier and calmer. These last few weeks I really saw a change in him. I have the best doctors at the Home, they are men who know their stuff and are progressive in their treatments. They had seen steady improvement with Peterson and were beginning to feel hopeful that he would be able to return to normal life.

"His nightmares were easing, and they had been a burden to him for years. He was engaging in the various therapies we were offering; he would work in the garden, or on the cars. He was attending the lectures we hold in the afternoons and was working his way through the library shelves. He had even tried his hand at an art class a local lady comes in to teach. Last week he actually laughed, and it was a genuine, heartfelt laugh. I saw joy in his eyes. I really thought we were winning."

O'Harris shook his head.

"There was nothing to make us suppose he was dangerous, nothing," O'Harris let out a whistle of air. "He had never caused harm to anyone, even in the middle of his worst hallucinations, he never lashed out. I thought he was the gentlest soul in the house. I can't begin to imagine how this could have happened."

"You think maybe he slipped into an hallucination and lashed out at this woman accidentally?" Tommy asked. He had experienced partial hallucinations in his past, especially when he had just returned from the Front. He had always known in some part of him they were not real, but they were horrific, nonetheless.

"That is the only way this makes sense," O'Harris sighed. "Unless I completely misread the fellow. At least, if it was a moment of insanity, he shan't hang, but spend the rest of his days in a prison for the criminally insane."

"I can tell you now that Clara will want to be involved in this," Tommy said, trying to reassure him. "She will not let this rest until she has dug out the truth. How strongly do you believe in the possibility he did this?"

"I don't know," O'Harris closed his eyes and winced. "My thoughts are so wrapped up with the fear of what this will do to the Home and, I confess, I am angered that I might have been so gullible as to fail to see this coming. My pride is hurt and I am not thinking straight. I want him to be innocent, because I don't want people thinking my men are dangerous, nor do I want them looking at me as if I was the biggest fool alive. And that is not a good enough reason. I can't think clearly."

O'Harris was becoming agitated. Tommy kept his voice calm.

"All right, look, we shall figure this out. It's all a shock at the moment, but once we have our heads around it, we will be able to see a way forward. What has Peterson said so far?"

"Inspector Park-Coombs told me that Peterson was barely alive when he was taken to hospital. He was lucky, a man heard someone calling for help and came out of his yard. He saw Peterson on the ground and when he realised there was a knife in his back, he had the local doctor summoned. Naturally, the doctor said Peterson needed to be sent to the hospital and had an ambulance called.

"A police constable was alerted by the man who found

Peterson. It was obvious a crime had been committed. The constable whistled for more help and then the Inspector was sent for. That is when they searched the alley and traced back to the dead woman. Peterson was rushed to hospital and had to be operated on at once to carefully remove the blade. They don't think anything vital was struck, but had he been left any longer in that alley he would have bled to death too."

O'Harris stopped, looking at his hands which were trembling.

"Dare I say, if he had died, we might have been spared this nightmare?"

"No," Tommy told him, "had he died, we would have no answer to this mystery. Better he is alive and able to speak to us. So, what has he said?"

"Sorry," O'Harris shook his head, realising he had failed to answer Tommy's question. "Peterson was unconscious through the night, he came around this morning. There was a constable outside his room and as soon as he knew he was awake he sent for Park-Coombs. Peterson told the Inspector that he could not remember a thing. He went to the picture house and then started to walk home. He went through the alleys, but he does not recall the woman or even being stabbed. I'm not sure the Inspector believed him."

"Do you?" Tommy asked.

"You know as well as I do, Tommy, that men who have suffered a significant trauma often blank it from their minds. Such amnesia is not uncommon," O'Harris shrugged. "Does that mean he killed the woman? I don't know. I think Peterson is the sort of fellow who would be so horrified by any violent act he committed, that he would not pretend to have forgotten about it. At least, that is what I used to think."

"Don't start to second-guess yourself now," Tommy told him. "Innocent until proven guilty, remember?"

"It does look bad though, Tommy. The woman lying there dead, the only knife was in Peterson's back and he was covered in her blood. There is no sign of anyone else being there."

"That does not mean there wasn't another person," Tommy insisted.

"And yet, Peterson does look to have killed the woman," O'Harris could not get his thoughts away from that idea. "This was not how I expected to begin the day. I thought he had slipped away to hang himself or something. I was feeling bad enough about that."

"Don't condemn him, or yourself, until you know for certain what happened. I mean, why would he kill this woman? Outside of him having a severe hallucination, there would be no reason. He didn't know her, did he?"

O'Harris shrugged.

"And you said yourself he had never been dangerous when hallucinating before," Tommy added.

"No," O'Harris agreed. "He had never been violent. My nurses all agree he is a gentle soul."

"Then hold onto that thought and don't despair. Whatever the truth of this, Clara will find it out."

O'Harris let out a long sigh.

"I do hope so, Tommy!"

Chapter Five

Professor Montgomery left Clara alone to peruse Professor Lynch's papers. The box was restored to Mr McGhie, who hastily took it away to lock it up in his cupboard. He did not trouble Clara as she worked.

The papers were in a dreadful muddle. They spanned over thirty years; from the time when Professor Lynch first came to the Institute, to his final days. No one had organised them, they had simply been packed up in boxes and deposited in the library. Among notes on the orbit of Saturn, Clara found a receipt for tea leaves and tobacco, along with a letter from the Brighton Public Library informing Lynch that one of his books was overdue. There were shopping lists and half-written speeches for public lunches, things that should never have been kept among the papers of a professor. There was a handwritten prescription from Lynch's doctor, detailing two different medicines he wanted the man to try and a recipe for a herbal tonic at the bottom. She found adverts that had been snipped from the local newspaper for a variety of random items – a horse hair stuffed footstool; a medicine for baldness; two different brands of soap; a metal bath tub; and a small geology sample collection. They had obviously been important to Lynch but had no relevance to his papers.

Clara had to sift through this motley assortment before she was able to start working on the papers themselves. These consisted of observational notes, star charts, papers from lectures, papers that Lynch had written for academic journals, a variety of diaries (some personal, some detailing the movements of the stars) and a vast wad of correspondence, mainly to other astronomers, but also to friends and family.

There were ten boxes of material and Clara had no option but to sort them all, as there was no guarantee that all the papers from the 1880s, for instance, were in one box. She acquired one of the reading tables and began making piles. Sorting papers first by decade, and then by type. She placed all extraneous items to one side. It was not her place to deem if they were important or not, but they were not relevant to her search and most were undated and impossible to place in a pile. It was not until she came to the eighth box to sort that she found anything of an astrological nature. Up until that point, everything had been solidly scientific with no hint of horoscopes about them.

The box she found the astrological charts in was unmarked, just like the others, and gave her no hint of its contents. The papers were a muddle yet again and began with some material from 1893 on lunar eclipses. Just beneath those papers was a star chart that Clara almost overlooked – her eyes had stopped taking in information by now – until something made her give it a second glance.

On the paper was a large circle, with a smaller inner circle drawn within its circumference. The outer circle was divided into twelve equal segments which bore the symbols of the zodiac. The inner circle was also bisected by straight lines which radiated out from the centre. However, these were not evenly spaced, so some of the triangular areas were bigger than others. Clara thought of it like uneven slices of a pie. There were further symbols in the inner circle, all along the edge where it touched the outer zodiac rim. Clara was not at first sure what the symbols were, until she realised one was in the shape of a crescent moon and it dawned on her that they represented the planets and stars of the solar system. These planetary sigils did not lie evenly across the chart, instead most of them were grouped to the top left, while three were scattered about the bottom right.

Clara turned the paper over for a clue as to what the chart meant or when it was made. She was surprised to read the date 1840, written in ink on the back of the chart. There was also a date and time – 24 June, 1pm. It was the oldest paper in the boxes, and due to Clara's limited understanding of astrology, she was not sure what it meant. Could it be that Professor Lynch's fascination with astrology had a far older origin that anyone guessed?

She was about to begin searching for more charts, when she became aware of someone stood by her shoulder. Clara glanced up into the face of a man in his fifties. He was portly and rather bald, but he had a very pleasant smile on his face.

"I apologise for interrupting," the gentleman said, looking slightly bashful. "I am Roderick Evans, the bursar at the Institute. I heard the Director had hired someone to look through Professor Lynch's papers."

Roderick had a strong Welsh accent. He was looking at Clara with a hint of caution, as if he was worried she might prove to be a monster in disguise. Clara recalled Professor Montgomery had said the bursar was one of those who was keen to have Lynch's box opened.

"Clara Fitzgerald," Clara introduced herself. "Nice to meet you Mr Evans."

"You must be the first soul to go through those papers in two decades," Evans said, his attention drifting to the boxes of documents.

Clara sensed his unease.

"My understanding is that these have never been catalogued. They are not even arranged in date order. As you can see, I have been doing a little sorting," Clara waved a hand at the piles of papers on the table before her. "Fortunately, the late Professor Lynch was very good at dating even his mundane documents."

The bursar looked along the length of the table.

"Where those in the boxes too?" He asked, pointing at the pile of random papers Clara had sorted from the rest.

"Yes. It seems whoever packed these up just placed everything into the boxes without considering what it was. There are receipts for hair oil, prescriptions from the doctor, a shopping list or two and some papers that appear to be quick notes that must have meant something to Professor Lynch, but are cryptic to me."

"I feel rather awful to think of the mess these papers are in," the bursar did appear ashamed at what Clara had found. "They should have been sorted long ago. It really is disgraceful, but I am as much responsible as anyone else. These papers were placed here because it was felt they should not be lost, but then everyone forgot about them."

Clara smiled at him, trying to make him relax.

"Why don't you sit down and join me. I have worked through several boxes already and you can take a look at the papers I have sorted."

The bursar hesitated, though Clara was not sure why he was so anxious around her. He finally sat down on the opposite side of the table to her. He glanced at the nearest pile of papers which was from the 1890s.

"Oh, here is the official proposal for the replacement of our main telescope," the bursar picked up a set of papers clipped together with a rusting paperclip. "Our previous telescope was no longer powerful enough. Professor Lynch outlined in this document why we needed a new one and sent it to all of our benefactors. We rely heavily on donations to keep running. I remember this paper so vividly, as it was all the talk among the staff. I wasn't bursar then, of course, I was barely out of my student days."

The bursar started working through the papers and he

seemed to find something that interested him with each one. For a while he was distracted, and Clara carried on with her own sorting process, hoping to find more astrological charts or any papers that related to them.

Evans finally finished with his pile of papers and reached over for the astrology chart Clara had found. It was sat next to her elbow. He lifted it up and studied it, his forehead creasing.

"I found that among some papers on the supposed composition of the rings of Saturn," Clara said.

"It's a long time since I last saw this," Evans said quietly. "Do you know what it is?"

"An astrological chart," Clara said.

"Yes, but, more specifically?"

Clara didn't like to admit ignorance, but she really had no choice.

"I supposed it was a horoscope."

"It is old Lynch's birth chart," the bursar did not gloat over Clara's lack of knowledge. "This shows where the planets were at the exact time of his birth. The various positions are supposed to tell a person about themselves, their strengths and weaknesses and how they can improve."

"Then the date on the back is that of Professor Lynch's birth, not when the chart was created?"

"Yes," the bursar studied the chart for a moment more. "Lynch became interested in this sort of thing in his later life. He would draw up birth charts for people, if they wanted. I never had mine done."

"Did Lynch's interest in astrology begin when his health started to fail?" Clara asked.

The bursar pulled a face as he considered.

"I'm not entirely sure. It certainly increased as his sickness overtook him," the bursar glanced shyly at Clara. "You have been asked by the Director to prove this box business is all nonsense. You must think I am terrible fool for believing in that box."

"I am here to give an unbiased opinion," Clara replied,

trying to reassure him. "It would hardly be productive of me to have already formed an idea. I am looking into these papers to see what caused Lynch to create this box and if there is any reason to take it seriously."

"Professor Montgomery is very sceptical, and I can understand that, had events not occurred to change my mind, I would have sided with him. But I have seen the power of Lynch's predictions."

"Maybe you could explain that to me?" Clara asked.

The bursar cleared his throat, slightly agitated.

"Professor Lynch spent his last days working on horoscopes, they filled his every waking moment. People like Montgomery will say it was a desperate act of a dying man to give himself hope. I think he was trying to be as productive in his last days as he could be. He knew he had this power to make predictions from the stars. Lynch had finally understood the misjudged art of astrology after being critical of it for so long. I think he was trying to make up for lost time.

"Anyway, the week before he died, he presented me with three astrological charts and detailed written explanations for them. They all related to my future. He had marked on them the year when the events would occur and said they were not a gimmick, but a way of helping me to face obstacles in my life. I didn't truly understand just then.

"The first chart was for the year 1909. Lynch's notes described how in this year the planets would be aligned in such a way that a great shift in my career would occur and if I was quick enough to grasp the opportunities that came my way, great things would follow. It was in 1909 that the position of bursar opened up unexpectedly. I had never thought of applying for a clerical post at the Institute, I was content being a lecturer. But with the implication of the chart at the back of my mind, I decided to submit an application. As you can see, I succeeded."

"That was what first convinced you there was something in these charts?" Clara said carefully, not wanting to offend the bursar.

"Yes. The next chart was for 1915. This one predicted that the year would be the worst of my life. I would suffer greatly emotionally and physically. I should prepare myself by being up-to-date with my work and expect to be called away from my duties for the greater part of the year," the bursar continued. "It was not a very nice prediction and I ignored it right up until the final months of 1914, when I started to feel uneasy. I can't quite explain it to you, but I felt a little 'off'.

"I decided to do as the horoscope suggested and worked hard to make sure I had no backlog of paperwork on my desk. I was in my office late so many nights and began to feel worse and worse. I had just caught up with myself at New Year's 1914. The next day I became seriously ill. My doctor was rather stumped, but thought it was a complaint of the heart. He prescribed a great deal of bed rest, and I found myself having to neglect my duties as bursar.

"I thought I was going to die, those first months of 1915. I felt so weak and tired of life. My body seemed to be giving up. To make things worse, just before Easter I learned from my sister that my only nephew had been killed in the war. My devastation cannot be described. That boy was the closest thing I had to a son and we had talked about him coming here to the Institute to study astronomy. The war got in the way, as it did for so many young men, and then disaster occurred."

The bursar fell silent as the hard memories came back to him and broke him a little all over again.

"Lynch's astrological chart had predicted it all," he said at last. "I did suffer greatly emotionally and physically, but, by the end of the year, I was making progress and I recovered completely. My doctor still does not know what was wrong with me. Yet, because of that chart, I had made sure my office was in good order, my paperwork was all done and so my temporary absence was not as damaging as it might otherwise have been."

Clara could see how, on the back of such turmoil, Evans

would become convinced that the astrological charts held some sort of power. Even if their predictions were rather vague. If the chart had specified that Evan's nephew would die, or could have explained the nature of his illness and thus helped his doctor to heal him, she might have been impressed. As it was, it was like so many fortune telling scams – hazy guesses, easy to interpret in a variety of ways, and lacking in specific details. Clara did not say this aloud, however.

"What of the third chart?" She asked.

"Ah, well, that is dated for this year and it says that a great divide will threaten the place I am most fond of, and I must be strong in my convictions. You see, don't you?" The bursar's eyes lit up. "It is referring to the revealing of Lynch's box and how it has put a wedge between those of us who believe in it and those who do not. As for being strong in my convictions, that refers to my new found belief in astrology, more to the point, my belief that Lynch had a gift for seeing into the future using the stars. I must stick to this belief, no matter what."

Clara held her tongue and did not point out that, as Lynch had prepared his box and given strict instructions for when it was to be revealed, his horoscope for 1922 would be easy to write. He knew the future, because he had planned it, he also had enough clarity at the last moment to realise his box would create tensions within the Institute.

What Clara could not say was whether Lynch had believed in his powers, or whether this was some game he had played to test his colleagues. Maybe it was some long-drawn-out test of their gullibility he concocted on his sickbed. She needed to know more about the man behind the charts, more about Lynch and just why he fell into astrology.

Until she did, men like the bursar would continue to follow him doggedly, and potentially destroy the reputation and the future of the Institute.

Chapter Six

Captain O'Harris was agitated as they entered the hospital and asked if they could see Private Peterson. Due to the serious nature of the crimes Peterson was accused of, and the concerns about his mental health, he had been placed in a private room with a constable on guard outside. He was also allowed visitors outside the usual time, as the police would need to speak to him whenever they wished. Captain O'Harris had asked to be placed on the list of special visitors who Peterson was allowed to receive at any time. Inspector Park-Coombs, knowing how important this matter was to the captain, had agreed, and had also suggested adding Clara's name to the list.

The inspector was sympathetic to O'Harris' plight. He had been at the opening of the Convalescence Home and knew its significance to both O'Harris and to the men it would help. He didn't like to think that that would now all fall apart, but he was a cynic and feared that Private Peterson had condemned the captain's grand schemes. In any case, O'Harris and Tommy were allowed to go upstairs to Peterson's room.

The constable on the door knew them both and gave them a sad smile as they approached. Tommy was beginning to feel a dread about the kind sympathy everyone was bestowing on O'Harris; it made the matter seem ten times worse. At least O'Harris was too much in a daze over everything to notice the policeman's look.

They entered the room and found Private Peterson lying on his stomach in the bed, his head turned to the left as he lay on the pillow. He had become hot beneath the blanket of the bed and thrust it back, revealing the heavy bandages around his torso where his pyjama top had rolled up.

"Morning Peterson," O'Harris said briskly, managing to cast off his apprehension for the moment. "I would like a word. This is Tommy Fitzgerald, you have met before."

Peterson's eyes looked dull, only the fact they moved saved them from appearing lifeless. He stared between Tommy and O'Harris, seemingly oblivious to what had been said. This made O'Harris even more restless; Tommy grabbed a chair for him and placed it by the bed, to try to settle him. He grabbed another for himself. O'Harris wanted to pace, Tommy could see that, but it would not be helpful if he started. Tommy felt they needed to keep the conversation calm if they were to get anything from Peterson, and that meant preventing O'Harris' anxiety from becoming obvious.

"How are you feeling?" Tommy asked once he had convinced the captain to sit down.

Peterson's eyes drifted to him, there was a sense that he was not entirely aware of where he was, or even entirely awake.

"Fine," he murmured in a weak voice.

"You know what happened to you?" Tommy asked tentatively.

Peterson hesitated, then he screwed up his eyes.

"Someone stabbed me… in the back."

"Yes," Tommy replied. "We are trying to find out who did it."

"I don't remember," Peterson said rather quickly, in a way that made Tommy uneasy. The denial was too quick, too firm.

"You went to the picture house last night?" Tommy changed direction.

"Yes," Peterson answered.

"What was playing?"

Peterson grimaced.

"Nosferatu," he said. "I didn't like it."

"Not my sort of thing either," Tommy told him. "Did you watch the whole film?"

"No," Peterson said quietly. "Slipped out early..."

He shut his eyes and for a moment Tommy thought he had drifted off, but then he looked at them again and there seemed a new determination in his eyes.

"I want to know who did this to me," he said.

"Naturally," Tommy agreed. "Do you remember encountering anyone on your way from the picture house?"

"No," Peterson said, and he seemed to realise how unhelpful this was and groaned in despair.

"Why were you in the alleys?" O'Harris jumped in. "The quickest route from the picture house to the Home is by the main roads."

Peterson sucked his bottom lip into his mouth and chewed on it. He was holding something back, not wanting to speak it aloud. That made Tommy even more worried.

"Why did you go that way?" O'Harris persisted. "There has to have been a reason. We are trying to help you Peterson, this is serious!"

Peterson cringed at the captain's harsh tone. Tommy placed his hand on O'Harris' arm to quieten him. The captain did not mean to be fierce, he was worried, that was all – and he was worried as much for Peterson as for his convalescence home.

"We want to help you," Tommy told Peterson. "You may not be aware, but another person was found hurt in the alleys. A woman. Sadly, she died. The police think you may have stabbed her."

Peterson's eyes flashed with fear and he let out a moan.

"Did I?" He asked, though Tommy was not sure if he

was seeking an answer from them, or whether he was questioning himself.

Tommy chose to answer him.

"We don't know, not without unravelling the situation in that alley last night. We need you to help us, so we can help you. O'Harris is certain you are not a dangerous man. He doesn't think you would kill someone."

Peterson's eyes were more alive as he turned them on O'Harris. There seemed a hint of gratitude in them, as if he had never imagined someone else would believe in him.

"Thank you," he whispered, again it was not clear who he was speaking to. "I try to remember, but there is this big blank."

"Let's start with why you went into the alleys," Tommy nudged him.

Peterson took a deep breath, preparing himself for saying what he didn't want to.

"I was having one of my... episodes," he said.

Tommy glanced at O'Harris for clarification.

"Peterson suffers from occasional hallucinations," he said.

"No, not that," Peterson said softly. "I wasn't hallucinating. It was the other thing. The one where I feel so afraid and scared."

"Oh, a panic attack," O'Harris guessed. "They are nothing to be ashamed of, old man. As the doctors have told you, they happen quite a lot to men who served in the war."

"I have them," Tommy added, trying to build some trust and camaraderie with Peterson. "They are a horrid thing, makes me feel like I need to run away, but I am trying to run away from myself, which is impossible."

"That's it," Peterson said grimly. "When I get like that, I don't want to be around other people. I don't like how it makes me behave. I don't like people seeing me in such a state. I think it was that film that set me off."

Peterson gave a slight sniff as the events of the previous night began to come over him again. He might not remember the details, but he did remember how he felt.

"I should never have watched that film. But I thought I was better…"

"Don't beat yourself up about it," O'Harris said. He had calmed down now and was able to respond to Peterson without sounding hard or scared. "That's why you went into the alleys? To avoid people?"

"Yes," Peterson responded. "I thought I could avoid everyone. I don't know what happened after that, I swear. If I could remember I would tell you. I wish I knew what I did. All I recall is trying to walk, knowing I had to get away from something, and having this pain in my back."

"Did you take a knife with you last night?" Tommy asked him.

"Whatever for?" Peterson said in surprise. "I don't even own a knife."

"Peterson, if you can remember anything, it is absolutely vital you say so. Maybe it is something vague or seemingly random, that you don't think important, but it could be the key to all this for us," O'Harris said softly, but with urgency in his tone.

Peterson frowned.

"I… everything is gone, I…" he let out a hiss of air through his teeth. "I honestly don't remember a woman, you have to believe me, and I don't remember a knife."

"We believe you," O'Harris reassured him. "But, is there anything, anything at all that might give us an insight?"

Peterson fell silent again, his gaze settled on the corner of the bedside cabinet by his hospital bed and there was a moment when Tommy wondered if he had slipped into a sort of daze. Then he blinked and looked at them.

"I think I might be going mad, it was perhaps because of the film I had just watched…" he trailed off.

"You can tell us anything," O'Harris insisted.

Peterson took a deep breath.

"I just keep remembering this word over and over in my mind. I can hear it being shrieked as if by a woman. But it makes no sense," Peterson shut his eyes tight and gave a groan. "I see snatches of the film too, when I close my eyes, I see that monstrous creature again. I… I think I may have started to hallucinate."

"Old fellow, don't say that to the police," O'Harris said quickly. "They will interpret that as a confession of guilt. They will say you attacked this woman while you were hallucinating, and you will not be able to argue against it. I have seen you hallucinate, Peterson, you have never been violent during those episodes. I have never been fearful that you would cause harm to anyone. Don't assume your own guilt before you know what happened."

"But this blank in my memory," Peterson was becoming tearful, "it has to mean something, doesn't it?"

"It means you were scared," Tommy interjected. "It means that something bad happened and caused you such shock you have erased the memory. It does not mean you were responsible for a murder. There had to be someone else there, someone who hurt this woman and you. The trauma of it all has created this amnesia. You must have heard about that happening to men at the Front?"

Peterson tried to nod his head, but couldn't while he was lying on the pillow. Instead he spoke.

"Yes. I've heard about it."

"You were vulnerable because you were having a panic attack. Whatever happened was so upsetting in the context of the situation that your mind has consigned it to some back space of your memory to protect you. Only, it has made things more complicated," Tommy wasn't sure he was explaining things correctly, he was no psychologist. He just wanted to help Peterson and cause him to relax enough to recall something more of that night. "It was like with my legs. You know, they stopped working after I was shot, I just could not feel them at all. They seemed to not exist. The doctors told me there was nothing mechanically wrong, but I refused to believe them. I did not want to admit it was something to do with my mental state. And then a very clever doctor persuaded me that it was true, and that it was nothing to be ashamed of. Because of him,

I can walk again. My brain had created this block in my mind, because of the horror of my injuries, and we had to break that block. It will be the same with your memory, Peterson."

Peterson was listening, but he did not seem convinced. He had spent a lot of time with various doctors, some more sympathetic to his plight than others, over the last few years. They had talked about a lot of theories, tried to explain what was wrong with him; the problem was, none of them had fixed him.

"I don't think I can help you," he said at last.

"It's about helping you," O'Harris gently corrected him. "What was the word you thought you heard? The one that keeps repeating in your head?"

Peterson cringed.

"I don't want to say. It really is crazy."

"Let us decide that, we are not going to judge you. We are here as friends," O'Harris paused. "I don't want to see you forced into a lunatic asylum for the rest of your days because of a lapse of memory. I stand by my conviction that you are not dangerous. In all the time since you have been home and suffering these problems, you have never once been violent. Your own doctor and mother assured me of that, and I have seen enough of your problems in the last few months to concur with that opinion. Please, Peterson, do not give up on yourself."

Peterson buried his head into the pillow. His fingers closed around the corner of the bed sheet and crumpled it up in his fist.

"I want to believe you, but I don't trust myself. When you can't remember what you did, you start to doubt your own actions," he mumbled.

"I don't doubt you," O'Harris leaned forward and touched his arm. "I have never doubted you. I want to help, give me the opportunity to do so."

Peterson winced, but he slowly turned his head back towards them.

"What does it matter anyway? They say I am crazy, so

if I tell you what I heard and it sounds mad, well, you will not be surprised."

"You are not mad or crazy," Tommy promised him. "No more so than myself or Captain O'Harris."

"Trust me, old boy, I know about amnesia," O'Harris added. "I forgot who I was after my crash, for a whole year."

Peterson let out another hiss.

"As I say, it is probably something from that film. I just keep hearing this woman shouting in my head over and over a single word," Peterson gave out a tense laugh, that had no joy in it. "Monster."

He paused and then held O'Harris' gaze.

"She yells monster."

Chapter Seven

Clara returned home in time for tea. She hung her coat and hat on the hall stand and hummed to herself as she wandered into the front parlour, where she found Tommy and O'Harris deep in conversation. O'Harris leapt up at the sight of her and pulled her into his embrace, which surprised Clara for a moment.

"I am so glad you are here," he said. "We have to talk; a terrible thing has happened."

Over the next half-hour, while Annie brought in scones and tea, O'Harris laid out the saga of Private Peterson and the murder in the alley. Clara listened without interruption, a frown on her face that grew deeper as the sorry affair was laid out before her.

"So, you see the pickle we are in," O'Harris finished.

"I like Private Peterson," Annie said quietly. She had poured out tea and was now sat in a chair near them. Annie served as housekeeper and cook to the Fitzgeralds, but she was more like a friend and had recently become engaged to Tommy. The circumstances sounded complicated on paper, but had taken such a natural and logical progression that neither Clara, Tommy nor Annie found anything odd about them. "I've met him at the Home when I take the cookery class. He has a light hand for pastry. I don't think a violent man could be so good at it."

Annie had volunteered to run a cookery class at the Home, much to everyone's amazement. She had explained that she wanted to be helpful and to feel she had a purpose. The classes had proved extremely popular, because Annie had a knack for bringing out the best in even the worst cook.

"Peterson didn't kill anyone," Annie said firmly.

No better recommendation could come for the man than from the quiet, humble, but utterly honest Annie. There were few people in this world she would give such a staunch defence to. Annie did not make such statements lightly.

"The trouble is proving that," Tommy said. "Peterson can remember nothing, and I think it unlikely that will change. Even if it did, the police will probably not believe him. From what they can see, there were two people in that alley and one of them is dead. Peterson's guilt seems certain to them."

"Poor man," Clara said sympathetically. "And all he can recall is the word monster?"

"Yes," O'Harris nodded, "and I am inclined to agree with him that the word is something from the film he watched and of no importance."

"I don't rule anything out until I am absolutely certain," Clara corrected him with a smile. "It does seem odd though. Why would anyone be yelling 'monster'? You might call someone a monster, I suppose, but as your last words? Why not call for help? Scream murder? It's puzzling. Anyway, have you spoken to the police further?"

"No," O'Harris admitted. "Other than to have Inspector Park-Coombs tell me where Peterson was and the situation. My priority was getting to him. He is my responsibility."

"Of course," Clara smiled at him to let him know she completely agreed with his decision. "I think there is a lot here we don't know and that we need to unravel. It is easy to blame a man with Peterson's problems for a murder without asking the important question of why? Why would he suddenly become violent and attack this woman? It was not in Peterson's nature. He had never displayed violent tendencies before. Just because the man suffers hallucinations and panic attacks, should not make him immediately considered a violent murderer."

"Not forgetting the mystery of the knife," Tommy added. "Peterson says he did not take a knife with him to the picture house, that he does not even possess one. There is no reason to doubt that. Which then begs the question, where did the knife appear from? If the woman had it, then how did Peterson get hold of it?"

"There is a lot we don't know as yet," Clara observed. "I would like to get a full report on Peterson's mental state from the doctors at the Home, John."

"Of course," O'Harris quickly confirmed. "You will find nothing to suggest we had any concerns that Peterson was a risk."

"I'll obviously speak to Inspector Park-Coombs and see what the police have so far uncovered. The Inspector might seem brash, but he is not uncaring and he does believe in justice. He will not see an innocent man condemned of a crime," Clara paused. "That does leave me with a problem over the Professor Lynch case, it will be hard to divide my time. Tommy, could you do the leg work on that case for me?"

"Well, I am your assistant," Tommy grinned. "What do you want me to do?"

"Firstly, see if Lynch's doctor is still alive and ask him about the professor's illness. Professor Montgomery wants proof that Lynch had lost his marbles in his final days and that explains his obsession with astrology," Clara said. "Personally, the old man's papers gave no hint that he was suffering from senility. He started exploring astrology in 1898, at a time when he was still writing incredibly complex scientific papers on the movements of the planets. I can find a paper he wrote on lunar eclipses dated the same day as he drew up a horoscope. Something tells me this man was not going crazy."

"There are a lot of people out there who believe in astrology, who you would not call crazy," O'Harris pointed out.

"Very true," Clara agreed. "For that matter, I know of academics who believe a scientist who believes in God is utterly mad. They consider science and religion mutually exclusive. No, I have a feeling I may have to disappoint Montgomery on that front. But we shall see."

"What can I do, Clara?" O'Harris asked. "I want to help Peterson."

"Have your doctors assess him," Clara said. "We need a professional opinion on his mental health. It would not hurt to delve deeper into his background and to see if anything like this has happened in the past. I don't want any surprises."

"Of course," O'Harris agreed. "Anything else?"

"You might want to start talking to a good lawyer, just in case," Clara didn't want to worry him further, but she felt it was best to be prepared.

"And I am going to make sandwiches and cake for Peterson and take them to him daily," Annie said firmly, as if someone might try to persuade her otherwise. "Hospital food is not sustaining. He is going to need all his strength."

Annie never failed in her staunch belief that good food was the answer to all of man's woes. Clara knew she would keep a good eye on Peterson and if anyone was going to find a way to break that memory block, it would be Annie with her cucumber sandwiches and caring manner.

"Right, we have a lot to do," Clara said. "And no time like the present. I want to see the place this all happened for myself. Do you two want to come?"

O'Harris and Tommy were quick to agree. With promises to Annie that they would be back for dinner, they set out to find the crime scene. O'Harris had been told by the police roughly where the incident took place and they could work out the rest by following Peterson's route back from the picture house. There were only a couple of places where he could have slipped into the back streets of Brighton from the main road and once within them, there was only a handful of ways to go. As it happened, they came across the spot where Peterson had fallen, first.

The rough bricks of the alley were stained a deep, brassy red where Peterson had lay bleeding. There was a further dark smear against the wall, seemingly caused as he dragged himself along. The trio stopped by the spot and stared at it.

"Who found him?" Clara asked O'Harris.

"The Inspector did not tell me the man's name. He is one of the residents of the houses here," the captain answered.

"Let's follow Peterson's trail," Clara said.

It was not hard to retrace the desperate escape of the wounded man. His injuries had meant he had not been able to go very far before he fell. He had been travelling along a straight alley with a brick wall along one side. On the other, several side alleys led to the backyards of various houses. Peterson had not veered from his route; the occasional red handprint, or smear of blood marked his progress and there were drops of blood on the ground. Clara took note of it all as they walked.

They came to a point just a few hundred feet from where Peterson had fallen, where the blood trail veered from the straight route it had so far taken and disappeared down a side alley. Here, at the corner of the intersection, was a lot more blood. A large dark brown patch spread across the ground, the stain dried and soaked deep into the stone and dirt of the alley. There was a further stain on the wall and splatters of blood had sprayed across a wider area. There was no doubting this was the scene of the crime.

Clara took a good look down the alley, at the back gates of at least a dozen houses, split between the two sides of the narrow pathway. How many people lived in those houses? This was a poorer area of Brighton and it was unlikely that a single family occupied each house. It was far more common for three or more families to rent the properties, occupying a single floor each. The poorest may even rent just a room or two, or share a floor with others in an equally struggling position. What this all meant to Clara was lots of eyes and ears to hear and see a commotion in this back alley. Yet, as far as she was aware, no one had come forward to say they had seen the attack.

"The police found the woman?" Clara asked O'Harris.

"That's what the Inspector said."

Clara pulled a face. Such an attack did not happen in silence. The police were working on the theory that the female victim had stabbed Peterson in her dying moments. You would think people would have come out to see what was happening, unless they knew better than to do so, and that raised a whole new array of questions.

"There is something wrong about all this," Clara said.

She took a few paces down the alley and glanced about at the houses. It was only late afternoon and she could hear children playing in the distance and people in the yards working, but no one had stepped outside to see what was going on, or why three people were inspecting the spot where a murder had been committed. There was always usually someone in a neighbourhood who was curious enough to take an interest. Clara had the feeling that curiosity was not a wise thing in this area of Brighton.

She came to a gate where she could hear someone sweeping in the yard behind and she knocked to get their attention.

"Hello? Excuse me?"

The sweeping stopped. There was a long pause, as if the person in the yard had frozen, and then the gate was tentatively opened. A young female face appeared in the narrow gap between gatepost and gate. The woman looked anxious as she peered out, Clara would go as far as to say she appeared terrified.

"Hello," Clara said with a friendly smile. "My friend was injured just down the alley last night and I am trying to find out what happened. I wondered if…"

The woman slammed the gate in Clara's face as fast as she could and then scuttled back to the house, her footsteps ringing on the hard ground of the yard. Clara frowned.

"What's the matter?" O'Harris called over.

Clara walked back towards him and her brother, mulling over the problem.

"She was scared," she said. "Too scared to talk to me. There is something happening here that clearly has people worried, and I dare say is connected to the death of this woman."

Clara observed the houses again, looking for signs that anyone was paying attention to what they were doing. Where were all the nosy neighbours? Where were the idle gossips and curtain-twitchers? For that matter, where were the people casually using the alley to go about their business? There should be people wandering around, cutting through from other parts of Brighton or heading for home. She had never seen an alley so deserted.

"I don't like this at all," Clara repeated herself. "I am even more convinced that Peterson is not responsible for this crime. I think he stumbled on something and got himself stabbed in the process."

"If only he could remember," O'Harris groaned, frustration coming into his tone.

"We shall have to do the remembering for him," Clara replied. "Come on, I have seen enough. I would like to talk to the man who helped Peterson, if we can find him."

They headed back the way they had come. Clara took note of all the blood stains again, working out Peterson's fraught journey. He had bumped into the alley wall here; fallen there. Here was the point where he could no longer walk and had to drag himself. It must have seemed an eternity to Peterson, but the entire ordeal probably only lasted minutes before he was found.

At the spot where he finally fell, Clara knelt down and tried to picture what it had been like. Tried to put herself in Peterson's place. No wonder he was so deeply traumatised by it all that he erased most of the episode from his mind. Clara could not truly imagine the pain and terror that had engulfed Peterson in that instant. He must have thought he would die. It was just horrible to consider. Clara had dropped her head and partially closed her eyes to get her mind around the scenario, when someone spoke.

"Who are you?"

Clara pulled herself from her thoughts at the sound of the voice. She looked up and saw a man stood in the gateway of the yard to her right. He looked angry rather than frightened, which gave her hope.

"We are friends of the man who was attacked last night and fell here," Clara explained to the man. "We want to know what happened to him."

The man folded his arms across his chest.

"Then you will be wanting to speak to me," he said sternly. "I'm the one that found him."

Chapter Eight

At first the man was reluctant to let them into his yard, let alone through to his house. He blocked the gate with the look of someone who won't be moved for anything.

"My name is Clara Fitzgerald," Clara hoped a polite introduction might ease the tension. "These gentlemen are my brother Tommy and Captain O'Harris."

The man turned his fierce gaze on each of them in turn. He was aged somewhere in his forties, possibly early fifties, and wore the dull, but tidy clothes of a labourer. His waistcoat had been patched a few times and had one button that was odd to the others. However, all his clothes were very clean and there was a pride to his appearance that suggested a man with standards.

His hair was rapidly running to grey, and he had a very square face and a firm jaw. He bore himself confidently, unlike so many who skittered about the alleys and called these houses home. Clara could see why he would be a man to go to the aid of someone else.

"The gentleman you found injured in this alley, his name is Private Peterson, and he does not remember anything that happened. We want to try and find out who hurt him," Clara added.

"The police came here and searched the alley," the man responded, his tone cold. "They found a woman dead, stabbed. They didn't say it, but I got the feeling they thought your friend killed her."

"We don't believe that," O'Harris added hastily. "Peterson is not a violent man and he had no reason to hurt the woman."

The man in the yard frowned, clearly trying to decide what he believed about the situation and what he did not. Finally, he gave a nod.

"I'll talk to you for a bit, but I don't know much. I never saw anything."

"Thank you, your help will be much appreciated," Clara said with relief. "What is your name?"

"Just call me Robert," the man replied. "We ought to talk inside."

Robert led them through the yard, which was typical of the yards of working-class homes. It was paved over and contained the dustbins for the house and a tin bath hanging on a wall. A clothes line ran from the back of the house to the corner of the wall that skirted the yard. Nearer the house there was a long low outhouse, which Clara assumed contained a toilet and probably the coal store. Robert led them past this and through a green door that led into a narrow corridor. On their left was a dark staircase leading up, on their right a kitchen offered a glimmer of somewhere more cosy and pleasant. Clara had been struck by how this whole area seemed to exist in shades of brown and grey, a splash of colour, even just some flowers or green grass, would not go amiss to brighten things up. Clara felt that living in this area for too long could have a very depressing effect on a person.

Robert motioned for them to step into the kitchen. There were two women within the small space, which was dominated by a compact range oven and a welsh dresser that must have had to come through the kitchen door in pieces, considering the size of it. The women were stood either side of a wooden table making pastry. They had been talking and were startled at the sight of visitors.

"This is my wife and my mother," Robert introduced the women quickly. "These people are friends of the fellow I helped last night and want to know what happened to him."

The older woman, who must have been in her seventies, had pure white hair scraped back into a bun, and scowled as this information was imparted.

"I told you not to go out there," the woman snapped at Robert.

"Yes, you did, and I said I can't leave a fellow to bleed to death," Robert responded in a flat tone that suggested he had had this argument several times already and was really not bothered in continuing it.

"I don't know what you hope to discover," the old woman turned her gaze on Clara, "but you would be best off forgetting about it all."

"Why is that?" Clara asked her.

"Because no good comes of interfering with these things," the old woman puttered. "People who get themselves into trouble have to sort things out for themselves."

"If you let me talk to these folks in peace, they'll be gone before you know it," Robert said to his mother.

"And what about dinner? Who is going to sort this pastry?" His mother barked at him.

"It will only be for a few moments," Robert stood his ground. "I don't know much, anyway."

The old woman cast another sharp look at Clara.

"It's a bad business, made worse by people poking their noses into it. But if you won't be told..." with her head held high, as if she knew best and would be proven right in the end, the old woman stalked out of the kitchen.

Robert's wife had been silent during the argument, but Clara had seen the intense way she had studied them all and sensed her quietness was far from being due to a lack of confidence. She just had nothing to add to the debate. She held Robert's gaze for as long as it took to leave the kitchen and follow his mother. There was a message in that look, one that Clara suspected meant Robert should be careful what he said.

Robert lit a lamp on the dresser. There was a gas light hanging from the kitchen ceiling, but it was not yet dark enough to warrant turning it on. The old lamp, with its cheap paraffin oil, sufficed to take the edge off the dull shadows of the room. Robert moved the lamp to the table and rested his hands on the wooden surface, just avoiding the flour being used in the pastry making.

"You'll have to excuse my mother, she is worried," he said.

"I get the impression that is quite a common thing around here," Clara replied.

"You noticed that?" Robert tilted his head.

"Most places you go where something like this has occurred, people are only too keen to peer out their windows and stand on their doorsteps taking a look. They all have an opinion on what happened," Clara said. "In contrast, I sensed that everyone here was very keen to keep out of sight. I have to wonder why that is."

Robert shrugged.

"We are quiet folk, minding our own business," he said.

Clara knew there was much more than he was saying but badgering him was unlikely to get information. The reaction of his mother to their presence, told her that something was amiss in the neighbourhood and people were anxious and scared to talk.

"How did you come to find Peterson?" Clara asked him instead.

Robert repeated his shrug.

"I heard someone calling for help. I was in the yard, cleaning my work boots, when I heard this man calling out. He sounded awful, so I went to the gate to take a look and he was lying on the ground, trying to drag himself along."

O'Harris cringed at this information. Robert noticed his expression.

"It did seem bad," he agreed. "I hurried out and saw that

the man had a knife in his back. My wife had been in the kitchen and saw me leave the yard through the window. She followed me and I told her to go fetch a doctor. There is one a few streets away. He came and instantly said we had to summon an ambulance."

"Did other people come out to assist you?" Clara wondered.

"Not at first, then when people realised I was out there, and the doctor appeared, they started to take a look. We didn't know about the woman, of course," Robert was solemn. "My wife managed to find a police constable while she was fetching the doctor and sent him this way. He said he would have to call for more help considering the nature of the incident. Before we knew it, there were a lot of people in the alley."

"And the police searched the area?" Clara asked.

Robert nodded.

"They followed the blood trail backwards. I watched them at first, but I had things to do. I was back cleaning my boots when I heard someone shouting. I guess that was when they found the woman."

"Do you know who she was?" Clara asked.

Robert shook his head quickly. Clara noted that he did not meet her eyes, and she suspected he was lying.

"Did no one see what happened?" She persisted.

"I guess not," Robert answered.

"Seems to me, everyone keeps very much to themselves around here," Tommy mentioned casually. "Usually the alleys behind houses are busy places. People cutting through them, friends talking across them as they work in opposite yards, children playing. Seems strange that no one was around to see anything."

"That's just how it was," Robert replied, still not meeting anyone's eyes. "I really don't know anymore than that and I am sorry for your friend. Will he be all right?"

"Depends on whether the police continue to consider him a murderer or not," O'Harris said darkly.

"Has anything happened like this before, in the area?"

Clara tried another approach.

"What do you mean?" Robert shuffled his feet, it might have been an unconscious movement, but Clara sensed he was uneasy at her question.

"I mean, have there been stabbings in the area before? Is it something people worry about?"

"People worry about a lot of things," Robert avoided her question. "You never really know who is about. People prefer to be indoors and safe in their beds at night."

"You mean this is not a place people should be wandering about after dark?" Clara pressed him.

"I didn't say that, I mean, things can happen anywhere, can't they?" Robert was becoming agitated. "Look, I really have told you everything I can."

"And that is much appreciated," Clara let the matter go, she knew when she was only going to push a person into aggressive silence. Robert didn't want to say anything more right there and then, but that did not mean he would not talk later, when things had calmed down.

"Yes, and I really appreciate what you did for Peterson," O'Harris quickly jumped in. "He has been through so much and didn't deserve to be attacked, at all. He really is a gentle soul."

"Did you say he was a soldier?" Robert asked tentatively.

"He was a private in the last war," O'Harris explained. "He went through some rough times, but then, didn't we all?"

"I was in the war," Robert said. "Those were dark times. You expect to come home and everything to be... different."

"Only, the war comes back with you," Tommy finished for him.

Robert pursed his lips together.

"When I heard him calling, your friend, it made me ˻ː ˹ ˌ ˻se times in the trenches when you would hear ˌalling out for help. It makes your stomach go ˌhen, so often we were not allowed to leave the trenches to help a mate, the officers wouldn't allow it. And then, when you were allowed, so often you found your mate dead and you asked yourself, what if I had been a moment sooner? Just a moment or two?" Robert sagged his head. "You don't forget things like that. It's a part of the reason why, when I heard that voice, I couldn't sit by and ignore it."

"Your mother would have preferred that you did," Clara read between the lines.

"My mother worries a lot," Robert said. "I tell her that we can't live our lives in fear, not if it means leaving others to suffer. He had lost a lot of blood, your friend. I'm amazed how far he dragged himself. Sheer determination, that was."

"Again, we very much appreciate that you went to his aid," Clara smiled at Robert, then she pulled one of her business cards from her handbag. "If you remember anything that might be useful, or maybe if you hear something, this is how you can contact me."

She pushed the card across the table towards him. Robert did not pick it up at once. He looked at the slip of card as if it might bite him.

"It says you are a private detective?" He said, with a hint of accusation in his voice.

"I am," Clara answered. "But I am also a friend of Private Peterson, and I hope to use my experience to unravel this mystery. Else, someone stands to get away with murder."

Robert said nothing, he was just staring at the card on the table.

"We can let ourselves out," Clara told him in a cheery voice. "We have disturbed your dinner arrangements too long."

They headed out into the corridor and to the yard. Clara half-expected Robert to follow them and tell them something he had suddenly 'remembered' about the attack on Peterson, unfortunately he did not appear and Clara was a touch disappointed. She didn't like it when she was wrong.

They stepped back out into the alley, which was still eerily deserted. There was not even a stray cat prowling about.

"Something is wrong about this place," Clara glanced up and down. "People are worried about something and have learned to mind their own business."

"You think that is why Peterson was hurt? Because he stumbled across something he shouldn't have?" O'Harris asked.

Clara was worried by the hopefulness in his tone.

"I don't know why Peterson was attacked," Clara explained. "I just know that something feels odd about this whole situation. People are scared of showing too much curiosity, or being seen in this alley. You ask me, there is a person going about causing a lot of anxiety to this neighbourhood. Whether that makes them a potential killer, I am not so sure."

"But you will figure it all out, won't you Clara," O'Harris' face fell as he picked up her uncertainty.

"I'll figure it out," Clara promised him, though she was worried just what sort of answer she might discover. "There are lots of questions, but I shall solve them all."

O'Harris relaxed.

"What now?" He asked.

"Well, I shall have to talk to Inspector Park-Coombs, but it is getting too late for that right now. I think it is best if we go home and start afresh in the morning."

O'Harris didn't look so sure, however he did not argue. They left the alley and threaded their way back to the main roads. Clara was relieved to get away from the crime scene; the whole neighbourhood had a depressive feel to it that was hard to explain. Whatever was going on in the district, she didn't think it was anything nice.

Chapter Nine

Clara had two tasks to attend to the next day and was relieved that she had delegated at least one of them to Tommy.

Over the last year, Clara's private investigation business had expanded enormously, and she had more work on her hands than she was capable of dealing with. Clara never felt like she could turn down a case either; how could you decide if one person's conundrum was worthy of more attention than another's? The solution was to employ an able assistant and her brother Tommy, who was at something of a loose end after recovering from his war injuries, had been up for the task.

Tommy had never pursued his childhood plans of becoming an architect (he wanted to be a cowboy up until the age of twelve, but architecture held more promise), as the war had interrupted his studies and he had not been able to return to them afterwards. With his health restored, he needed something to do, a purpose in life that would, preferably, also increase the household income. It had taken Clara a long while to contemplate offering him a position within her business – after all, she was the business, and it seemed odd to have someone else helping with her work. But it made sense; it enabled Clara to keep up with all the work on her plate, while also offering Tommy something to do. They had talked about Tommy becoming a partner in the business, but Clara was not quite ready for such a leap.

She had taken so long building up her reputation and proving that a woman could run a business as well as any man, that it seemed a betrayal of herself to suddenly take on a male partner. Fortunately, Tommy did not take offence at being made her assistant, he just enjoyed having something to do.

Clara gave Tommy the task of finding Professor Lynch's old doctor and learning all he could about the astronomer's final illness, then she set off to speak to Inspector Park-Coombs.

The inspector and Clara had a strong working relationship; she avoided stepping on his toes and he avoided insulting her capabilities as a private detective. They helped each other and, as a result, Park-Coombs' success rate for solving crimes had risen above the national average and had impressed his superiors. Even so, whenever he saw Clara walk into the police station, his heart would sink a fraction. He knew the appearance of Clara meant there was trouble somewhere, and he was about to be dragged into it.

On this particular occasion, he had been expecting Clara to drop by the second she realised who the man found stabbed in the alley was. Park-Coombs had no doubt that as soon as he had finished speaking to Captain O'Harris and had appraised him of the situation, then the former RFC pilot could be seeking out Clara to resolve the matter for him. He even left instructions with the desk sergeant to have Clara shown to his office as soon as she arrived. Park-Coombs knew that Clara would not rest until she had spoken with him and it would be simplest to get everything over and done with.

Clara, in turn, knew she would be anticipated and was not surprised when the desk sergeant smiled as she entered the police station and pointed straight to the stairs.

"Go up, he is expecting you," he said.

Clara glanced at the staircase, then gave the sergeant a nod and headed up. She knew exactly where Park-Coombs' office was and was soon knocking on his door.

"Come in."

Clara entered and Park-Coombs lifted his head from the paperwork he was sorting through to acknowledge her.

"I was expecting you sooner," he said.

"I was on another case," Clara explained. "By the time I learned of what was going on, it was too late to come and see you."

Clara wandered into the office and took a seat opposite Park-Coombs without being asked.

"This is a messy one."

"Not least because of your friend O'Harris being involved," Park-Coombs nodded. "I didn't like to say to him, but he opened himself up for this potential disappointment when he started that Home."

"Are you suggesting you thought something like this would happen?" Clara said in astonishment.

"I didn't think it would be so dramatic," Park-Coombs explained. "I just had this feeling he was asking for trouble when he opened a place for men with troubled minds. It's really an asylum, isn't it?"

"It is far more complicated a situation than such a label will give credit to. In any case, I do not believe that O'Harris' guests are murderers."

"How do you explain Private Peterson?" Park-Coombs said, with obvious glee at finding a flaw in her conviction. "The evidence is pretty clear."

"Really Inspector? What evidence is that?" Clara asked.

Park-Coombs' satisfaction diminished as he realised Clara was about to counter every point he made in favour of Peterson being the suspect.

"The knife in his back," Park-Coombs began, but then instantly regretted speaking the words.

"And yet, Peterson did not own a knife," Clara observed.

"And he was stabbed in the back, a task virtually impossible to do yourself."

"We have a theory for that too," Park-Coombs said quickly.

"That the woman was carrying the knife and stabbed him?" Clara suggested. "Do you have proof the knife belonged to her?"

Park-Coombs hesitated, which was all it took for Clara to pounce.

"If we cannot connect the knife to either of the victims, then we must ask where it came from."

"Peterson's memory loss is all too convenient," Park-Coombs quickly pointed out.

"Personally, I would call it inconvenient," Clara replied. "By failing to remember anything, Peterson puts himself in a position of appearing guilty and hiding something, while also being unable to defend himself by stating what really happened."

"But Peterson has these hallucinations, he confessed to them. He was distraught when I questioned him and said when he has these moments, he doesn't know what he is doing. I'm not saying the man is a natural killer, but when he is hallucinating he is back at the Front, anything could happen. Maybe he thought the woman was an enemy soldier? Maybe he thought she was attacking him and he was defending his trench, doing his duty?" Park-Coombs raised the issue that was going to be the real sticking point in this case. If they could not find out what happened, then everyone was going to say that it was a very sad instance of a mentally ill man going crazy. It would save Peterson from the noose, but he would spend the rest of his life in a lunatic asylum, and it would be the end of O'Harris' Home.

"O'Harris has a team of expert doctors looking after these men, and they are all in agreement that Peterson is not dangerous. He has never shown signs of violence during one of these episodes," Clara felt the argument was weak, but she had to state it. How many people would say the same about someone they knew who suddenly killed another person? It was a stock response which would hold no water in a court of law.

The inspector's face told her he was unimpressed by the statement.

"Things change, people change. Maybe, in the past, people have always been careful around him during these episodes, so he did not feel the need to react violently. Maybe this woman, in fear of her life, pushed him away or shouted at him, and that tipped Peterson over the edge?"

Clara was silent, because that was a possibility none of them could deny.

"But, if she had this knife, why didn't she use it first?" Clara asked the question that was bothering her. "Imagine, Inspector, I am that woman and you are Peterson. He is coming down the alley, acting oddly because he is hallucinating, though I must stress neither we or Peterson know that he was hallucinating, he may have just been having a panic attack. Come on, get up."

Park-Coombs gave a long sigh, then rose and came around his desk to face Clara.

"Now, I have a knife," Clara picked up a pencil from the desk to represent a knife, she held it out before her. "Assuming I am scared of you, as you approach I'll thrust the knife at you to keep you away."

"Which could be when Peterson grabbed hold of it," Park-Coombs reached out and grabbed the pencil. "Then he struck out at the victim."

He thrust the pencil at Clara's stomach.

"Now, the blade went in with some force and lodged, so Peterson lets it go," Park-Coombs gave the pencil back to Clara. "He now turns away, the woman wrenches the knife from her belly with her last strength and stabs him in the back."

Clara obeyed his scenario and prodded the pencil into the Inspector's spine.

"You see the problem with that, don't you?" She asked him.

Park-Coombs turned back around and raised an

eyebrow.

"If the knife went in so deep that Peterson could not pull it straight back out, then what are the chances that a dying woman, bleeding heavily and in terrible pain, could?" Clara said.

"People have these sudden spurts of strength," Park-Coombs said dismissively.

"To wrench a knife from yourself and thrust it hard enough at a man, who is already walking away from you, that it lodges deep in his back?" Clara was unconvinced. "That requires a lot of effort from a person who was clearly not in a position to do something so energetic."

"I imagine you have another theory," Park-Coombs folded his arms across his chest and waited to be impressed by Clara's take on the case.

"Honestly, Inspector, I don't have anything other than speculation. My instinct says there were other people in that alley and that Peterson stumbled upon something he shouldn't have. Did you not notice how reluctant people were to talk in that area?"

"I find in places like that its normal for people to not want to talk to the police," Park-Coombs huffed.

"But it was more than that. The alleys were deserted, how many alleys behind yards in neighbourhoods like that do you know which are not actively used? Where were the people going about their everyday lives? Where were the children playing? Why did no one find that woman's body until so long after Peterson had been found and taken to hospital? Do you see what I mean? These alleys are like main roads, if something happens, someone sees it or comes across it pretty quickly."

Park-Coombs mellowed.

"I do know what you mean," he said. "I grew up in a similar area, not quite so poor, but with lots of houses together and an alley running behind the yards. There was always someone in that alley, day and night. I used to lay in bed and hear old man Frazer crashing about in the alley, dead drunk and singing to himself. His wife wouldn't let him in the house when he had had a drink, so he would sleep in the alley and be stumbled over by the dustmen or the coal man."

"Exactly, Inspector, life spills over into those alleyways. People acquire it as a means of expanding their own meagre living space, especially when they only have a room or two to call their own. But those alleys last night were so barren, so empty, it was unsettling."

Park-Coombs thought about this for a while.

"Did you notice how there was nothing stacked in them, either? Aside from the bins we found the woman behind, there was nothing in that alley. No stacks of wood, no broken furniture, no dumped rubbish or broken glass."

"No old drunks littering the ground," Clara added.

Park-Coombs smiled.

"That too," he nodded. "It was almost as if it had been cleared for a purpose. How odd."

"I noticed that people seemed scared," Clara said. "They seemed fearful. Even the man who found Peterson and was prepared to speak to me, was very reluctant to say much. And his mother made some odd remarks about not getting involved in other people's problems. Have you had any reports of trouble in that area?"

"Not for a few years now," Park-Coombs rubbed his moustache. "Used to be a time that place was the resort of thieves and pimps. Wouldn't be many weeks we were not out there having to sort some trouble. Now you mention it, it has quietened down considerably. Hadn't given it a thought before, we are so busy and it is a relief to not have to worry about a place."

"It is almost as if someone has cleared out the area of troublemakers and scared the locals into being more law-abiding."

"Which raises that awkward question of – why?" Park-Coombs was becoming intrigued, Clara could see he was at last coming around to the idea that something more was going on than first met the eye.

"Whatever is going on in that neighbourhood, we need

to delve into it. It may be the only way to save Peterson," she said.

Park-Coombs held up a hand to pause her.

"I am not ruling Peterson out as a suspect any time soon. There might be something going on in that place, but that does not mean your friend could not have lost his head and stabbed a woman. We have already discussed how it might have happened."

"And how difficult that would have been," Clara pointed out.

Park-Coombs was not defeated.

"We both know that weirder things have happened. I've seen a dying man running away from a crime scene on a broken leg. In those heat of the moment situations, people can do the unexpected."

"Then I shall just have to prove you wrong," Clara replied. "And that means knowing more about what happened that night. There is the woman, of course, who was she? And I would like to see the knife for myself."

"Then we should go to the morgue and chat with Dr Deáth," Park-Coombs walked to a coat stand by the wall and collected his jacket. "He should have some information for us by now."

The Inspector held his office door open for Clara and they headed off to find the coroner.

Chapter Ten

Tommy had been left in charge of locating Professor Lynch's old doctor. There was no knowing if the man was still alive after all these years, but if he was, he might be able to provide insight into the last days of Lynch, the astronomer turned astrologer. Clara had taken a note of the doctor's name on the prescription she had found in Lynch's papers, and Tommy had compared this to a street directory he had found in what had once been his father's library. Tommy and Clara still lived in the house they had grown up in. Their parents had been killed during the war; a terrible misfortune while they were visiting London and a German Zeppelin came over and dropped bombs.

At the time Tommy had been serving with the army at the Front. Clara had suddenly found herself alone. She had coped by volunteering as a nurse and playing her part, and then Tommy had come home severely injured and Annie had joined them as a housekeeper and to help with Tommy, and life had changed yet again.

There were still echoes of their parents about the house, however. Including the library, which was on the top floor of the property and dominated the length of the attic. This had been the domain of their father, who used it as an office, a reading room and a retreat from the everyday world. Tommy and Clara rarely went up there these days, except to fetch a book. It felt like they were trespassing on their father's private space when they entered the attic, even though he had been gone so many years. You could still smell the smoke of his pipe in the rooms.

Tommy had slipped in, found a directory from 1909 and opened it on the table in the library, only to start to feel uneasy – as if he was being watched. He kept looking over his shoulder at the battered, red leather armchair his father had refused to let go, and which had sat in his library ever since. Tommy was a little bit superstitious, he was prepared to admit that to himself, and after trying to overcome the sense of someone else being in the room with him for several minutes, he had to give up and head downstairs with the directory.

In the familiar, comfortable territory of the parlour, he flicked through the street directory looking for the doctor's name.

Dr Ralph Finnigan had been the man to see Lynch through his last illness. Clara had found a number of notes, prescriptions and invoices from him among the random papers that had been kept after Lynch's death. Though they were hardly relevant to Lynch's astronomy career, they were useful to her. They gave her a link back to the past. Without those scraps of paper, it was uncertain she would have been able to discover who had been Lynch's doctor twenty years ago.

Professor Lynch had died in 1902. Tommy had not been able to find Dr Finnigan in the 1900 directory in his father's library. The next edition they had was for 1909, so he was just hoping Dr Finnigan was still practicing in that year. He was in luck; Dr R. Finnigan was listed along with the address of his surgery under the 'professionals' section of the book. Of course, after twenty years the surgery may have moved or closed, but it was a start. There was also an alphabetical list of residents in Brighton at the back of the directory – you could look for someone based on their occupation, street address, or name. Tommy found a number of Finnigans listed, and two were noted as doctors. He took down both addresses as they were a starting point, at least.

With this information to hand, he headed out to see if Dr Finnigan was still alive and remembered Professor Lynch.

~~~*~~~

The address of the surgery was in a road Tommy knew, but he did not recall the practice. When he arrived and located the correct building, he found it was now an undertaker's shop. That seemed ever so slightly ironic. He went in, nonetheless, to see if anyone remember Dr Finnigan. The shop exterior was very fittingly painted black, with the shop name written in gold Gothic style lettering. A window display showed a range of coffin fittings, mounted on a tiered stand covered in green baize. Weeping cherubs perched at each end of the display, with a row of crepe squares in various grades of black laid out between them.

Tommy felt a little uncomfortable as he entered the premises. The interior was lit by electric lights, as the shop window was completely blocked off for the purposes of the display and also, Tommy guessed, to give customers additional privacy while making arrangements. A gentleman in a black suit sat behind a tall shop counter, there was little else in the front room, except for some framed scripture quotes on the walls which Tommy imagined were meant to be comforting to the bereaved.

"How may I help you?" The shop clerk asked in a quiet, respectful tone.

"Sorry, I'm not here about a funeral," Tommy hastened to explain. "I am trying to find a gentleman named Dr Finnigan. He used to have his surgery in this building."

The clerk frowned.

"I've only known this place as an undertaker's," he said.

Tommy was disappointed. Dr Finnigan had clearly retired a long time ago.

"But let me ask Mr Burke, he is the director of this establishment and may remember the gentleman you are referring to," the clerk was very keen to assist and disappeared through a back door.

Tommy caught a glimpse of coffins as the door swung shut. There would be a showroom out the back for all the funeral paraphernalia people would need to buy. Even though Tommy knew there were no bodies in those coffins, that they were display items and would likely never hold a corpse, he felt a shiver go down his spine.

"Someone walked over my grave," he muttered to himself, rather wishing he had not been left alone in the dimly-lit room that was feeling more and more like something out of a Dickens' novel.

He was relieved when the clerk returned with an older gentleman.

"This is Mr Burke," the clerk introduced the older man.

"You were asking about Dr Finnigan?" Mr Burke said.

"I am trying to find him," Tommy nodded. "I'm afraid, the only addresses I have for him are probably terribly out of date."

"May I ask why you are looking for him?" Mr Burke asked cautiously.

Tommy had not expected the question and did not have an immediate answer, fortunately, like his sister, he had a quick imagination.

"My dear great aunt has just passed over," Tommy said. "She lived in Brighton until 1902 and was a patient of Dr Finnigan. She made a private request to the family for some of her personal belongings to be distributed to people she wanted to be remembered by. Dr Finnigan helped her through a serious illness and she remembered him all these years. She wanted him to have a pocket watch that had belonged to her late husband. It is not worth a great deal, but it is a sentimental gift. I have been charged with distributing these little bequests. Unfortunately, my great aunt did not leave details of where to find Dr Finnigan."

"I find that is often the way," Mr Burke said sympathetically. "Was it a local funeral?"

"No," Tommy quickly added. "She had moved to Ireland to live with her daughter. She was nearly ninety, you know, when she passed. I happen to be her sole relative in the south of England, so I have been asked to take care of things here."

"Naturally. Older people become very sentimental and develop strong attachments," Mr Burke said, sounding as if he was talking about an animal rather than a person. "You have my sympathies for your loss."

"Thank you," Tommy responded.

"Unfortunately, Dr Finnigan has not had a surgery here since 1911. I believe that was the year he retired from medical practice," Mr Burke continued. "I took over the lease for this property in 1912."

"Oh dear," Tommy didn't have to try hard to look glum at this news.

"I can give you Dr Finnigan's address, however. At least the last one I have for him," Mr Burke folded his hands together as he spoke. "We were asked to forward any post to him that might arrive here by mistake. Even three years after he had given up the surgery we were still receiving letters for him. Would you like the address?"

"Would it be in Honeysuckle Avenue?" Tommy asked, taking the slip of paper from his pocket where he had written down the two addresses belonging to a Dr Finnigan. "Or Beresford Drive?"

"Ah, you have already done some research?"

"I took a look at an old street directory," Tommy replied. "My great aunt didn't leave any real details."

"You will find Dr Finnigan in Beresford Drive, if he is still alive, of course. Not that we have heard any different. We certainly have not had cause to arrange his funeral," Mr Burke's tone suggested he would be affronted to discover another undertaker had been employed to deal with the doctor's final affairs.

"Thanks anyway," Tommy told him, before leaving the shop.

He pulled the old street directory from his pocket and consulted the map in the back to work out where he needed to go next. Fortunately, Beresford Drive was not far from where he was. Dr Finnigan would not have wanted to walk a great distance to get to his surgery.

Tommy walked to Beresford Drive in fifteen minutes and found the house easily enough. All the houses in the row were grand Victorian buildings, with tall bay windows and great chimneys rising from their roofs. The one listed as Dr Finnigan's home address had a white pebble path leading to a front door with colourful stained glass panels. The lawn was immaculate, as if someone had gone on their hands and knees and trimmed it with scissors. Tommy felt a little intimidated by the grandeur of the place. He wondered if Clara ever felt that way, and then guessed it was unlikely. Clara was rarely intimidated by anything.

He walked to the front door and knocked. Only a few moments passed before a woman appeared. She was wearing an apron over her skirt and had the appearance of a housekeeper.

"Sorry for the intrusion," Tommy said quickly, feeling awkward, "I am trying to find Dr Finnigan."

"He's working at the hospital at this time of day," the woman told Tommy.

Tommy frowned.

"I was under the impression he had retired?" He said.

"Oh, you are looking for the old Dr Finnigan?" The housekeeper's eyes lit up with understanding. "I thought you might be after his son, who is still a practicing doctor. You best come in, I'll have to ask Mrs Finnigan before we let the old doctor see any visitors."

Tommy was shown into a front room and was then abandoned. He stood uneasily near a large fireplace, listening to the irritating tick of a grandfather clock that continuously reminded him of how long he had been there. How did Clara manage to intrude on other people's lives with such confidence and ease? Tommy felt very nervous, even though he was not doing anything wrong or sinister. All he wanted to do was speak to the old doctor, so why did he feel as if he was there to impart bad news or something similar?

A middle-aged woman finally appeared in the room, just as Tommy was wondering if he could bear the anticipation any longer. She had a smile on her face which made him feel better.

"I understand from Nancy that you want to speak to my father-in-law?" She said.

She was a kindly-faced, plump woman with a pair of gold spectacles hanging from a chain around her neck. Tommy relaxed.

"Yes, I know it is rather out-of-the-blue," Tommy said sheepishly. "What it is, is that I am trying to find out information about Professor Lynch, the astronomer. I am tracking down anyone who knew him when he was alive."

"Ah, so someone is writing a biography of the man? About time, he made some truly important contributions to the field of astronomy," Mrs Finnigan clapped her hands together in delight.

"You knew Professor Lynch?" Tommy asked her.

"Only by reputation and through the stories my father-in-law has told. He was good friends with the professor."

Tommy tried not to appear too excited as he realised he was on to something at last. If anyone would know if Lynch was of sound mind in his final days, it would be one of his closest friends, who also happened to be his doctor.

"Could I speak with Dr Finnigan?" Tommy asked.

Mrs Finnigan's enthusiasm waned a fraction, she glanced over her shoulder towards the big staircase in the hallway of the house.

"Time has not been kind to my father-in-law," she explained sadly. "Mentally he is as alert as ever, but physically he is very unwell. He is embarrassed by his infirmity and rarely sees visitors these days."

Tommy tried to mask his disappointment.

"I really need to speak to him, to better understand Professor Lynch," Tommy insisted. "He need not be embarrassed, I have known what it is to be an invalid. After the war, I was crippled and it took a long time for me to learn to walk again. I still have a limp. I know how frustrating it is to be confined by the limitations of a weak body."

Mrs Finnigan listened keenly and seemed to mellow.

"Why don't you come upstairs and we shall see what my father-in-law says?" She suggested.

Tommy followed her up the staircase and towards a front bedroom, which was brightly lit by one of the tall bay windows. It was a huge room and served as the entire world to the ailing Dr Finnigan. Here was his sitting room, his bedroom, and his bathroom, all in one space.

Dr Finnigan was visible through the partially open door, sitting by the fireplace in a bath chair. He was hunched forward, reading a newspaper, his hands gripping the edges of the pages like the talons of a bird.

"Father?" Mrs Finnigan approached him. "Father? This young man wants to speak with you. He wants to ask you about Professor Lynch."

Dr Finnigan turned in his chair and looked towards the door. His eyes were bright as buttons, even as his body failed him.

"Professor Lynch?" He said, then he smiled. "It's about that damn box? Isn't it?"

Chapter Eleven

The morgue was in a separate building to the police station and was built below street level as a natural means for keeping the rooms chilled. This was especially essential in summer, when the only other option to natural temperature control was expensive mechanical refrigeration systems. In hot weather, storing the dead could quickly run up the electricity bills.

Fortunately, Dr Deáth was rarely troubled for storage space. There were not that many murders or suspicious deaths in the town to cause the narrow, brick chambers he placed bodies in to end up over-subscribed. Dr Deáth was kept busy, but not to the point where he was concerned about the bodies piling up. In fact, he sometimes went over to the hospital morgue and helped there when they were overwhelmed. As the coroner cheerfully said, he liked to keep busy.

Dr Deáth was just in the process of sewing up the torso of a young woman who was laid naked on a metal table. He glanced up as he heard Clara and Inspector Park-Coombs enter.

"Heart attack caused by a blood clot in the main artery," he informed the inspector casually. "Could have happened at any moment. Nothing anyone could have done."

"The woman collapsed in the street yesterday," the inspector explained to Clara. "Was all very puzzling, seeing as she was apparently young and healthy, so of course the police had to take an interest."

"Just one of those things," Dr Deáth said with a shrug. Death did not trouble him greatly, it was just a part of life and one he approached with a sunny attitude. He did not see tragedy or release when he studied his corpses, he saw facts and details, and he recorded them for others. "How can I help you?"

"Its about that stabbing the other night. The woman in the alley," Park-Coombs said.

"Our Jane Smith?" Dr Deáth nodded, he had given the corpse the token name they used for unidentified people. "Why don't you go into my parlour and put the kettle on? I shall be with you in just a minute and we can talk."

Clara and the inspector wandered into the coroner's cosy parlour, set just behind the morgue. It always felt odd to Clara stepping from the white, clinical tiles of the morgue, into this warm, carpeted room, that looked like a snapshot of a Victorian lady's sitting room. The walls were covered in a dark red wallpaper, with flowers picked out in velvet, and the fireplace was constructed of a deep brown wood and pond weed green tiles. There was a bookcase and several low side tables lining the walls and positively overflowing with what Clara could only term knick-knacks. They were not the usual seaside souvenirs or porcelain shepherdesses most similar collections comprised of, but a macabre assortment of anatomical items – odd small bones in class cases, wax models of various body parts, a collection of framed illustrations of diseases of the lungs, a porcelain phrenology skull with a pair of glasses perched on its nose, and a variety of similar items. Clara guessed they all meant something to Dr Deáth, but the chaos with which they were arranged on the side tables made her brain itch. She also observed that nothing had been dusted in quite some time. It was a far cry from the immaculate, almost barren morgue in which Dr Deáth conducted his work.

Inspector Park-Coombs was grumbling to himself as he dug out the kettle from beneath a stack of medical journals.

"I keep threatening to get him a cleaner," he told Clara as he headed into a bathroom that opened off the parlour and filled the kettle with water from the sink. "Trouble would be finding someone brave enough to work here. Takes a certain kind of person to be comfortable cleaning around the dead."

Clara thought what Annie would say about undertaking such a task. She suspected the appeal of sorting Dr Deáth's vast collection into some sort of order would be enough to override any anxiety Annie had about hanging around corpses. Then again…

The inspector returned with the kettle and hung it in the fireplace. There were two armchairs either side of the hearth and Clara took one, while the inspector sat opposite. The kettle was just beginning to whistle when Dr Deáth appeared.

"Now, how may I help? Oh, hang on a minute," Dr Deáth spun on the spot and went to a cupboard near the door. Opening it, he produced a large, yellow tin, that bore the text in bright red of 'Mr Mercer's Rat Formula, for the dealing with all types of pest. Contains Arsenic.' Dr Deáth popped off the lid of this tin and held it out towards Clara and the Inspector. It contained homemade biscuits.

"Help yourselves."

"Isn't that a slightly risky place to store them?" Park-Coombs flicked his moustache anxiously at the sight of the tin.

"I sterilised it thoroughly," Dr Deáth said with a grin of amusement. "And if rats can read, this tin will certainly fox them. Clara?"

"Thank you, but not right now," Clara refused politely.

"Suit yourselves, it really is fine," Dr Deáth returned the tin to the cupboard. "Now, you want to know about the stabbing?"

"We don't yet know who the woman is," Park-Coombs elaborated. "No one has come forward to say a relative or friend is missing, and the woman did not have anything on her that suggested a name. Have you found out anything more about her?"

The coroner settled back against a sideboard opposite them, displacing a couple of his collectibles, and began to speak.

"Let's begin with the obvious. She was aged between thirty and forty, of average build and well fed. Her teeth were badly stained with nicotine and she had lost two at the front. There was evidence of old bruises on her arms, but I'm not sure what that would imply. It didn't happen when she was stabbed, they were older than that and had faded. Possibly someone had held her hard, but it might also have been the result of a fall. The bruises were too faint to be clear on what had caused them.

"Aside from that, the only sign of violence on her was the knife wound to her belly. It was a deep stroke that perforated the intestines. Even if she had not bled to death, there is a good chance she would not have survived. Once the intestines are pierced the body is exposed to all sorts of nasty things, and you can guarantee peritonitis."

Clara winced at the description, in sympathy with the woman.

"How long would it have taken for her to die?" She asked.

"A main artery had been nicked, I doubt it was long. Maybe a few minutes?" Dr Deáth answered. "There is no exactness to it, but she would have been unconscious very quickly. Interestingly, if the knife had not been removed, she might have lasted longer, the blade acting as a sort of plug. Once the blade was withdrawn, she really had no hope."

"Would she have been able to fight with her attacker after she was stabbed?" Clara continued.

Dr Deáth considered before he answered.

"Nothing is certain in these situations, people do remarkable things. But shock from the blow and the pain, not to mention the fast loss of blood would have made any lengthy struggle impossible. My guess would be she collapsed pretty quickly."

Clara cast a look at the inspector, but he ignored her.

"What can you tell us about her lifestyle?" Park-Coombs asked. "Anything to suggest who she was would be useful."

Dr Deáth munched on one of the biscuits from the rat poison tin.

"Going by my observations, I would say the woman had been a frequent victim of violence. There were marks and cuts that suggested old wounds that had healed, and I noticed a slight peculiarity with one eye that I thought might have been caused by a severe blow to the head. Of course, she might have been in a road accident or something else to explain it.

"As I said, her teeth were stained and she had lost a few. There was no scent of alcohol about the body and the liver looked healthy. The lungs, however, were blackened and slick with a sort of yellow sludge I would find it difficult to describe. There was obvious evidence for Tuberculosis, and I would say it was quite progressed, though not to the point where she was losing weight as a consequence. I would give a cautious prognosis of another five years or so before the disease concluded its deadly task, were I a doctor of the living."

Dr Deáth finished his biscuit.

"There were also clear signs of venereal disease, sorry to be graphic Clara, but I know you don't get upset by such talk."

"You know it takes more than medical terms to shock me," Clara assured him. "I assume you are saying the woman was a prostitute?"

"I am, though I can't rule out that the condition might have been given to her via a legitimate lover. She had no wedding ring, so did not appear to be married. But she might have been living with someone," Dr Deáth became thoughtful. "She had not been with a man that night, of that I am certain, but it would not surprise me if she was a good-time girl. Her hands were not those of someone who had done a lot of hard labour with them, like a servant or fisher-girl. She didn't look like a shop girl, which leaves me wondering how she made a living, being unmarried, as I said."

"This is not getting us closer to working out who she is," Inspector Park-Coombs looked glum. "You have just described a number of women around Brighton, in very similar circumstances."

"Oh, there was one thing," Dr Deáth looked pleased as he remembered himself. "She had a tattoo on the inside of her thigh. It was the word or name Rose, with a ring of thorns around it."

"Her name?" Park-Coombs frowned. "Why have your own name tattooed on your leg? To help you remember it?"

"What about the knife used to stab her?" Clara asked. "Was it the same as the one in Peterson's back?"

"Ah, yes!" Dr Deáth disappeared from the room.

Clara glanced at the inspector who hefted his shoulders in a shrug. The coroner returned within a few moments holding a blade in his hands.

"Now this is a thing of beauty," he told them with a sigh that expressed his awe at the object in his hands. He was like an art collector purring over an Old Master. "This is an 1855 hunting knife, made to be issued in Indian to officers in the British Army. It is ceremonial rather than functional, though as we have seen it can be quite vicious. This knife is based on similar ones used in the local region for dispatching hunted animals, and I have read about ones made of silver or gold and presented to local maharajahs as a gift. The blade is partially serrated, to enable it to be used for skinning carcasses. It also has an upward curving tip, reminiscent of the Persian scimitar.

"The handle is made of mahogany with insets of ivory.

The blade is finely tempered British steel with the date of manufacture noted on it. Only fifty of these blades were ever made and were given to a select few officers who had been influential in quelling an Indian rebellion in 1855. I saw one of these come on the market a few years back. It sold for fifteen guineas."

"I never knew you to be a connoisseur of knives," Park-Coombs said with just a slight hint of concern for his coroner's sudden fetish.

Dr Deáth was amused.

"You may have noticed I have an array of blades at my disposal for use during my work. I understand the intricacies of knives, their different functions and the way they are made. Not to mention, in my line of work it is helpful to know about different weapons that might be used against a person," the coroner paused. "But this is extraordinary. This is not the sort of knife you see used in street crime. It is an heirloom, a collector's piece. To find this in a man's back simply beggar's belief."

"Why would you use such a costly knife, when you could buy a cheap switchblade," Clara nodded.

"Exactly. This makes me think that the person who was carrying it was doing so for a reason. This is a knife to respect, to mark out a man. They were made for that very reason. Back in 1855, if you saw a British officer with one of these on his belt, you knew he had been involved in some pretty fierce fighting and had helped quell a rebellion," Dr Deáth breathed in through his teeth, making a hissing sound. "Whatever your thoughts on such things, you can't deny that this knife represents power – a power a person is happy to enforce violently."

"Hmm," Clara mused. "It seems to me Inspector, that the knife is going to be the key. Find out how that ended up in Brighton and we might be a step closer to discovering who wielded it and why."

The inspector said nothing, he had cupped his chin in his hands as he looked at the knife.

"Inspector?"

"I was thinking, that's not the sort of knife a working-class lass carries around with her," Park-Coombs said solemnly. "How would she get hold of it? It's not the sort of thing young Private Peterson would have access to either. Which makes me conclude that you are right Clara, someone else was in that alley, someone we have yet to find."

Clara was delighted to hear him say that, it would be a huge relief to Captain O'Harris to know that Peterson was no longer the police's prime suspect.

"You know, a thing like this you would not lose lightly," Dr Deáth turned the blade before his face, letting it catch the light. "I imagine the owner did not intend to leave it in Private Peterson's back. So why did they?"

"Something happened that caused them to run without reclaiming the knife," Park-Coombs surmised. "They could have easily caught up with Peterson and pulled the blade out. Something must have prevented them from doing so."

"Or someone," Clara frowned. "There is definitely something happening in that neighbourhood. Something that has everyone on edge. Peterson was unlucky to find himself tangled up in it all."

The inspector had not taken his eyes off the knife in the coroner's hand. A determined look crept onto his face.

"I wonder how many former British army officers who served in Indian retired to Brighton?" He said.

"Now that," Clara replied to him with a twinkle in her eye, "is just the sort of question I am very good at answering."

Chapter Twelve

"Dr Ralph Finnigan," the aged doctor held out his wizened hand. He could not unfurl his fingers, arthritis had crippled his joints, so Tommy clasped his crooked fist and shook it.

"Tommy Fitzgerald, thank you for speaking to me."

Dr Finnigan motioned for Tommy to take a seat, while his daughter-in-law departed to make them some tea.

"I would normally have refused, but when it comes to old Professor Lynch, I cannot resist," Dr Finnigan sighed. With a shaking arm he lowered the newspaper he was reading to a table before him. He found it difficult to unclasp it from his fingers. "I have become a shadow of myself. My body has withered into this appalling husk. Truth is, I hate people seeing me this way. I hate to think of them feeling sorry for me.

"You know how often I have been into the homes of the sick and dying and expressed my sympathy? I hate to think of it now, knowing how it must have angered those people to hear this young, healthy doctor, who knew none of their real woes, giving his stock response of how sorry he felt for them. What nonsense it was. Had I my time over, I would never say such awful platitudes. People don't want you feeling sorry for them, they just want their doctor to make them better, or at least ease their suffering. I sometimes wonder if there is an irony to all this."

Dr Finnigan lifted his hands and stared at the useless fingers as they clawed in towards his palms.

"I was crippled after the war. I was confined to a wheelchair," Tommy said. "I too despised it when people said how sorry they were for me. As if I did not have enough sense of my situation without someone else going on about how it made them feel bad. I was lucky, I recovered, but I still vividly remember."

"I sensed a kindred spirit in you when you stood at the door," Dr Finnigan grinned. "You didn't have that sad look in your eyes when you saw me, like most do. You didn't look at my sickness, you looked at me. That's why you are sitting opposite me and not out on your ear on the street."

Dr Finnigan chuckled.

"You know, it was my old friend Professor Lynch who said pity was the most merciless cruelty a man could inflict on another, when all it did was make him feel sorry for himself. I made a point of never pitying him, even as his final illness took its toll."

"And you knew about the box?" Tommy said. "It hasn't been made public knowledge as yet, so Professor Lynch told you about it?"

Dr Finnigan chuckled.

"He showed me it. Why, he would stagger from his death bed and make that thing. Piecing it together painstakingly. He told me he was going to have it put aside until twenty years after his death. Well, it has been twenty years, hasn't it?"

"That it has," Tommy nodded. "Did you know what it contained?"

"He never said," Dr Finnigan shook his head. "I don't think I ever really asked, either. I had this impression that it was a secret and it was not something he would talk about. In any case, I was usually busy attending to his needs. Towards the end, Professor Lynch required a vast amount of medicines and treatments to keep him in any sort of comfort."

"What was he dying from?" Tommy asked. "If that is not too blunt to ask."

"Blunt is preferable to me, and I am too old to worry about being sensitive about these things. Illness is not something we should avoid talking about from some false sense of tact and politeness. If we discussed these things more openly, I swear people would get treatment for things sooner and maybe they would survive an otherwise fatal disease. I may be optimistic with that, but how often did I see a patient whose symptoms indicated he had been ailing for months, but who had been too abashed to talk about his condition and had suffered in silence? Then, when he finally concluded he could suffer no more, he came to me and discovered he had left things too late," Dr Finnigan sighed. "Being a doctor is not an easy profession. Not if you care about people. Not if your patients are also friends."

Tommy had been nodding along to indicate his understanding. The doctor came to a pause and Tommy wondered if he needed to repeat his question, but Finnigan had not forgotten.

"Professor Lynch suffered from a digestive disorder most of his life," the doctor explained. "It was not immediately life-threatening, but caused him a good deal of discomfort and embarrassment. He suffered terrible pains and all sorts of inconveniences caused by his body's inability to process food. I suspected that some types of food were a trigger, but it was very difficult to narrow them down. I did end up devising a special diet for him, which alleviated some of the symptoms, but outside factors could start a relapse. I believed stress would trigger an episode, but at times he would have a flare-up and neither of us could determine what had been the spark. I was always impressed at how cheerful he remained, considering how debilitating the condition could be at times. He could spend weeks only going from his rooms at the Institute, to the lecture hall and back. He dreaded going further afield due to not knowing where a suitable bathroom might be found, and also from the general fatigue the chronic pain and nausea caused him.

"In the hotter summer months, dehydration presented a very real danger. Have you ever seen a man die of dysentery?"

"Unfortunately," Tommy grimaced. "During the war we saw quite a few cases. At times we seemed to have more men on the casualty list from dysentery than anything caused by enemy action."

"Then you can well understand how a man can fast deteriorate when his body is absorbing neither food nor water. I worried greatly about Lynch at times. At bad times he would drop considerable amounts of weight and be so weak as to barely be able to walk down the stairs."

"Yet, he kept his condition secret from everyone at the Institute?" Tommy asked in amazement.

"As I said, people are too shy when it comes to discussing sickness, especially the sort of sickness Professor Lynch was suffering. I dare say he felt ashamed of his body. He told me once that sometimes he felt dirty and feared he smelt. He would take a bath three times a day to try and erase that feeling."

"Poor man," Tommy tutted sadly.

"He was very good at masking it all. He gave the impression of being a recluse, so people would not question why he was always so keen to go back to his rooms," Dr Finnigan explained. "I don't think he ever told a soul. I was his only confidant on the matter."

"That seems somewhat sad, that he suffered so alone."

"Maybe he preferred people not to feel sympathy for him," Dr Finnigan suggested. "As I now know, pity can be wearying, it can make your ailments feel all the worse when someone else feels sorry for you. In any case, there were times when Professor Lynch was relatively healthy and could lead a normal life, for the most part. He lived for those times."

"Then his condition worsened?" Tommy guessed.

"I suppose the constant strain of sickness began to wear his body down. In his last four years the disease never seemed to leave him, there were no more periods of respite. I began to think it had turned cancerous. I had read a lot of literature on the topic in my efforts to help Professor Lynch, and I had come across a reference more than once that such serious bowel conditions could eventually turn into cancer. I had no means of proving my theory, however, only my observations," Dr Finnigan paused, his mind wandering back twenty years. "If another patient, with no prior history of bowel complaints, presented with Professor Lynch's symptoms and over such a period of time, I would have diagnosed a cancer of the digestive system. I did not immediately think of this when Lynch was ill, because of his prior history. However, as the time dragged on, I came to the conclusion that it had to be that, as he was not able to recover. He had always recovered before, therefore something must have changed to prevent him recovering this time.

"I tried so many different things. Digestive powders, pain relief, a simplified diet of chicken and potatoes, followed by a different diet of fish and oats when the first did not work. I tried purges and emetics, in case we could flush the sickness from him, as awful as I felt about doing so. But you become desperate. We dabbled with laudanum, which in most people has the side-effect of making them constipated, to no effect in Professor Lynch. I even began to go for folk remedies, had him eat dried, powdered clay as a binding agent, or concoctions of herbs. Simply nothing worked. He continued to fade away before my eyes, each day a little weaker, a little thinner, yet still with a warm smile on his face and an optimism to his voice I cannot describe. Sometimes, I wanted to sob at how bravely he bore it all."

Dr Finnigan fell silent and his aged eyes had, indeed, become wet with tears.

"I wonder where that tea is?" He said gruffly, trying to brush off his obvious upset.

"My next question is not easy to ask," Tommy admitted as gently as he could. "Did Professor Lynch's illness cause him to become mentally disturbed?"

"Mentally disturbed?"

"I mean, did he show signs of senility?"

"No," Dr Finnigan was aghast at the idea. "Who has suggested otherwise? Professor Lynch was as alert the day he died as he had been all his life. In fact, hours before he passed, we discussed a recent meteor shower that had fallen through the sky. Lynch had managed to observe it from his bed, peering out of the window with a small telescope."

"It is because of the box," Tommy said, seeing that he had disgruntled the doctor. "The contents, or rather the supposed contents, have caused quite a stir in the Institute. You see, when Professor Lynch left the box, he also left instructions stating that within it were contained various astrological prophecies concerning the future of the nation and a means for protecting England's future. It's all rather vague, but it has caused a rift at the Institute, between those who are inclined to think Professor Lynch had a knack for astrology and those who cannot believe a student of astronomy would dabble in such things."

Dr Finnigan listened intently, a frown forming on his face.

"I was aware of Professor Lynch's interest in astrology. We discussed it from time to time. I believe the charts he made gave him hope for the future. He did not believe in God, you see, but his illness made him desperate to see some sort of pattern in the way the world worked. I don't know, call it fate or call it delusion, but he wanted there to be a reason, a logic, for what was happening to him. He couldn't bear the thought that it was all for nothing, that it was a purely random fluke of existence that had caused him to be ill," Dr Finnigan glanced at his clawed hands. "People need to see there is a reason for things, it makes them feel better. Sometimes I find myself thinking, the reason I became this shell was to better understand my patients and to share that understanding with my son. He is also a doctor. You see, I have fallen under the same spell. I want to believe that everything happens for a reason."

"And that was why Professor Lynch made and studied astrology charts?"

"Yes. It was a hobby at first, then in his final days it became his comfort. He read into the charts what he wanted. I would go see him and he would declare that his latest chart indicated he had a long life ahead of him and that made him sure my next remedy would work."

"Then the box of prophecies, was created not for some joke, or because of senility, but out of this genuine belief that astrology charts could predict the future?"

Dr Finnigan shrugged.

"I don't know. Professor Lynch never discussed the matter with me, I just know how he felt about the charts he showed me. He wanted to cast my horoscope, but I wouldn't let him. I didn't like the idea of having hints concerning my future. Imagine if my horoscope had informed me of this?" Dr Finnigan lifted his almost useless hand and shook his head. "Some things are best not known. Why is this all being worried about now, anyway?"

"Professor Lynch left some very peculiar instructions about the box only being opened in the presence of the king and several bishops. There are those at the Institute who want to follow his wishes, and those who think doing so will irreversibly damage the academic reputation of the Institute," Tommy elaborated. "Among those who want the box dismissed, the hope is that it might be proved Professor Lynch was mad in his final days, and thus the box was a product of his madness."

"Well, I can assure them that was not the case," Dr Finnigan said stoutly. "I don't know what purpose Professor Lynch was serving with that box, but he created it while in full control of his faculties, and I would say as much to anyone who needs to know. Twenty years have not dimmed my memory. I can picture him on his final day. I saw him just a couple of hours before he passed. He wanted to discuss his telescope. He said the calibration was off and someone needed to check it. That was the concern on his mind. He said he had had trouble getting it to focus on the moon the previous night, let alone on more distant stars. I said nothing, but I believe his eyesight was failing him in those last hours. It was his body shutting down."

Dr Finnigan suddenly sat upright in his chair and shook his fist at Tommy in a fierce fashion.

"But he was not mad! How dare they insinuate that!"

"They are afraid, if people learn that Professor Lynch dabbled in astrology, it will destroy his academic reputation," Tommy replied, trying to be careful with what he said and not make the doctor angrier.

"Bah!" Dr Finnigan growled, his voice rising. "They don't care a jot for his reputation! It's all about them! It always has been!"

Tommy didn't know what to say to calm the aging doctor, who was now clearly upset. Luckily, at that precise moment, Mrs Finnigan arrived with the tea tray.

"What are you two talking about? You look grimmer than a tiger in the zoo!" She put the tea tray down with a firm clunk. "Whatever it is, I want you to talk no more over it. Have some tea and cheer up."

Tommy decided she was right. Talking further on the subject of Professor Lynch's sanity was not going to change Dr Finnigan's mind, nor his opinion. He gave an apologetic smile to the old doctor, who just glowered, but then he took a cup of tea and starting talking about the weather.

They were able to finish the conversation on mundane topics and everyone relaxed. Tommy left with a better understanding of Professor Lynch's last days. Somehow, he didn't think that was going to cheer Clara, however.

Chapter Thirteen

Colonel Brandt was always happy to help Clara. He had served in the army and retired before the Great War. He had always felt a slight pang of regret that he had been deemed too old to play his part in that conflict. Brandt was a bachelor, who had dedicated his life to serving his country and now felt rather lost and forgotten. His friendship with Clara broke up his otherwise unchanging routine of going from his house to his club and back again.

Clara found him at home that day, as he was suffering from an episode of gout that was making him feel most morose. He brightened when she appeared and joined him in his sitting room, which overlooked the garden and was warm with the autumn sunshine.

"The year is on the turn again," Brandt remarked as he pointed out a chair for Clara to take. "I always feel rather down at this time of year, like so much is concluding."

"Yet, there is a whole new season about to begin," Clara reminded him. "And while some things stop, other things come into action. The leaves fall, but the bushes burst into berry, and while the swallows leave, so other birds arrive. It is not things ending, it is things changing."

"You are always so bright about these things," Colonel

Brandt smiled at her. "I think too hard, I fear, and this damn leg is making me sour."

"Your housekeeper told me about the gout," Clara said. "You should have sent word, I would have come over sooner."

"Don't be silly, you have a life to lead and I am perfectly all right here. I am looked after," Brandt sighed. "It was my own fault, anyway. My doctor warned me that strawberries would trigger it off, he said he had seen it before. Gout isn't always caused by cheese and port, as we all used to think. No, it can be caused by fruit and vegetables too. And I am such a glutton for strawberries."

Colonel Brandt hefted his shoulders, as if to say – what can you do?

"No more of Annie's famous strawberry jam?" Clara teased.

"Don't you dare!" Brandt pointed a finger at her. "That's a court martial offence, madam!"

Clara laughed at his mock fierce look.

"Probably strawberry jam doesn't count anyway," she said.

"I should cocoa!" Brandt chuckled. "Now, did you come over to depress me about my jam privileges or are you on a case?"

"You know me too well," Clara's eyes twinkled. "Though, I do try to come to see you as a friend, and not just on business."

"But it is the middle of a weekday morning," Brandt pointed out. "That constitutes working hours for you."

"Fair point," Clara observed. "I was hoping you could give me some military advice, you have the contacts, after all."

"Ah, and in what capacity would you need it?"

"Ever heard of an Indian hunting knife made in 1855 for British Army officers who helped quell a rebellion in the country that year? It was a ceremonial thing, rather than practical."

"I have heard of it," Brandt nodded. "Actually, I knew a

fellow who had earned one. He was one of the youngest officers to receive a blade and he was just reaching retirement as I was entering the service. He was a colonel by then and he was a real old hard-nails who we all tried to avoid. He used to keep the knife on a stand on his desk. If you got called into his office for some misdemeanour, he would grab it up and point it at you. Vicious blade on that thing. I guess he is long dead now."

"Such a knife has been used to commit a crime in Brighton, and I am hoping to track down who it belongs to."

Colonel Brandt frowned.

"How odd! They were the sort of item people treasured. Not many were made, and they marked out those men who stood up to the rebellion," Brandt's eyes drifted to the garden outside his window. "There were many ups and downs in India in those days, still a few now with all these rumblings of the country wanting its independence. I'm not saying there wasn't bad business on our side, I've seen some things in my time that made me ashamed to be British, but that does not give a fellow the right to go after British women and children who have done him no harm.

"The 1855 uprising was a small one, in comparison to others, that took place in one province where a number of British families had settled, mainly army families. I heard it was a bloody affair and some real savagery took place. Women raped and children butchered. It was nasty, and the retaliation was even nastier. That's why the officers were given those knives, because the government was grateful they had stopped the situation spreading. Could have been really awful if it had. It was awful enough as it was. That sort of thing you have to be a tough fellow to survive and live with the consequences."

"Considering the time that has passed since that event, the person who used this knife is mostly likely a grandson of the officer who received it. Unless, of course, it somehow found its way into a pawnshop and was bought by a random individual," Clara said.

"Anything is possible," Colonel Brandt agreed. "But those blades are worth a lot today. A clever pawnbroker would likely realise the value of such a rare item. I doubt they would let it go cheaply to a street thug, not unless they were utterly stupid."

"As you say, anything is possible," Clara said, suddenly beginning to doubt her lead. "I am curious if any of the officers who participated in breaking the 1855 uprising settled in Brighton when they retired, or had family here. Might you be able to find out?"

Brandt nodded.

"I certainly could try, I do have contacts in various regimental societies who could help me. What was the nature of the crime, dare I ask?"

"A woman was stabbed," Clara said. "She died, and another man was stabbed in the back. Unfortunately, he cannot remember what happened. However, the knife was most certainly not his and it would be a very odd thing for a woman to be carrying."

"Odd for anyone to carry unless they meant to use it," Brandt added. "It is not a knife that is easy to conceal or which you would use like a pocketknife. I shall investigate and see what I can find out."

"That would be much appreciated. Now, I assume you are coming to Sunday dinner this week? All being well with the leg?"

"It will be well!" Colonel Brandt said stoutly. "Nothing shall keep me from Annie's best roast beef!"

After leaving Colonel Brandt, Clara made her way back to the scene of the crime. Once again, she noticed the unsettling emptiness of the alleyways in the area, it was as if people were afraid to use them. But why? Clara came to the spot where the woman had died and stared at the dark brown stains on the ground and wall where her body had slumped. She pursed her lips and frowned.

"Hey! Who are you?"

The stern voice came from her left and Clara glanced up. The man approaching her was in his early twenties, wearing a green-brown jacket and a bowler hat. He had the worst teeth Clara had seen in a mouth for some time and he was looking aggressive as he approached her. Rather than being concerned, Clara was delighted that at last someone was interested in talking to her, even if it was to threaten her.

"Good afternoon," she said, the time having just ticked past noon. She did not give her name. "Are you aware a woman died here?"

"What of it?" The man barked at her. "You are not supposed to be here!"

Clara frowned at him.

"How do you mean? This is a public right of way."

"You are not meant to be here, no one is!" The man loomed over Clara, trying to threaten her with his bulk.

Clara was far from deterred.

"Look here, I am from the council. We were informed that an incident occurred in one of our public rights of way. We manage these alleys as we do the roads, and it is our responsibility to ensure they are not obstructed or unavailable for public use," Clara said quickly. "Now I want to know who has told you this area is not open to the public, because it was certainly not the council. I have been sent here to see that the alley is still fully accessible. Who is spreading these lies that this alley is not for public use?"

"Listen lady, I don't care who sent you, you don't move on at once I'll be slamming my fist into your face," the man leaned further over her; he was a lot bigger than Clara.

Clara narrowed her eyes, she was scared, no doubt about that, but she was also stubborn.

"Then I shall be forced to instruct the council to close this alley and the ones surrounding it as they are a public health hazard. They will place barriers across the ends and then have the whole neighbourhood thoroughly inspected, and I have a feeling that would upset whoever you are

101

working for a great deal," Clara lifted her chin and sized up the thug. She was certain he was just a messenger boy. "How much would it mess up your business if you couldn't use these alleys, huh?"

"I'll beat you black and blue!" The thug persisted, but there was a flicker of uncertainty in his eyes and Clara was going to jump on that. He wasn't very bright, after all, and she could see he was worried he might be making matters worse.

"Not just a public health hazard," Clara continued. "I shall inform my superiors that the area is prone to flooding and needs to be dug up at once and new drainage installed. Such work could take, oh, I don't know, months, and there is a backlog on tasks, so it could be a good year before anything begins. In the meantime, measures will be taken to prevent anyone using this alley and permanently sealing it."

The thug rocked back as he started to process this information.

"I could kill you!" He snapped as one last volley.

"And how would that help?" Clara asked him sarcastically.

The thug didn't seem used to being confronted and he had run out of arguments. He still loomed over Clara and had his hands balled into fists, but he wasn't sure what to say.

"I see," Clara said. "I think you ought to tell whoever it is who employs you that people are taking note. Murdering that woman was a very bad idea if you wanted to keep a low profile."

"They caught the murderer," the thug snarled.

"The police know he could not have done it," Clara laughed. "Only a simpleton would imagine he was responsible."

"There were no witnesses," the thug growled, caught up in Clara's game now. He had not even realised he had just admitted that he knew a good deal more about the murder than an innocent person should. "No one saw anything."

"You don't need witnesses to unravel a crime," Clara told him calmly. "Anyway, that is the police's business, I am just here to make a report for the council."

Clara produced a notebook from her handbag and made a pretence of writing something down.

"Does no one ever use this alley?" She looked about her as if she had just noticed how quiet everything was. "Hmm, if that is the case, the council may consider acquiring the space for some other purpose. This is a very wide alley, after all, big enough for a cart to go down. We could use that space to significantly extend the household yards."

"What are you saying? You'll take away the alley?" The thug was looking worried, which told Clara all she needed.

"Honestly, it is too big. If it was being used more productively we could overlook that issue, but as it is so clearly ignored by the residents I think the wasted space could be repurposed. In fact, we could dispose of this alley altogether and interlink the gardens for the purposes of getting dustbins out. That would also resolve the public right of way issue you were complaining about."

The thug's eyes widened.

"What complaint?" He asked in alarm.

"The one you just made about people wandering through this alley, I assume you are concerned about crime? In recent years there has been a suggestion that these alleyways encourage illegal activities and the council is considering removing the majority of them. Your complaint further indicates this is a significant issue," Clara continued to pretend to make notes.

"I made no complaint!" The thug shouted.

"Do not worry, it will be taken in complete confidence. You inform your boss we are listening to the concerns of our residents."

"Look here, don't go telling the council anything!" The thug grabbed Clara's arm and his fingers dug in.

"I think you better let me go," Clara told him coldly and with the voice she used to use on difficult patients in the hospital. Tommy described it as her schoolteacher voice. "I think you better let me go right now, don't you?"

There was something in that tone, it suggested an awful lot of nastiness could follow if things did not go Clara's way. It usually reached deep down into a fellow and found his inner schoolboy.

The thug slowly released her.

"I have seen enough," Clara told him, her tone stern. "And trust me, you have provided me with all I need to know. Good day!"

She stormed off, her legs feeling a little shaky as she departed the alley. She didn't look back. She didn't dare.

Chapter Fourteen

Clara went straight to the police station and found
Inspector Park-Coombs. Her initial bravado was wearing
off and she was now feeling very shaken and a little unwell.
It was only once she was safely out of harm's way that it
had occurred to her how much trouble she could have been
in had the thug not reacted to her words and her aura of
authority. He could have killed her, he certainly could have
harmed her a good deal, and there was not much she could
have done about it. Clara was not someone to be cowed
easily, but she was disturbed that she had narrowly avoided
a great deal of trouble.

She asked the desk sergeant for the inspector. A few
months ago that would have been an ordeal in itself, but
the old desk sergeant had been replaced by a younger
constable. It had first been temporary, but the removal had
so dented the former desk sergeant's ego that he had
decided to leave the force rather than face the barbs of his
colleagues over his behaviour – he had managed to offend
a very senior police officer and nearly landed them all in a
lot of hot water.

The desk sergeant noticed Clara's demeanour was not

her usual confident self.

"Are you all right Miss Fitzgerald?"

"Just had a bit of a scare, that's all," Clara said. "I would like to discuss it with the Inspector, it's very important."

The desk sergeant used the telephone behind him to let the inspector know she was there. The police station had both an internal telephone system and an external one for use by the general public to summon them. Not that most people had access to a phone, unless it was in a public place, but it was useful for the areas further away from the town where a constable was not readily to be found at the drop of a hat.

"I'll make you a cup of tea," the desk sergeant told Clara after he had passed on her message. "Why don't you come sit in the back office, rather than out here."

Clara was grateful for his sympathy and to be allowed to move from the waiting area of the police station into the larger, open room at the back, where the various ranks of police had desks and tables to use for writing up the endless reports they always seemed to be doing. There was also a large rank of wooden filing cabinets.

"Hello Clara," Brighton's sole female police officer, Sarah Butler, greeted Clara warmly. "You look pale."

"It's been a difficult day," Clara sighed.

The desk sergeant made sure Clara had a chair and then went to make the tea. Sarah drifted over.

"Someone upset you?" She asked in her gentle Scottish patter.

"I was in the alley where that woman was murdered and I was accosted by a man," Clara explained. "He was very threatening and clearly did not want me to be there."

"Did he hurt you?"

Clara touched at her arm where the thug had gripped her.

"Not really. I was scared more than anything."

"This is a bad business," Sarah said with a worried look on her face. "The Inspector has me going through the files concerning that neighbourhood, it is noticeable that in the last couple of years the reports of incidents in the area have tailed off. At first that might seem a good thing, but in their place, we have reports of disappearances."

"Disappearances?"

"It took me a while to see the pattern," Sarah explained. "But nearly every one of the former troublemakers from that area have vanished at some point. They have been reported missing by family members and never shown up. It is like someone got rid of them."

"That is very odd," Clara agreed. "Either we have a remarkable vigilante on our hands, or someone is up to something and they don't want the police accidentally stumbling across it because of a lowlife drunk or drug addict causing trouble. They get rid of them, clear the scene. For what?"

"It all adds up to something very strange," Sarah agreed. "I'm still going through the reports, and I am going to send out a notice to other police stations to see if any of these people have appeared in their territory. I think someone may have scared them away."

"They must be damn scary," Clara observed.

Sarah raised her eyebrows.

"You tell me, Clara."

At that moment, Inspector Park-Coombs appeared in the room. He saw Clara sitting down and a frown formed on his face.

"Has something happened?"

"Nothing I won't recover from," Clara promised him. "I have had a rather unpleasant encounter with a thug who attempted to threaten me. I was in the alley where Peterson and that woman were stabbed."

"The murder alley," Park-Coombs understood. "Why was this fellow threatening you?"

"He didn't want me there. I was only looking around, trying to get a better feel for the place. I had barely been there a moment before he came up to me and demanded I leave, and then made threats of violence when I refused."

"You should have just left Clara," Park-Coombs told

her, his frown deepening.

"No one tells me what to do, Inspector," Clara said stoutly.

"Would you recognise this man if you saw him again?" The Inspector asked.

"Absolutely!" Clara declared. "I would have no difficulty picking him out."

Park-Coombs turned to Sarah.

"Can you get the photograph album of known Brighton criminals? We'll have Clara take a look through it."

The desk sergeant arrived back just then with a cup of tea for Clara. He nodded in passing to the inspector and returned to his post.

"I don't like hearing you have had trouble," Park-Coombs leaned back on a nearby desk.

"It is part of the job," Clara shrugged. "Had I thought I would be so accosted, I would not have gone to the alley alone."

"Yes, you would have," Park-Coombs smiled at her. "Clara Fitzgerald does not back down from bullies, and she does not like feeling beholden to a man for protection."

"She does not like feeling scared, either," Clara remarked. "But that is beside the point now. There is definitely something occurring in that alley, something that great efforts are being taken to protect and keep secret. I believe those alleys are being used as trackways for some purpose, and that is why people are not being allowed in them. They have to be kept clear to avoid disrupting whatever business these people are about and to prevent people witnessing it. Any thoughts on what that might be?"

"A few," Park-Coombs said. "Drugs naturally springs to mind, but that would not require the alleyways to be kept empty."

"I would like to know who the murdered woman was and why she died. I think that could be the key, along with discovering where the knife came from," Clara mused. "I was intending to visit Brighton's tattoo parlours to see if anyone recalled doing that tattoo on the woman's leg. It looked a professional job, not something done roughly at home."

"There was a certain artistry to it," Park-Coombs rubbed his chin thoughtfully. "I'm not keen on tattoos, but I've seen enough in my time to say that one was created by someone with a flair for it. But it could have been done years ago."

"Maybe," Clara shrugged. "What else do we have to go on?"

"I'm going to have my lot canvas among the local prostitutes, see if anyone is missing. The girls aren't keen on the police, but they are even less fond of one of their number being murdered. Any time a good-time girl gets stabbed, their friends start worrying about Jack the Ripper being in town," Park-Coombs explained. "We'll try all we can to identify her."

"What about putting a photograph, or maybe a drawing of her in the paper?" Clara suggested. "Someone might recognise her."

"Not a bad idea," Park-Coombs smiled. "I'll see what our resident sketch artist can come up with, PC Hobbs has a talent for drawing we exploit heavily."

Sarah returned with the photo album and handed it to Clara.

"Sir," she said to the inspector, "considering the seriousness of what happened today, might it be advisable for Clara to continue her investigations with the presence of a police constable at her side?"

Clara flicked her eyes up from the album, unsure about all this.

"A joint operation between ourselves and Clara?" Park-Coombs mulled over the idea. "That is not a bad thought. Clara, what do you say? We have a mutual goal in mind and clearly there is a lot of danger surrounding this matter. I would prefer if you had an official presence with you when you start investigating deeper."

"I usually find that people who won't speak to the police,

will speak to me," Clara said carefully. "I'm not sure a police constable constantly with me will make my job easier."

"It will make you safer, however," Park-Coombs pointed out. "And these people who are running this affair are not the sort to talk to anyone, whether they are civilian or police."

Clara was still hesitant. She cooperated with the police, as it suited them both to share information and to be on the same side, but she liked her independence.

"I have Tommy and O'Harris," Clara pointed out.

"O'Harris is too biased in this matter, I don't want him involved in any investigation," Park-Coombs swiftly said. "It's in his own best interest if he does not interfere. There is still a fair chance Peterson will end up being tried for this crime and if a prosecution counsel learned that evidence collected for the case was done so with the involvement of Captain O'Harris, who naturally has a vested interest in seeing Peterson acquitted, then we shall have a lot of problems. It could destroy any defence case you put together."

Clara could understand that. She wasn't sure O'Harris would, but she did see that keeping him at arms' length from the investigation was in everyone's best interest.

"I still have Tommy," Clara insisted.

"And you will need him to be working independently on this case if you want to find all the information you can," Park-Coombs reminded her. "No, you need someone whose sole purpose is to watch your back."

Clara wasn't convinced, but she could also see she was not going to get away with refusing the inspector's suggestion.

"I would like to volunteer," Sarah spoke up. "I recently completely the woman police constable's self-defence course with flying colours."

"I believe the exact words of your instructor were 'heaven help the criminal who gets in the way of PC Butler's truncheon,'" Park-Coombs said. "But in this regard that is probably a fine thing. Will you accept PC

Butler as your assistant in this matter, Clara?"

Clara knew she had no choice.

"Do I get to use a truncheon while I am working with PC Butler?" She asked.

"No," Park-Coombs told her firmly.

"Pity, well then, I guess you best be my temporary assistant Sarah, seeing as I shall need someone to batter the odd thug or two," Clara replied.

"I shall be delighted to work with you," Sarah beamed. "And any of them wee blighters threatens you again, I shall give them a Glasgow kiss to remember me by."

"That was not on the self-defence course," Park-Coombs said hastily.

"Aye, but I grew up in a fishing village where you learned to fight with boys sooner than you learned your letters," Sarah grinned. "Clara won't come to any harm while I am around."

Clara was amused, she also felt a bit better knowing she would have someone keeping an eye on her. She had been flicking casually through the photo album, glancing at the criminals inside. Most were simply not brawny enough to be the thug who threatened her, though she did make the effort to look at all their faces. She suddenly came to a photograph and paused, tapping her finger on the edge of the picture. Inspector Park-Coombs noticed.

"Is that the man who attacked you?" He asked.

"No," Clara peered at the picture harder. "This is the man who introduced himself as Robert and who helped Private Peterson. At least I think it is. He looks a lot younger here."

Park-Coombs took the album off her and removed the photograph she had identified from the paper tabs holding it in place. He turned it over.

"This picture was taken in 1911," he said. "If it is the same man, he will be a decade older. Fellow's name is Robert Hartley and this is interesting."

"What is?" Clara asked keenly.

"The note on the back says we picked him up because

he was a member of the Seashore Boys, a gang who were a real nuisance at the turn of the century, always causing mischief. They had a knack for stealing off pleasure yachts coming down for the season. They were more active in Hove than here," Park-Coombs examined the photo again. "They would sneak aboard yachts when they were anchored off the coast and shakedown the occupants for their valuables. They were cunning, but we caught up with them eventually.

"Robert Hartley was one of their fences. Used to take the goods and sell them on in London. He got ten years in prison, which we felt was rather lenient, but he was treated as an accessory rather than one of the main players."

"And now Robert is living in a neighbourhood where a new gang is ruling the roost, or so it would appear?" Clara pondered. "Maybe that is why he was the only one prepared to slip out and help Peterson. He may even have contacts with this new gang. What happened to the rest of the Seashore Boys?"

"The main ringleaders got thirty years apiece, the rest of the members – we picked up a dozen in total – are doing a variety of sentences, most of them ten to fifteen years, so some will be out now like Robert. Though, so far, I've not picked any up in connection with any criminal trouble in the town. They may be keeping their heads down, but it won't last, it never does with these folk."

"I think I need to talk to Robert again and see what he really knows about this mess," Clara said. "He seems one of the few people not afraid to defy whoever is behind this mystery."

"Robert was a tough blighter," Park-Coombs nodded. "Never killed anyone, but hard-as-nails. If anyone is prepared to take no-nonsense from this gang, it will be him. But you have to be careful Clara, he may be working with them."

"That's all right Inspector," Clara smiled. "I have Sarah to watch over me."

Chapter Fifteen

Clara returned home, feeling she needed to take a little time to regroup before she returned to the alleyways and spoke to Robert Hartley. She found Tommy in the front parlour, which she was pleased about as she also wanted to learn what he had discovered concerning Professor Lynch.

"Did you find Dr Finnigan?" She asked him.

Tommy looked up from the newspaper he was reading.

"I did," he smiled. "He was very helpful and talked to me for some time, but the news won't please Professor Montgomery."

"Dr Finnigan did not consider Professor Lynch to be suffering from senility or madness, then?"

"He said he was as sharp as a knife right to the end," Tommy paused, an aura of sadness coming over him. "Professor Lynch suffered from a serious health complaint for much of his life. It was incurable and led to him being a virtual prisoner at the Institute. He managed, for the most part, to continue his duties and he told no one of his sickness. Ultimately, it worsened and took his life. My opinion, an opinion I think Dr Finnigan shares, is that Professor Lynch needed to find some comfort during his troubled existence, and that came through his astrology. It gave him a sense that there was more to this life, some sort of order and reason that he could not see. Cold science could not help him in the end, so he turned to the stars."

Clara understood such a need, during her time as a volunteer nurse she had seen many people trying to seek a logic, a reason for their illness or injury. Some sought God, others talked of fate, serendipity or similar vague and distant ideas. Why should Professor Lynch be any different? Had he found the Church in his last years, none of his colleagues would have blinked an eye.

"Did Dr Finnigan know what might be in the box?" She asked.

"No," Tommy replied. "He saw it, but he was never shown the contents. He felt it was a secret."

Clara sat down in a chair opposite Tommy.

"Which leaves me unsure how to proceed," she said. "How can I discover what is in that box without opening it?"

"What if you did open it?" Tommy said.

Clara frowned.

"That is the last think Professor Montgomery wants. He doesn't want this to become public knowledge, which it would do if the Institute was to ask the King to attend such a ceremony."

"That isn't quite what I meant," Tommy had a sly look in his eye. "What if you were to get hold of the box yourself and open the contents?"

A smile crept onto Clara's face.

"Steal it you mean?"

"It would not be stealing if you had the permission of Professor Montgomery. He is the Director of the Institute and ultimately responsible for all the property within. If he gave you permission, it would not be illegal, just an insult to some of his colleagues."

"I like that idea," Clara agreed. "I have visions of us prowling about the darkened corridors of the Institute with torches. How exciting."

"Well, you always enjoy going to places you are not

meant to be," Tommy teased her.

Clara pulled a face, then laughed.

"First things first, I'll need to see Professor Montgomery again."

Clara glanced at the time and was thinking about whether she could reach the Institute before they closed for the day, when the doorbell rang. Tommy rose to answer it.

"O'Harris," his voice carried through from the hallway. "You look worried."

Clara was on her feet and heading for the front door at once. In the hallway she spied O'Harris and saw exactly what Tommy meant. His face was ashen, and he looked as though he had not slept a lot recently, worse, his expression seemed to suggest the world was coming to an end, or at least his world.

"I had to come see you both," he said. "Private Peterson has confessed to the murder of that woman."

"You need to come in and sit down," Clara took his hand and led him through to the parlour. "Tommy, can you ask Annie to make some of her special 'consolation' tea?"

Tommy disappeared to the kitchen. Clara showed O'Harris to the sofa in the parlour and then sat beside him and clutched his hand.

"Why would he confess?" She asked him.

"I don't know," O'Harris looked bleak. "He refuses to talk to me."

"This has just happened?" Clara said. "I was only at the police station a short while ago and the Inspector mentioned nothing of this."

"He probably didn't know. Peterson wrote out his confession and handed it to the constable who has been assigned to watch over him. The constable had it send to the Inspector, who telephoned me a few minutes ago. I drove over here as soon as I heard, I just don't know what to do Clara," Captain O'Harris quivered with anguish as he contemplated the end of everything he had worked for. "I keep thinking of the enormity of it all and it scares me. Peterson will either hang or spend his life in a lunatic asylum for criminals. I have failed him, I have failed his family who beseeched me to help him. With that failure, so comes the end of my convalescence home, so ends the future hopes of the men I was aiding. I have failed everyone. Who will dare set up a similar project after this? It could be years before help is once again offered to these men and many don't have that sort of time."

O'Harris' hand clasped tightly to Clara's. She rested her other hand on his hunched shoulders and rubbed them gently.

"This is not over, not yet. I do not believe Peterson killed that woman. Events today have made me certain of that."

"Events? What has happened?" A flicker of hope came into O'Harris' eyes, enough to make Clara wish she had not said anything, she was still far from resolving this case.

"It is not something to worry about…" she began.

"Clara, what happened?" O'Harris insisted. "You have to tell me."

Clara sighed.

"I was threatened by a thug in the alley where the woman died. He seemed very concerned I should not be looking at the scene of the crime."

"You were threatened, are you all right?" O'Harris instantly became concerned.

"I am absolutely fine, but there is something going on in that neighbourhood and I think that was the reason why that woman died. I am also certain she did not die at the hands of Peterson."

"I should come with you when you investigate further," O'Harris quickly added. "I shall not have people threatening you!"

Clara gently smiled, touched by his concern. She brushed a hand against his cheek.

"I know," she said softly. "But you cannot be part of my investigation. The Inspector has made that plain. Your presence could compromise Peterson if this ends up going to court."

"I don't understand, how could I compromise him?" O'Harris' eyes burned with intensity and he set his lips into a firm line.

"Because you naturally wish to see him proven innocent. You are biased towards him, of course you are, that is not a criticism, just an observation. The Inspector feels if you were to be involved in my investigation, and this matter was to end up in a court of law, a cunning prosecution counsel could argue any evidence I gathered was biased in Peterson's favour and have it dismissed."

"I would never do that. I will be completely neutral!"

"I know," Clara told him, squeezing his hand. "But the prosecution would attack your involvement nonetheless. For the sake of Peterson, and for the future of your convalescence home, you must keep your distance from my investigation. I shall regularly inform you of what is happening, of course."

O'Harris groaned, despair coming over him again.

"I don't know how much longer this can be kept from the newspapers. I saw Gilbert McMillan sniffing around the hospital."

"I shall have a word with him," Clara promised. "He owes me a favour or two."

"This is going to come out eventually," O'Harris said miserably. "I have had to explain what has gone on to the men and staff, it was only fair. They have seen the police on the doorstep and noticed the absence of Peterson."

"What did you tell them?"

"That Peterson had been stabbed and that he was in the hospital. That a woman had also been stabbed and Peterson could not remember a thing about the incident. I didn't add that the police were considering him a suspect," O'Harris rubbed a hand over his eyes wearily. "I may need to now."

"Say nothing that you do not know to be completely true," Clara told him firmly. "You do not know that Peterson hurt that woman and whatever the police are speculating you must stick only to the absolute facts.

Peterson was stabbed, a woman was stabbed. That is all you know for sure, and that is all you will say."

"They'll learn the truth eventually," O'Harris protested.

"You think Peterson guilty?"

"No!"

"Then the truth they will eventually learn is that he was wrongly accused of this crime committed by someone else," Clara pointed out. "You are slipping into despair. Give me a chance to resolve this."

O'Harris looked at her and gave out a shaky sigh.

"I am not handling this well."

"How are you supposed to handle this?" Clara asked him curiously. "This is a unique and difficult situation. Do not criticise yourself so harshly."

Annie appeared with her consolation tea, which consisted of a strong brew laced with a lot of sugar and a drop of brandy, accompanied by a large slice of cake. Cake made everything better, in Annie's professional opinion. She placed the tray of items before O'Harris and pressed the cup of tea into his hands.

"I want to see Private Peterson," she said suddenly, her face hard and holding back a lot of emotion.

"Annie…"

"No, Clara, I want to see him. I like Peterson. He has attended every one of my cookery classes and he has an exceptional talent for fine pastry," Annie said this fast before she could be contradicted. "I want to see him and find out what all this confession nonsense is about."

"Maybe you will have better luck than me," O'Harris sipped his tea. "He won't speak to me."

"Annie…" Clara tried again.

"Don't try to persuade me out of it!" Annie said quickly, her voice trembling a little.

"I wasn't going to," Clara lightly laughed. "I was going to say I think that might be a good idea. Peterson needs to know he has friends who are looking out for him. He might also be more willing to explain himself to you, than to me or O'Harris. I barely know him, and he needs a friend right now."

Annie relaxed, her shoulders sinking as the tension slipped from her body.

"He is a good lad," Annie persisted. "Quiet, a little shy, haunted, no doubt, but he has a good heart. I won't have anyone say otherwise. I don't think he would hurt a soul willingly. I think it was because they made him fight and shoot people in the war that he is so damaged now. They broke his soul, Clara, and that is not easy to fix."

Clara found herself touched by Annie's insight and her staunch defence of Peterson. Annie saw things as they were, and when you won her loyalty – which was not easy to do – you had it for life. To have Annie so convinced Peterson was innocent made Clara even more certain he had done nothing wrong.

"I am going to find out the real culprit of this crime," Clara told both Annie and O'Harris. "I swear to that. Peterson just has to be patient and wait for me to do what I can. Please explain that to him Annie."

"I will," Annie promised.

"Tell him, I am on his side too," O'Harris added. "I believe he is innocent and would not hurt a woman. I do not think he has suddenly regained his memory and discovered himself a killer. I think he has been made to feel guilty and confess."

"The Inspector would not do that," Clara said, feeling she should defend Park-Coombs.

"Maybe not on purpose, but something has pressed Peterson into making this statement," O'Harris was less sympathetic to the police. "Park-Coombs has always had one eye on the home, thinking the men there are dangerous. When he arrived on my doorstep to tell me about Peterson, I saw it in his eyes that he felt he had been proved right."

"You are judging him too cruelly," Clara countered. "Park-Coombs may have his faults, but he would not wish ill on your men. And he would not like to think one of them was a killer. He is looking into this matter thoroughly, don't worry."

"You have your opinion of him, I have mine," O'Harris said coldly. "Now, I want to know you will be safe in your investigations, Clara. Will Tommy go with you from now on?"

Tommy had been loitering behind the sofa, listening to the conversation but with nothing of his own to add.

"What is this?" He asked.

"Clara told me someone threatened her today," O'Harris said.

"Clara!" Tommy reacted with alarm.

Clara inwardly groaned; this was why she did not tell them about such things.

"There was a slight incident, but I handled it," she said. "In any case, Park-Coombs has assigned me a police constable to accompany me during my investigations."

"Who?" O'Harris demanded.

"Sarah Butler," Clara said, feeling he was being over-protective. She appreciated his concern, but she was able to look out for herself and make decisions over her own safety.

"Sarah is a woman!" Tommy said loudly.

"Your observational skills are truly improving," Clara replied coolly. "Sarah is also trained in self-defence and is mean with a truncheon. To top it off, men always underestimate women and that leads to their downfall."

Her last comment was pointed and shut Tommy up. O'Harris looked less convinced.

"I don't want anything to happen to you," he took Clara's hand in both of his. "A woman is already dead, I couldn't bear it if you came to any harm."

"Then you are in luck, for I don't intend anything to happen to me," Clara responded. "Sarah is going to be watching my back and I am not so bad at looking out for myself. I have ruffled some feathers and that is good news. It means I am heading in the right direction."

O'Harris lowered his eyes from hers. He looked drained.

"Go home," Clara told him. "Get some rest and have faith in me."

"I trust you Clara," O'Harris said in a voice barely above a whispered. "Please, solve this. For Peterson, and for the rest of us."

Chapter Sixteen

Captain O'Harris' arrival had delayed Clara, not that she would begrudge him her time, it just meant that she arrived at the Institute only a few minutes before it was due to close its doors to the public. The door porter was reluctant to let her see Professor Montgomery and it took some persuading to convince him to ring the academic and see if he would make time for Clara.

"He has to think about his dinner," the porter grumbled as he picked up the telephone. "It gets served at half-six prompt."

Clara was sure, if it was necessary, the kitchen staff at the institute would keep a plate aside for the professor, though she didn't say it. Like a university, the institute incorporated several buildings for accommodating both students and their tutors. Most of the higher staff, and certainly the professors, had suites of rooms on site. It was essential, as otherwise they would have to find accommodation further afield and would have the complication of travelling back and forth to the Institute each day. It was a self-contained world. A vast refectory enabled students and academics to have their meals without leaving the grounds. It was easy to see how

Professor Lynch had been able to exist within the walls of the Institute and never stray further away. It was also possible to see how this had enabled him to mask his illness from his colleagues.

The porter finished his phone call and turned back to Clara. In a begrudging fashion, he said;

"Professor Montgomery says he will see you. You can go up at once, you know the way."

The porter than removed himself from his little office and made a point of locking the front doors. Clara left him to it, heading upstairs to see the professor.

Montgomery was pouring over paperwork as she knocked on his open door. He waved her in.

"You have news?" He said, as Clara closed the door behind her.

"A little, but it will not cheer you," Clara explained, approaching his desk and taking the chair before it. "Professor Lynch's old doctor is still alive and remembers his patient well."

"Old Dr Finnigan is still going?" Professor Montgomery said with some surprise. "I thought he must have died years ago. He was a good friend to Professor Lynch. Took care of him right up to the end. What did he have to say?"

"In the opinion of Dr Finnigan, there was nothing about Professor Lynch's manner in his final days to suggest he had lost his rationality," Clara explained carefully. "His last sickness would not have caused mental decay either. According to Dr Finnigan, Professor Lynch was as sane on his last day as he had ever been."

Professor Montgomery fell silent; that was not the news he had wanted to hear.

"Did he say anything else?" He asked, a faint hint of hopefulness in his tone.

"He did. Professor Lynch had suffered a debilitating digestive complaint most his life, which he had managed to hide from everyone until his final sickness. This condition caused Lynch a lot of misery and suffering. Dr Finnigan feels he turned to astrology to find a way to carry on through this hardship. It gave him the sort of strength others find through God," Clara paused. "I don't think you can judge that as an act of insanity. Rather, it was Professor Lynch's attempt to find some sort of reason for his sickness. He was trying to make peace with his suffering."

Montgomery was silent a while.

"I always suspected that Professor Lynch was unwell long before he was confined by his final illness, but he never confided in me. If I ever asked him, he informed me he was quite all right," he said. "There were little things, times when he seemed to lose weight and looked very pale and sickly, but he never missed a lecture, at least not until his last year. We all have periods of sickness and you don't tend to think about it being something serious. I suppose I was always very busy, too."

"Professor Lynch did not want you to know about his condition," Clara explained to him. "You were not being negligent as a colleague and friend, not when he preferred people not to know. He didn't want sympathy, he just wanted to get on with his life."

"Did he suffer a lot?" Professor Montgomery asked, his voice tight in his throat.

"Dr Finnigan said that, sadly, at times he did suffer greatly. The fact he carried on at all is quite remarkable."

"He never ate his meals in the refectory," Montgomery recalled. "And he would never accept an invitation to a private dinner in someone's rooms. He said he liked to eat alone, it aided his digestion."

"And it prevented you seeing the struggles he had with his stomach," Clara nodded. "But, I think all this secrecy ate away at him. He began to wonder why he had been cursed with this complaint. It is a natural thing, we all have done it when some misfortune occurs to us. We ask why we were singled out for this bad luck and not someone else.

"For Professor Lynch, finding an answer that brought him some sort of comfort, required turning from the foundations of his scientific background and moving into astrology. He saw a pattern to the stars that made him feel better, made him think there was a rhyme and reason to it all."

"And the prophecies?" Montgomery asked.

"They gave him hope. Despite all his sickness, I don't think Professor Lynch wanted to imagine he was dying. The astrological charts suggested he would recover and thrive; that enabled him to endure. Professor Lynch's life revolved around the stars in the night sky and they were what he turned to when he needed hope."

Professor Montgomery took this all in with a great deal of thought.

"Then, he was not mad, as such, deluded, perhaps," he said

"I would rather say it was a sort of desperation, a way of being able to keep going. At the end of the day, that has been the purpose of superstition and belief throughout human history. When the scientific world failed Professor Lynch, he needed to find something to comfort him," Clara hoped she was explaining her point successfully to Professor Montgomery, she sensed he was not a man to understand belief of any sort easily. It was not a part of his mental make-up. "I'm afraid this does not assist us with the prophecy box. Proving that Professor Lynch was perfectly sane, if misguided, when he constructed it, does not change anything."

"Yes," Professor Montgomery said thoughtfully. "What do you suggest?"

"That is quite difficult under the circumstances," Clara said carefully, knowing that what she was about to propose was not going to go down well. "My feeling is that we should endeavour to open the box ourselves, to preview its contents. It is the only way we can make a true decision on what to do next."

"Mr McGhie would never allow it, nor the bursar," Professor Montgomery shook his head.

"That was why I am proposing we open the box without their knowledge," Clara explained.

Professor Montgomery was surprised by the idea and that left him temporarily speechless. He stared at Clara as if she had just suggested they make a trip to the moon and back before supper.

"You mean, steal it from the library?" The academic muttered uneasily, dropping his voice as if there might be someone listening to them.

"It would not be stealing if I had your permission. Your authority overrides that of the librarian and the bursar, it also can countermand the request of a dead man. For the sake of appearances, it would be best if the box was opened at night when the librarian was not present."

"Then there is an element of subterfuge in this?" Montgomery seemed amazed at the thought. "And if we succeed and learn the contents of the box, what then?"

"That is the problem you have been faced with since you hired me. You wanted me to discover what was in that box, so you could then decide how to handle matters. You hoped I could prove Professor Lynch insane, and thus get you off the hook for making a decision, but things are not going to be that easy," Clara knew she was being blunt, but there was little other option. Professor Montgomery had few choices left and that she had to make plain. "Once you know the contents of the box, you can make a wiser decision. Maybe there will be something inside that will warrant a grand opening, such as a new scientific discovery Lynch made in his final days."

Montgomery's eyes widened as such a possibility embedded its way into his brain.

"You mean, maybe he identified a new star and wrote about it, but did not have the strength to reveal his discovery publicly?" Montgomery gasped, such a notion would warrant the full attention of the press and the authorities. "But why hide it in a box for twenty years?"

"To create a legacy? A means to be remembered by?" Clara shrugged. "Why supposedly write prophecies and hide them for twenty years? I think it safe to say we cannot know what was going through Professor Lynch's mind in those last days."

Professor Montgomery turned his head away from Clara, contemplating everything she had just told him.

"I suddenly feel there was a lot I did not know about Lynch," he said softly. "I thought I understood him, I thought I could have told you exactly who he was. But now… he was so sick and never told me. What does that say of our friendship?"

"He didn't want you to know about his illness and to worry. He didn't want or need your sympathy. He just wanted to be able to talk to you as a fellow astronomer," Clara said, though honestly she could not say what Professor Lynch wanted, she just knew what to say to console Montgomery. "You were colleagues, men of science, and he did not want that tarnished by thoughts of his sickness. You know, sometimes an ailment can take over a person's life and it is nice for them to get away from it by being with people who know nothing about that problem."

Montgomery seemed to accept this explanation. He was still quiet, struggling to get his head around these new revelations, but less perturbed than before.

"You have made some excellent points, Miss Fitzgerald, but I cannot authorise the stealing and secret opening of Lynch's box without giving the matter considerable thought. This could cause a good deal of consternation among the Institute staff, were it to get out," Montgomery was solemn. "While I come to a decision, I request that you speak with as many of the staff who formerly knew Professor Lynch as possible. There may be someone with information, which will result in us being able to avoid resorting to subterfuge."

"All right," Clara said. "I shall see what I can do, but I think that ultimately we shall need to open that box."

"I understand, but the situation is complicated," Professor Montgomery took a deep breath. "I am traipsing on the memory of a man who was well liked here. I am also contradicting the beliefs of some of my staff. It might alarm me how many of them have become besotted with the idea of this box and its prophecies, but I still have to be careful how I handle all this. The last thing we need is a permanent rift among the senior staff, that could spell as much disaster for us as a public opening of this damn box."

Montgomery clenched his fists, beside himself at the problems mounting up before him.

"Why did he do such a stupid thing?" He demanded of Clara. "He was wise enough to see the trouble this box would cause. Why do it? That does not seem to me to be the Professor Lynch I knew."

"It could have been an innocent thing," Clara pointed out. "He might not have contemplated how this would affect everyone."

"Well, it is far from the man I knew," Montgomery grumbled. "Find me some logic to this mess, Miss Fitzgerald."

"I am endeavouring," Clara promised him.

Professor Montgomery rose, a signal that their meeting was at an end. Clara rose also.

"To imagine resorting to creeping around in my own teaching establishment…" Montgomery tutted to himself. "You don't know how often I think about that box being consumed in a fire, or being lost in the archive room, permanently. Was there nothing in the papers you looked at to explain it?"

"Nothing," Clara told him. "I found the papers largely to be purely scientific, though there were a handful of astrological charts. But nothing concerning that box. Had Dr Finnigan not mentioned being shown the box by Professor Lynch, I should have almost begun to wonder if it was his work at all."

"What?" Montgomery latched onto the stray comment as if it was a life raft. "Someone else made the box? As in a hoax? A way of challenging the Institute's reputation and dominance in the field of astronomy?"

"I never said that," Clara hastened to add. "I said, had Dr Finnigan not seen the box in Lynch's rooms, I might have contemplated the chance of it being a fake."

"But, supposing it was made by someone else? Or at least its contents and that nonsensical letter supposedly from Lynch about the twenty year wait before opening it," Montgomery was rushing through his words. "Then, this whole thing could be a monumental hoax! Yes, Miss Fitzgerald, you must find who has created this forgery and reveal them!"

"You have the wrong idea…" Clara tried to protest, but Montgomery was already edging her towards the door.

"This could explain everything, and it would make things a lot easier," the academic continued. "Once you have discovered who is behind this, I shall be able to get the Institute back on track. Heads may have to roll."

Montgomery shuffled her out of his office and refused to listen to her as he departed for his dinner. He had come to his conclusion over the matter and nothing would change his mind. Clara gave up and headed for home. If all astronomers were as stubborn and singled-minded as Professor Montgomery, she could see why this box was causing such consternation.

Chapter Seventeen

Annie had brought a tin containing homemade raisin and lemon biscuits to the hospital for Private Peterson. She clutched it to her chest like it was a shield as she entered the building and approached the reception desk. The last time Annie had been here was when she was having emergency surgery for appendicitis. Just the smell of the hospital foyer brought back vividly the memories of her sudden collapse and subsequent eventful few days in hospital. She was determined never to go through such a thing again.

At the reception desk she clung to her biscuits in the vain hope they would somehow protect her from her anxieties and stop the hospital from seeming such an intimidating place. If needs be she could lift the lid, sniff the biscuits and be instantly reminded of her safe kitchen and all her familiar things. She fought her nerves, however, she was doing this for Peterson.

"May I help?" The receptionist asked.

"I've come to see a patient, Private Peterson," Annie explained. "She knew it was just at the start of visiting time and there should be no problem with her being allowed to see him, but she still felt worried she might be turned away.

The receptionist went through a book listing current patients and finally came to Peterson's entry.

"You can locate him on the second floor, in a private room," she said. "There is a note here to say he is to be limited on visitors."

"I have permission from Inspector Park-Coombs," Annie said quickly.

The receptionist studied the page a moment longer, seemingly making up her mind as to what to say. Finally, she relented.

"I think the note means he is limited to how many people can visit him in a day," she concluded. "He has been through a serious trauma and needs a lot of rest."

"Of course," Annie said with a nod. "He shall come to no harm from me."

The receptionist had lost interest, there was a queue of people behind Annie and they were growing impatient. She said Annie could go upstairs and paid her no more heed.

Annie found her way to Peterson's room and saw that Constable Maven was on duty outside. She automatically opened her tin of biscuits and offered him one.

"Thanks, miss," Maven said with clear delight, Annie's cooking resulted in many friendships. "No more trouble with chicken thefts?"

There had been a brief spate in the neighbourhood of chickens disappearing from backyards. Annie had been so concerned that she had herded her flock into the outhouse and had insisted on sleeping there with them.

"No," Annie told him. PC Maven was one of the constables who had been assigned to patrol the area for a few nights and see if he could catch the chicken thieves. Annie had made him tea and sandwiches. "I'm guessing your presence scared them off."

"Hopefully," Maven said with a boyish smile. He looked too young to be a police constable. "Still, better chicken thieves than this business."

He tossed his head towards the door of Peterson's room

to indicate what he meant, then he bit into his biscuit.

"Poor fellow sounds insane," he said. "Reckon a shell dropped too near him during the war, or something. I hear him talking to himself sometimes, and I look in and he is sound asleep. But he keeps talking."

"What does he say?" Annie asked.

"All sorts of things, some of it you can't understand, but one time he was calling out for someone called Jimmy for nearly half-an-hour. Seemed to me he was trying to look for the fellow, in his dreams, like," Maven shrugged, this was all a bit beyond his limited understanding of psychology. "Could be he was dreaming he was back at the Front, that's what I reckon."

"Could be," Annie nodded.

"And Jimmy was a comrade who never came back from an assault," Maven had clearly been mulling this all over. "I dare say that's it."

"Sounds likely," Annie agreed with him. "Well, I better get in to see him before visiting hour is over. Have another biscuit."

Annie left Constable Maven munching on a second raisin and lemon biscuit as she pushed the door to Peterson's room.

The soldier was staring blankly at the floor. He lay stock-still and his eyes didn't blink. Annie felt a chill run down her spine as she saw the state of him. He looked to have lost all hope and to have hidden away into some safe part of his mind as a defence against the demons. She wasn't even sure if he was aware she had entered the room. Annie placed the box of biscuits on the cabinet beside his bed.

"Peterson?" She said, softly. "I brought some biscuits. These are the ones I promised you the recipe for."

Peterson said nothing, his gaze fixed statically on a floor tile. Annie stifled a sigh of despair, she had to be positive for his sake.

"I wanted to talk with you, about all this nonsense about the woman and the knife," she said, wondering if he heard her. She carried on, nonetheless. "I'm going to be plain. I do not think you would hurt anyone, I would stake my life on that, and I don't think you would kill a woman. I don't understand why you would confess to such a thing. It is simply not you."

There was no reaction from Peterson. Annie started to feel a little despondent.

"Clara is on the case, anyway. You know, this brawny fellow threatened her life when she went poking around and that has to be clear proof that something is going on in those backstreets. I think that man was responsible for the death of that woman, not you," Annie kept speaking as it made her feel better hearing her own voice. "I don't know why you were in that alley, or how everything occurred, but I do know you are not the sort of man who would stab a woman. I have seen your skill with pastry, don't forget. That takes a light hand and an even temper. You don't have it in you to stab someone."

Peterson had still not reacted and Annie was beginning to fret whether he was actually alive, his stillness was scaring her. She reached out and touched his arm, then clasped his hand in hers.

"Why won't you talk to me?" She asked him, feeling relieved that his hand was warm. "Won't you eat a biscuit?"

Annie looked at her box of goodies. It was rare that such a gift would not rouse a person from despair, that made her fear Peterson was already too lost to be saved. Feeling agitated, Annie grabbed up a biscuit and began nibbling on it herself.

"Why would you make a confession?" Annie repeated. "Did you suddenly remember something? Or did someone pressure you into it? Because I don't believe you did this and so there is nothing to confess, but if you think you are somehow helping everyone by confessing, you are not. If you can't remember what happened, you can't feel guilty over it. There is no point."

Annie felt a little pressure in her hand from Peterson

twitching his fingers.

"I want you fit and out of here in time for my next cookery class," she continued. "I was going to show you all how to make jam. There has been a glut of strawberries, O'Harris tells me. The greenhouses at the Home are positively bursting. There shall be so much strawberry jam you will be eating it until next Easter. Maybe you can send a jar to your mother, she would like that."

Peterson's eyes flickered and this was enough to give Annie hope she was heading in the right direction.

"No one has told her yet what has happened. We didn't want to worry her unnecessarily. Hopefully this can all be resolved before she needs to know anything," Annie paused. "You know, you owe it to her to hang in here. To not take the easy path of succumbing to your demons. Your mum knows you are not a killer. She would be broken through and through were she to discover you had confessed to this crime. You wouldn't want that."

Peterson's fingers twitched harder this time.

"Your mother needs the truth, she deserves that. Not some confession you were persuaded to make because you can't remember what really happened. She is going to be so worried about you."

Peterson made a noise at the back of his throat. It could have been a moan, or it might have been a sigh. Annie felt she was reaching him.

"I want to know why you made that confession," Annie persisted. "Did you suddenly remember something? You have so many people on your side, Peterson, so many people wanting to help you. Give us the chance."

Peterson made the strange noise again. Annie wasn't sure if he was trying to speak.

"Do you want to sit up?" She asked him.

Peterson slipped his hand from hers and pushed himself onto his side. He winced as pain pressed into his injured back, but he could breathe more freely on his side, and he could talk.

"Why did you come, Annie?" He said weakly.

"Because you are a friend and I like you," Annie told him in her blunt fashion. "And I can't imagine you murdering a woman you had never met before."

"I was having one of my moments," Peterson said bleakly.

"You have never attacked anyone during those moments before," Annie pointed out. "Why would this time be different?"

"I don't know," Peterson said softly. "I just feel this guilt in me. As if I failed to do something or did something I shouldn't have."

"Then you still don't remember what occurred?"

"I had this dream and in it there was the woman, the one I stabbed…"

"The one who was stabbed," Annie corrected him. "We do not know you stabbed her."

"In my dream I stabbed her," Peterson said miserably. "She was running down the alley towards me. I felt afraid, I can't explain why, but that is how I felt, and suddenly there was a knife in my hand and I lashed out at her."

"You confessed because of a dream?" Annie said, aghast.

"It was so vivid, and I have dreamed about things before and later they proved to be things that had happened."

"We all have dreams like that," Annie said. "But we also all dream about things that have not happened, that could not physically occur. I have dreamed I was a bird and flew over the houses of Brighton, that was not based upon reality."

"This felt real," Peterson countered.

"And you have never had a dream like that before?" Annie pressed.

Peterson fell silent, unable to answer her question.

"Exactly," Annie said firmly. "Dreams are just our brains firing off crazy ideas. You have been thinking about this matter so much, no wonder you dreamt of stabbing that woman! It does not mean it happened. After all, your dream did not explain how you came to have the knife, or how you ended up stabbed in the back."

Peterson did not know what to say.

"I know you feel guilty. I know you are terribly afraid you did this thing but confessing helps no one. It does not get us any nearer the truth. Clara believes you are innocent, and Clara is good at these things."

Peterson fixed Annie with his gaze.

"You don't really know me, Annie. I killed people in the war. A man can't come back from that."

"You are not a killer," Annie promised him. "Thousands of men served in the war from this country alone. They are not all walking around in danger of killing a perfect stranger at any moment. Please, stop thinking the worst of yourself."

Peterson clearly did not know how to do that.

"You have to hold on," Annie pressed him. "You mustn't be afraid. Clara will find the truth."

Peterson was thoughtful a while, then he spoke.

"Annie, why do you care what becomes of me?"

"You silly thing!" Annie groaned. "Because I like you, because I think you are a good person who could have a future ahead of him, if only you would start to believe in yourself. And trust yourself. You have allowed these episodes to rule your life for too long. You live in fear of them, when you really don't need to."

Peterson was silent again, rolling his head into his pillow.

"I can't take back my confession," he almost sobbed.

"You can," Annie told him firmly. "In any case, Clara is going to prove it could not have been you."

Annie paused.

"Do you not remember anything about that night?"

"I don't know. Things become… strange. I don't know which bits are genuine and which bits I imagined or dreamt."

"Don't fret over it," Annie advised him. "Clara is very clever at these things. She can solve anything."

Annie touched his shoulder lightly.

"You've got to stop hiding from yourself," she said. "Maybe its time you embraced your demons."

"Embraced them?" Peterson said appalled.

"Yes, accept them as a part of you, instead of fearing them. After all, you've been fighting them all these years without success, what would it hurt to try a different approach?"

"You mean well Annie, but you don't understand," Peterson shoved his face deeper into his pillow.

"Maybe I understand better than you think," Annie told him. "Maybe you're not the only one with demons to fight."

Somewhere deep in the hospital a bell rang; it was the end of visiting time. Annie gave a sigh; the time had flown past.

"I'm going to come and visit you again," she told Peterson as she rose.

"Don't Annie, I just want to be left alone."

"And what good will that do?" Annie asked him sternly. "You will lie in this bed moping, trying to piece together what happened that night, hating yourself for being unable to remember and then hating yourself for having these problems in the first place. I won't allow that."

"I'll tell the hospital I don't want visitors," Peterson said sourly.

"You try that young man and I shall contact your mother immediately," Annie said, refusing to give in.

"Don't do that," Peterson said hastily. "I don't want her to know about what happened."

"Nothing has happened," Annie reminded him. "Except some horrible person stabbed you, and we are going to find who they were and why they killed that woman too."

"And if I really did it?" Peterson asked her with his voice trembling with fear.

"At some point you are going to have to take a leap of faith," Annie squeezed his shoulder. "You will need to trust not in Clara, or in me, or in Captain O'Harris, but in yourself. I can't make you believe in yourself, no one can.

That's a decision for you to make, and you alone."

Peterson said nothing. Annie had to leave, she wished she could stay, she wished she could heal the young man in the bed. But what she had said she knew to be true; the only person who could truly help Peterson now was himself.

Chapter Eighteen

Clara returned to the alleyways. She had Sarah with her, dressed in plainclothes rather than her uniform. Sarah had her truncheon concealed up the sleeve of the big overcoat she was wearing. They walked to the backyard of Robert Hartley's house and let themselves in. There appeared to be no one around to witness their arrival. It was dark, the autumn nights folding in fast. The alley was filled with deep shadows that could conceal anything, as it was, they did not even conceal a cat or mouse.

Clara knocked on the back door and imagined the sound caused consternation to the residents inside. After a long pause, which almost suggested the house was empty, the door was tentatively opened by Robert's wife. Her eyes widened as she saw who was outside.

"Sorry to disturb you so late in the evening, Mrs Hartley," Clara said, "but, I would like to speak to your husband again."

Mrs Hartley clearly did not know what to say. She stood in her hallway, glancing between the two women, before finally retreating inside. She left the back door open, enabling Clara and Sarah to hear the fraught conversation that now took place between her and her husband.

"That woman is outside again!"

"What woman?"

"The one who came earlier asking about that lad who was stabbed."

"I told you not to interfere with that, Robert!" That was the fearsome voice of Robert's mother.

"What does she want?" Robert asked in a more cautious tone.

"Does it matter? I'll get rid of her!"

"Mother!"

The senior Mrs Hartley appeared in the hallway and marched towards Clara and Sarah with a face like thunder. She was a stout, powerfully built woman, the sort who spent her days performing manual tasks, some of them quite unpleasant. She was not to be argued with in a hurry.

"You can clear off!" She told Clara with a wave of her hand.

Clara did not move.

"I need to speak to Robert," Clara insisted. "Something is happening in this neighbourhood which is more than just the petty crime everyone is used to. This is serious and I need all the information I can get. Else a young man may be accused of a murder he did not commit."

"What does that matter to me?" Mrs Hartley demanded. "I don't have time to trouble myself with the problems of strangers. You have to look after yourself and your own in life, that's it."

She said her statement with finality, intending that to be the last word. Clara refused to accept it.

"I am doing exactly that, looking after myself and my own. The young man who was stabbed in the alley is my friend, and my own life has been threatened in this affair. I take a very dim view of such things," Clara folded her arms, she could be as stubborn and fierce as the next woman. "Someone has caused me a lot of trouble and they are about to discover that I don't like that. They hurt someone I care about, they came after me, and that makes me all the more determined to deal with them. I shan't stop until I know exactly who is behind this crime and what has been going on."

Robert had appeared in the hallway. He was standing back from the doorway and as there was no light in the corridor, he was almost hidden in the shadows, but he was there.

"Mother, let them in," he said calmly.

"We don't need any trouble," Mrs Hartley turned around on her son and barked. "You don't need trouble."

"We are already in trouble," Robert said without any hint of regret in his voice. "The moment I went out into the alley, we were in trouble."

"I told you not to go outside!"

"I was tired of hiding!" Robert snapped at her. "I was tired of this fearfulness. I was never afraid of anything and I am not now! That lad needed help and I was damn well going to give it. Never let it be said that old Robbie was one to let a boy die behind his house without trying to save him."

"You are a fool," Mrs Hartley wailed at him, her ferocity disappeared in the face of her anguish. "You will be the end of us all!"

"I'm not going to hide anymore," Robert said quietly, and there was to be no arguing with him, that was plain.

"You always were selfish Robert Hartley!" His mother snapped at him, before storming back into the kitchen and slamming the door behind her.

Robert stood facing his unexpected guests solemnly.

"You better come in."

He showed them into the only other room on the ground floor. Had the house been in full use, it would have been a parlour, but the Hartleys (like so many in the neighbourhood) could not afford to rent an entire house and so they existed in two rooms. The kitchen at the back and the parlour at the front, which served as bedroom and sitting room to them. They were luckier than those living on the other floors, as they did have a kitchen. Robert's mother had insisted on it. The people living further up had to make do with cooking in their fireplaces or eating all their meals cold.

The parlour contained a double bed with an iron frame squashed against the back wall and parallel to the fireplace. A second, smaller bed, was set against the wall near the door and partly obscured the front window. There was little room for any other furniture, though a chest of drawers was wedged into a corner and there was a wooden chair by the fireplace, shrouded in discarded clothes. Robert walked to the fireplace and turned around. He motioned for his guests to sit on the bed, if they wished. Clara preferred to stand, and Sarah was loitering in the background as a watchdog for trouble.

"Thank you for speaking to me again," Clara said to Robert, wanting to get him on her side first.

"So, you've been threatened?" Robert asked her.

"Yes. Earlier today I went back into the alley to see where the murder of that poor woman occurred. I was accosted by a brutish fellow who threatened me if I failed to leave at once."

"This is a dangerous business, you should not get involved," Robert said.

"On the contrary, it is for that reason I intend to become involved. Someone is making life a misery for the people around here and they have caused harm to my friend, now they have threatened me and that is like a red rag to a bull," Clara said staunchly. "I don't like bullies and I don't like being threatened."

"I would call you a fool, but maybe you have more backbone and sense than the rest of us," Robert gave a weak laugh.

"What of you? You were prepared to defy them to help my friend," Clara pointed out.

"Well, I am still waiting to see what comes of that," Robert said with a tense smile.

"I went to the police after I was threatened," Clara explained to him. "I was shown a book with photographs of convicted criminals in it, in case the man who threatened me was in there. I didn't find him, but I came across your picture. You were with the Seashore Boys."

Robert gave a snort of laughter.

"For my sins," he said. "They cost me years of my life, rotting away in prison while my wife and mother did the best they could to survive without me. I only ran with them because it was safer to work with them, than stand against them."

"You know about gangs, Robert," Clara said quietly. "You know how they operate. Why aren't you working with this new gang?"

"Because I am honest now," Robert said with a growl. "I learned the hard way where gangs take you. I don't intend to ever go back to prison."

"But you know about this new gang? You are prepared to defy them."

Robert turned his head away and stared at the bed, as if there was something there that had caught his attention. When he looked back his face was grim.

"I keep out of their business, that's for the best. They want the alleys to themselves, so be it."

"What do they want the alleys for?" Clara asked.

Robert shrugged his shoulders.

"I don't ask, and I don't look."

"Then why did you go out the other night and help my friend?" Clara demanded. "You must have known he had stumbled onto the gang's turf and paid the price?"

Robert had crossed his arms over his chest and hunched his shoulders. He was a man who was used to keeping quiet and minding his own business, but something had come over him the other day, some element of pity and empathy that had forced him to face his own anxieties. He had been holding his tongue and staying out of the way, but it had tested his patience and pride. It had rankled to be obeying some gang, most of whom were too young to remember the Seashore Boys and what they stood for. Robert might have his regrets, but he had never forgotten how it felt to have that power behind you, to be part of something that others feared and respected. Now he had no power and it nipped at him, nipped like the cold of a January morning and sapped his soul.

"Sometimes, you have to do things," he said. "It was a split-second decision."

Robert huffed.

"I had a brother, you know? Younger than me. One day he stumbled onto a rival gang and they went for him. He never was the brightest, always in the wrong places at the wrong times. They beat him up and left him for dead. He crawled along the ground down an alley, calling desperately for help. But no one came out to him, they were all too afraid to interfere," Robert met Clara's eyes. "He was just alive when a police constable heard him calling and found him. It was too late. He died on the way to the hospital. The doctors said to my mother, if only he had been found a little sooner they might have saved him.

"Do you know what a cruelty that is to say to a grieving mother? The Seashore Boys took it as an insult against them and a few nights later we raided our rivals' territory and wiped them out. It was revenge, but it did not bring my brother back. It did not make me feel any better. I just kept thinking, if someone had had the guts to step out of their house and help him, my brother would have lived. He had done nothing, he was not even a part of the Seashore Boys. We never did figure out why he was in that alley that day.

"When I heard someone calling for help, it made me think of my brother. My mother said don't go, and I found myself imagining that all those years ago, some other fellow was told the same by his mother or wife and left my brother to die. I couldn't bear it. I couldn't be that man and so I went outside."

"You have earned my everlasting gratitude for that act of kindness," Clara said, meaning every word.

Robert shrugged.

"Maybe I repaid a little debt to my brother that night. Maybe I salvaged a piece of my soul, or maybe I've sentenced us all to death."

"These gangsters know you helped my friend?" Clara asked him.

"They saw me," Robert answered, without appearing to be bothered by this statement. "When I went out my yard gate, one of the gang was coming towards your friend. He wasn't hurrying, because his victim could not get away. I figured he was after the knife in your pal's back. He stopped when he saw me. We met eyes and there was this moment he didn't know what to do.

"You see, they know I was in a gang, they've heard whispered stories. They know I was in prison and that gives me a little clout around here. I keep out of their business and they leave me alone. In that instant, I was more of a problem than that knife in your friend's back. I didn't move or back down, and the other fellow did."

A slight smile curled Robert's lips.

"There is a rumour around the neighbourhood that I killed the leader of a rival gang back in the day. They say it was because he stopped my wife and threatened her. It was never proved I did it, but everyone knows. Actually, I've never killed anyone and that's the truth."

"But the rumour keeps you safe," Clara understood.

"Yes," Robert grinned at her. "It's why I started it in the first place."

Clara was amused at his cunning.

"Can you tell me anything about this gang?" She asked.

"Nothing, really," Robert shook his head. "I have been keeping out of their way. I don't need trouble and, on the whole, they have caused no real harm. People are scared, but people are always scared. This murder, that was different…"

Robert's grin had gone.

"They had never killed before, at least, not in such a cold-blooded fashion. This takes things in a new direction and one I don't like," Robert became maudlin. "Once the killing begins, then no one is safe. This can't go on, something must be done."

"Are you aware that a number of individuals who used to live in this neighbourhood and who were known to the police for minor criminal offences, have disappeared?"

"No," Robert replied. "I don't mix with those people, but it doesn't surprise me. Whoever runs this gang is paranoid about being seen and about being caught. Makes sense he would get rid of anyone who might grass on him, given the chance."

"What of the woman who died? Has anyone said who she was?"

Robert sucked in his lips and became quiet. Clara guessed he knew something, but he was debating what to say. He finally spoke up.

"There are always rumours, but you can't rely on them being true. You might like to ask at a boarding house down by the docks called the Sailor's Rest. People say the woman was known there, that she went by the name Rose Red, but that's all. What she was doing here I don't know."

"Thank you," Clara told him warmly. "You have been of far greater help than you realise."

Robert snorted.

"Let's hope we both don't come to regret it."

Chapter Nineteen

Clara decided to take some time in the morning to go back to the Institute and interview some of the academics. She had considered passing the task to Tommy, he was keen to keep on the case, but she wasn't sure Professor Montgomery would be pleased if he discovered she was not personally questioning his colleagues. Clara compromised by promising Tommy that once she had finished at the Institute, they would head together to the docks to track down the Sailor's Rest. There was still no news from Colonel Brandt on the possible owner of the knife, which meant they had only one lead in the matter of the murder in the alley.

"I've spoken to the bursar and the librarian," Clara explained to Tommy as she left for the Institute. "They both firmly believe in this box containing prophecies. Professor Montgomery said he would compile a list of other members of staff who were contemporary with Professor Lynch and leave it for me at the porter's office. After twenty years, the list is not likely to be long."

Clara was right. When the porter grudgingly moved from his chair in his office and retrieved the list, it contained only two extra names. One was for a lecturer and the other for the head porter at the Institute. Clara decided to start with him first.

"Where would I find the Head Porter?" She asked the ordinary porter in his office.

"This time of day, probably doing his rounds of the staff quarters, ensuring all is well," the man said. "What do you want with him?"

"Just a quick word," Clara said. "Shall I just pop upstairs?"

She knew the presumptuous remark would instantly ruffle the porter's feathers.

"Certainly not! Staff quarters are off-limits to anyone who is not a staff member!" He said fiercely. "I shall let the Head Porter know you wish to see him. Professor Montgomery has said I must accede to your every request, more's the pity."

"Really?" Clara said in delight. "Every request?"

The porter narrowed his eyes at her, indicating what he thought to her jest and reminding her she wasn't to take liberties. He was like so many low-level little men who worked in colleges and universities – given an ounce of power, he clung to it vehemently and with a pugnacious dedication. It made him slightly obnoxious.

However, the porter did manage to get a message to his superior and half-an-hour later he appeared to talk with Clara. He motioned for her to join him in an empty side-room where they could speak in peace.

"How may I help?" He asked Clara.

"I am talking to everyone who knew Professor Lynch," Clara explained. "I believe you were a porter here in his day?"

"I was," the Head Porter admitted. "I was just a young man then. Is this about his box?"

"It is," Clara said.

"Everyone has been talking about a young lady going about the Institute, asking questions concerning the box that has just appeared in the library," the Head Porter replied.

"What do you make of the box and its supposed contents?" Clara asked.

The Head Porter became stoical.

"It is not my place to question what the senior staff do," he said, slightly snootily.

"Yet, you will have an opinion," Clara nudged him. "This conversation is just between us, you can tell me anything."

"My opinion is hardly relevant," the Head Porter said with an air of indignation. "Professor Lynch was a wise and clever man. His loss to the Institute was hard. I am sure if he felt the box was important it was."

Clara was disappointed.

"What if it is true it contains prophecies Professor Lynch wrote?" She asked.

"I do not see what you want me to say? The professor must have thought these things important and that is that."

The Head Porter pulled a pocket watch from his waistcoat and checked the time.

"I must depart, I have a lot of things to do," he said.

He left Clara alone in the room and she had the impression he had disliked every moment of their conversation. She might not have learned much, but his attitude did tell her that Professor Lynch was well-liked by those who knew him, and no one wanted to speak ill of him. Professor Montgomery looked to be on his own when it came to questioning Lynch's last gift to the Institute.

"Never mind," Clara sighed, she had one last person to speak to.

~~~*~~~

Professor Hobart was the lecturer in advanced mathematics for the Institute and Clara caught him at the tail end of a lesson. The door to his classroom was a little open and she stood in the hall trying to follow the complicated mathematical problem the professor was revealing to his students. Clara understood that to correctly calculate star movements, trajectories and orbits required a solid foundation in mathematics and she would not have considered herself incompetent in the subject, but the vast and seemingly endless equation Professor Hobart was explaining was lost upon her. It began at one end of a very long blackboard and did not finish until it reached the other end, and there were lots of letters involved as well as numbers.

Clara took a deep breath and consoled herself that such an equation was not necessary to her own career choice, and it was jolly good that there were at least some people in this world who understood this stuff and could practically apply it.

The big bell in the Institute's clock tower chimed on cue, and Hobart dismissed his class. Clara stood aside to let everyone file out, intrigued to see that none looked as baffled as her by what they had just heard, then she slipped into the classroom.

Professor Hobart was scrubbing the equation from the blackboard.

"Just a moment," he said, without looking behind him.

Clara waited patiently until he turned around.

"Oh," Professor Hobart was surprised to see her, "I apologise, I thought you were a student come to ask me a question."

"Clara Fitzgerald," Clara introduced herself, discreetly closing the door at her side. "I had hoped to take a moment of your time to ask about Professor Lynch? I believe you knew him?"

"I was one of his students," Professor Hobart smiled proudly. "The professor encouraged me to take up teaching, he saw I had an aptitude for explaining complicated problems to people."

Clara imagined that was probably true, if the 'people' already had a strong foundation in mathematics.

"Why are you asking about the professor?" Hobart paused, his smile fading.

"You have heard about the box that was discovered in

the library?" Clara asked him.

Hobart had the blackboard eraser in his hands and he twisted it around anxiously.

"I have. I haven't really paid that much attention though," he didn't meet Clara's eyes.

"I hardly have to explain to you, Professor, the divide this box has caused among your colleagues. I have been asked to investigate its contents and determine what should be done with it."

Hobart looked uncomfortable.

"Professor Lynch was a brilliant astronomer," he said in a tone that implied he would not be shaken on that belief. "I admired him. I admired his intelligence and dedication to the investigation of the universe. He never once mentioned prophecies to me."

"Never?"

"No," Hobart was firm. "If you ask me, someone is spreading rumours about him, to tarnish his reputation."

"Why would anyone do that? Especially his former friends?"

"I don't know, but I can't believe he would dabble in astrology. He was a man of science, he did not believe in hocus pocus stuff."

Hobart forcefully put the blackboard eraser down on his desk and Clara reflected that he would now have a chalky patch right where he sat.

"I am neutral in this debate," Clara told him, hoping to calm him a little. "That is the whole purpose for my being here. I have been asked to determine if there could be any validity to this box business and whether an official, formal opening should be pursued."

"Is that a possibility?" Hobart looked appalled. "If it is, I shall protest it to the utmost. You can't have such nonsense going on in an Institute of science, Professor Lynch would be appalled, I am sure of that."

"You really think this box is a fraud?"

"I am certain of it," Professor Hobart was adamant. "The man I knew would never create such a thing and purport to see into the future."

"What if, at the end of his life, Professor Lynch was looking for some sort of comfort? Something to cling to in this time of distress?" Clara pointed out.

Hobart shook his head.

"Professor Lynch understood that our time on this earth is finite and then we return to dust. He had left his legacy, of that he could be proud. He would not have dabbled in mysticism. Never!"

~~~*~~~

Clara made her way back to Professor Montgomery's office, feeling she had achieved very little in the last few hours. It seemed that Professor Lynch had been a man who presented a different persona to different people. To his students he was a robust man of science, to his doctor he was a man riddled with disease and trying to cope with his suffering, while to certain of his colleagues he was a prophet. There was no obvious answer to the riddle of his box based on what she had learned from those who had known him.

Professor Montgomery welcomed her into his office with a hopeful look on his face. Clara was sorry to disappoint him.

"If ever there was a man who presented a different facet of himself to different people, it was Professor Lynch," she began. "Your bursar and your librarian are certain he was a master astrologer with a knack for interpreting the stars. Your Head Porter refuses to make any comment, except that Professor Lynch was a man he greatly respected. Professor Hobart is appalled at the idea his mentor would even consider astrology and considers the box a fraud. And then there is Dr Finnigan, who saw a man on the brink of death clutching at straws and admired him for his strength of will and determination. I have no clear answers for you, Professor, and I don't think I shall gain anymore from just talking to the people who knew Lynch."

Professor Montgomery was despondent with this assessment.

"You are sure you looked through his papers thoroughly?" He asked, desperately.

"Yes and came across a mixture of genuine scientific papers and astrology charts. There was a thesis on Halley's Comet sandwiched between Lynch's birth chart and a later horoscope. All I can tell you from those papers was that Lynch was a man of contradictions."

Montgomery groaned.

"This is awful. I have nothing I can use to stop the librarian and bursar pursuing their idea of a public opening of the box. Even if I refuse to allow it to happen, they can stir up a fuss and talk about the box. How will I ever be able to face our benefactors and sponsors again?"

"There is my other idea," Clara reminded him.

"A secret opening of the box?" Montgomery clasped his hand to his forehead and cradled his head for a few seconds. "Is that what I am reduced to? Sneaking about in my own institute?"

"It will give you more options if you know what the box contains," Clara said. "As I suggested before, supposing it contains a final paper of such importance to the science of astronomy that it will revolutionise the discipline? Then, a public opening would be in your favour."

"You are trying to offer me hope Miss Fitzgerald, but what if the box contains more astrology charts?"

"Then at least you will know," Clara said. "And then you can argue against the opening of the box with greater conviction. Without knowing what is in that box, you are open to doubts and that is a disadvantage."

"I have no doubts that box should not be opened publicly!" Montgomery protested.

"Even if it were to contain an astronomy paper, as I suggested?"

Montgomery hesitated. Clara could see him working out the consequences of the public unveiling of an important work by the late Professor Lynch, one of the most well-remembered and beloved academics at the Institute. The publicity for his college would be of great importance and would enable him to find further funding and students. It could only benefit the Institute. Montgomery gave a little wistful sigh as he imagined such a fantastic result.

"You know how to charm a man, Miss Fitzgerald," he said softly. "You know how to speak to his inner accountant and give him hope. You are saying that Lynch may not have filled this box with nonsense, but with something of benefit to the Institute?"

"I honestly do not know," Clara replied. "I am just trying to impress upon you how difficult it is to make a correct decision about this box without knowing what it contains."

"And Mr McGhie will never let it be opened privately, at least with his knowledge," Montgomery said thoughtfully. "That is for sure."

"A secret inspection of the box's contents is the only thing I can think of to help you," Clara told the professor. "I have explored every other avenue I can think of without success. There is nothing among Lynch's papers to hint at the box and none of the people still here who knew him had any knowledge of the box's contents. Not even Dr Finnigan, who must be considered the person closest to Lynch in his last days. He saw him daily, but was never told the secret of the box."

"Lynch was a very private man," Montgomery agreed. "I see now that he kept an awful lot to himself. I thought I knew him well, but plainly I did not. Had I been more understanding of his astrology, maybe he would have spoken about the box to me."

"Or maybe not," Clara consoled him. "He wanted this last great secret, a sort of legacy. He wanted people to be talking about him years after he was gone. I think I see this as a sort of immortality, a means of proving he was not forgotten. Perhaps, in the end, he feared his academic contributions would not be enough to secure his place in history."

"You think that a possibility?" Montgomery smiled to himself. "I can see that, yes. This box business is a way of keeping Lynch's memory alive, and he thought it up himself."

"Where does that leave us?" Clara asked him.

Professor Montgomery had to stop and think again. It was plain he was reluctant to make a decision, yet also plain he had no choice.

"I suppose we are opening that box," he said. "Tonight, I don't want to waste anymore time on the matter."

Chapter Twenty

Her work done at the Institute, for the time being at least, Clara and Tommy headed for the Brighton docks. Ships and boats were always coming and going from Brighton's shores. Some were fishing craft, others were passenger ships or pleasure yachts. They needed to dock somewhere and there needed to be places for them to be repaired or just overhauled at the end of a long season. The Sailor's Rest supposedly catered as a boarding house for seamen without a place to stay when their ships were berthed at Brighton, but, in reality, there were not that many non-local sailors entering the docks, and the seafront hotels and boarding houses further inland soaked up travellers to Brighton looking for a place to rest their heads. As a result, the Sailor's Rest had diversified.

Clara and Tommy found the boarding house on a backstreet, opposite a fish warehouse. The cobbles of the old road sparkled with fish scales, as children lacking shoes dashed about in a game of tag. A faded notice in the window of the boarding house indicated it had rooms to let and a bell rang as Clara pushed open the door.

A woman emerged from the door of a sitting room as Clara and Tommy stepped into the hallway. She stared at them through thick, black glasses which made her eyes seem enormous.

"I don't cater for outside workers," she told Clara firmly. "If the gent wants a lass, I'll supply one with a room."

Tommy stifled a chuckle at the implication that Clara was a working girl come to look for a room to share with her client. Clara managed to take the whole thing in her stride and didn't even blush.

"Clara Fitzgerald, private detective, this is my brother Tommy," she introduced herself to the woman, who looked surprised by the information. "I am looking into the murder of a woman that happened the other night and it has been suggested that the victim was called Rose Red and that she worked here."

The woman's mouth gaped.

"What are you talking about?" She demanded.

"A woman was killed in an alleyway, she had nothing on her to identify who she was," Clara explained. "But there was a tattoo on her leg of the name Rose surrounded by thorns. I am trying to find out who she was and also who attacked her. The rumour is she went by the name Rose Red and resided here."

"Why do you care what happened to her?" The woman asked, acting defensive.

Clara was patient.

"I don't like to see a murderer escape justice," she answered. "I care because someone hurt her, someone took her life and no one, not even a working girl, deserves to have their time on this earth cut short by an act of violence. I can't say who did this without first knowing more about the victim. I hoped you could help me."

The woman had dipped her head and was looking bleak.

"No one much cares what happens to us round these parts. We are expendable," she muttered.

"I care," Clara promised.

"You would be the first," the woman snorted. "I get trouble from time to time and do I ever get help from the police? They don't come near us. Too afraid, I reckon, or just haven't got the time for us."

"Well, I am here now, and I am not the police. I just want to find out who murdered Rose Red."

The woman gave her a strange look.

"There's the thing, you are going to have a hard job."

"Why?" Clara asked.

"Because Rose Red is not dead," the woman snorted with amusement. "Rose is my sister. Rose, love, come out here!"

A second woman emerged from the sitting room. She bore a remarkable resemblance to the woman in the alley, aside from being very much alive and well.

"There has been talk you are dead," the first woman told Rose.

Rose grinned at this information, revealing that she had a gap in her front teeth.

"Now, don't that just tickle you!" She laughed. "Do I look dead?"

"No," Clara found herself smiling too. "And I am very relieved about that, but that leaves me still baffled as to who that woman was in the alley."

"What woman?" Rose asked her sister.

"A woman was killed. Whereabouts did you say?"

"Near the picture house," Clara elaborated. "No one knows who she is, but she had this tattoo on her leg of the word rose…"

"…surrounded by thorns," Rose Red finished the sentence.

Her eyes had gone wide and her smile had disappeared completely. Clara realised she was trembling.

"You know who she is," she said.

"I need a cigarette," Rose started patting her pockets, her sister hastily produced a cigarette from her open skirt pocket and handed it over.

"Matches," Rose muttered, turning around and heading back into the sitting room.

Her sister looked as surprised by the development as

Clara and Tommy.

"I need to speak to her," Clara implored the woman.

There was a moment when the woman hesitated, then her own curiosity got the better of her and she stood back so Tommy and Clara could go through to the sitting room. She followed behind.

The room was small and swamped by a sofa and an armchair placed near a small fireplace. The walls were lined with pictures, most of them very old. They were prints cut from magazines, some pasted directly to the wallpaper, others cheaply framed. There were no photographs, but the mantelpiece and the windowsill heaved with tatty ornaments, the sort you could buy for a penny on the pier or won at the fair when it was in town. The room smelt of fried food, mainly fish, and tobacco smoke.

Rose had lit her cigarette and now paced back and forth in the narrow space between the sofa and the wall.

"I can't believe all this," Rose said. "You are sure about that woman's tattoo?"

"Yes," Clara said gently. "Everyone thought she was you. There is a striking resemblance."

Rose Red nodded.

"Then there is no doubting it," she paced faster, puffing out cigarette smoke as fast as she could. "The woman in that alley, the one you thought was me, goes by the name of Jenny. I don't know if that's her real name, or what her last name is."

"Why did she have the name Rose tattooed on her leg?" Clara asked.

Rose came to a halt, the hand holding the cigarette slipped to her side, while her other arm was clasped across her waist as if she was hugging herself.

"Jenny and me…" Rose stopped, rocking on her heels. "This business… and you know what I mean by that, right?"

"I am aware of the work you do," Clara said. "And I am

not here to judge, only to find out who killed Jenny."

Rose's eyes flicked to Tommy.

"Don't feel right having a man listening to this," she said gruffly. "Men only ever brought me and Jenny trouble."

"I can leave," Tommy said graciously. "If you would prefer."

Rose did not say anything. Tommy took that as a hint and headed back for the hallway. Now it was just the three women in the sitting room. Rose had smoked so hard she had nearly finished her cigarette and she looked at its stub anxiously. Her sister noticed her unease and quickly offered her another. Rose seemed to relax a fraction as the new cigarette was lit.

"This life, it wrecks your nerves," she told Clara. "I can't sleep without my sister Ethel nearby."

Ethel, the woman with the glasses, clasped her hands before her and watched her sister sadly.

"Ethel looks out for me. She doesn't do what I do, don't ever think she does. Ethel is virtuous. I never would let her do this," Rose was talking quick and pacing again. "But you have to survive, don't you?"

"Yes," Clara said sympathetically. "The world can be a very cruel place, when you are a woman with no money and no prospects."

"You understand that," Rose smiled at Clara, like they were comrades in this domestic war. "It's a tough life. Bet it's hard doing what you do?"

"Oh, that it is," Clara shrugged. "Men rarely see me as anything but an interfering woman who should go get herself a husband rather than muddle in their business. That just makes me more determined to prove I am as good, in fact, better, than them."

Rose's grin had returned.

"I like you. Do you really want to find out who killed Jenny?"

"Yes. I will do all I can to discover what happened to

her."

Rose relaxed a fraction further.

"I knew Jenny for years. We shared the same streets, often walked together. That was before Ethel started this place. Ethel was not like me, she was always a sensible girl," Rose smiled fondly at her sister. "She got married to a seaman. During the war he served on one of those patrol boats looking for German submarines. They helped to sink one too, but Ethel's husband was killed."

"He was a brave man," Clara turned and told Ethel.

Ethel gave a shrug and dropped her head, shy at the compliment.

"You got prize money for sinking submarines, and the share Ethel's husband would have had went to her and she started this place to keep a roof over her head," Rose gave a sad sigh. "She said I could come and work here, you know, proper work. But the place has never been that profitable, so I started to provide certain guests with extras again."

Ethel gave a soft sob.

"It is not your fault, love," Rose stepped out from behind the sofa and clutched Ethel's hand. "You've tried so very hard for me. Don't cry."

Clara felt she was imposing on this moment between the two sisters and wondered if she ought to leave, but Rose was looking at her again.

"That brings us to Jenny," she said. "When I left street-walking we lost touch. I can't say I have seen her in years."

"Would you recognise her, if you did see her?" Clara asked.

"No need, that tattoo tells me its her," Rose gave Clara a knowing look. "This business, you tend to develop a dislike for male company, but you still want company. Back in the day, me and Jenny were thick as thieves, we went everywhere together, looked out for each other. One time we met this Chinese sailor who could do the most beautiful tattoos and we had one each. Mine says Jenny, and Jenny's said Rose, and they were ringed in thorns. They were our secret, no one else would know what they meant, would they? The fellas never knew our real names, so they could not know what those tattoos stood for.

"And then I left Jenny. It sounds rotten, it wasn't like that. I was going to start a new life and when the time was right, she would join me. It just… never happened. I wasn't there to look out for her. Not in the end…"

Tears ran down Rose's face. Ethel clasped her hand tightly and they drew together like two desperate waifs tossed into the world's ocean, hopeless and frightened.

"Life is so cruel to women like us," Rose cried. "We never stood a chance."

Clara stepped closer to Rose.

"I shall discover who did this to Jenny," she said. "I shall make it my duty. But, I must know more about Rose's life these last few years. Who could I speak to about her?"

Rose shrugged.

"We lost touch," she sniffed. "I don't know. I don't know…"

"What about her mother?" Ethel nudged her sister. "She might know."

Rose wiped tears from her eyes.

"She might," she admitted. "Jenny's mother never took to me, don't know why. Not like she had done any different with her life. She drinks heavy. A right gin fiend. If you want to find her, I would suggest trying some of the local doss houses first, or a pub doorway. Jenny tried to rise above that, but she started to fall into drink too."

Rose became silent. Her tears had stopped. She only had so many left to shed these days.

"How did she die?" She asked.

"She was stabbed," Clara explained. "I think she was in a place she was not supposed to be. Did you always walk around the alleys by the picture house when you worked together?"

"Yes, they were our hunting grounds," Rose gave a bitter laugh. "Men falling out of the picture house near enough on top of us, and before it was a picture house, it was a cheap music hall. Those alleys were always full of girls and men looking for girls."

"Not these days," Clara said darkly.

Rose gave her an enquiring look.

"What do you mean?"

"Someone has made a point of clearing them out, and it isn't the police. They are empty, no one dares step foot in them and if you do, you'll get threatened with violence until you leave. I discovered that myself."

Rose glanced at her sister.

"That… that is the oddest thing. Those alleys were always so crowded with people. Most of 'em were lowlifes, but there would be children and women, some like me and Jenny, and some just housewives having a natter. Me and Jenny would walk down them arm-in-arm, calling out to all the people we knew as we went past. No one judged us."

"Why would anyone want the alleys empty?" Ethel asked quietly, her eyes screwing up in anxiety behind her glasses, which made for a strange sight.

"Maybe so they can conduct their business without hindrance?" Clara replied. "Someone wants no witnesses and no one getting in the way. And they are prepared to act violently to ensure that."

"Oh Jenny," Rose sniffed. "Why did she have to get mixed up in that?"

"I'm sorry," Clara said. "I really am. I hope I can figure this out and put your friend's killer behind bars."

"Do that," Rose nodded. "You've got to. Maybe we are just common working girls, and maybe we aren't worth the time of day to the police, but we still have feelings, we still want to live. Ain't no one cares about us."

Clara took Rose's hand and held it firmly.

"I care," she swore. "And I will do all in my power to bring justice to Jenny."

"You ain't like the rest," Rose embraced Clara and sobbed softly in her ear. "You have a good heart. If you need to ask me anything, anything at all, come back at once. I want to help find Jenny's killer."

Clara gently hugged her back.

Chapter Twenty-One

There was a message when Clara finally arrived home from Colonel Brandt. He had been asking around among his contacts and had discovered that a former army major, who had served in India, had retired to Brighton in 1876. He had been part of the force sent to quell the 1855 rebellion and had been decorated for his bravery. He had earned one of the special hunting knives. He was also long since dead, having passed away in 1891. However, Brandt had learned through his colleagues that the major had had a son and it was possible the knife had remained in the family as an heirloom. Or it might have been sold, pawned or stolen at any time since the major was awarded it. Clara just had to hope someone had been sentimental. Since she was short on leads, it certainly would not hurt to track down the major's family and see what they knew about the knife.

Her father's collection of old trade directories was once again to prove useful. He had been slightly obsessed about buying them throughout his adult life, much to Clara's mother's mild disapproval. No one needed that many directories. Clara, however, thanked her father's odd collection. It helped her enormously, and she was continuing the family tradition, buying up the latest trade and street directory as soon as it came out.

They had an edition for 1890, the year before the major died. His full name had been Major Edward Basildon, and the street directory specified his address as 18 Lovall road. Clara fetched a map and was interested to note that Lovall Road was not far from the crime scene; just a couple of streets over. She pointed this out to Tommy.

"Coincidence or clue?" She asked him.

"Depends if his descendants still live in the area," Tommy pointed out.

They also discovered that in 1890 a second Edward Basildon was living in Lovall Road, a few doors down from number 18. Clara tapped her finger on the name.

"Has to be his son," she said to Tommy.

Tommy fetched a street directory for ten years later and found Lovall Road. He traced his finger down the list of residents.

"Edward Basildon," he pointed to 10 Lovall Road. "Assuming he is Major Basildon's son, he could be in his seventies by now."

"Old enough to have a son and a grandson of his own. How many Basildons live in Brighton?"

Tommy flicked to the back of the directory and checked out the name list again.

"Only five are listed for 1900. Hang on, let's get the newest directory down."

Tommy fetched the 1921 Jolley's Street Directory from a shelf. Clara had yet to use it, though she had scrolled through the section for her own street to assure herself that she had been correctly listed. She had also paid for a full-page advertisement in the directory, as you never knew who might look in there.

"Still only five Basildons listed," Tommy told her. "Edward Basildon is still living in Lovall Road, the other Basildons are in different parts of Brighton."

"Well, I think we know who are going to be paying a visit to," Clara said.

~~~*~~~

An hour later they found themselves in Lovall Road. It was a quiet place lined with terrace houses. The front doors of the houses exited straight onto the pavement, but some homeowners had compensated for the lack of a front garden by placing flower boxes on the sills of their front windows. While the houses were far from extravagant, the road had an air of respectability and everyone appeared to be trying their best. Number ten was at the top end of the road and Clara had to pass number 18 to reach it. She glanced at the former home of Major Basildon, noting that the window was dominated by a canary cage, two bright yellow birds hopping about inside.

"Seems a humble place for an army major to live," Tommy remarked.

Clara was distracted from the canaries.

"I suppose anyone can find themselves a little short of money," she said.

"Short enough to sell a highly valuable dagger?" Tommy suggested.

Clara made a hissing noise by sucking backwards through her teeth.

"I hope not, or else this is another dead end."

They came to 10 Lovall Road. A bicycle was propped against the wall, partly covering the bottom of the deep window. Clara knocked on the door.

They waited only a moment before a woman answered. She was in her forties and therefore unlikely to be the wife of Edward Basildon – unless they had misjudged his age.

"Hello," Clara smiled politely. "My colleague and I are from the British Army's Historical Research Society. We work at compiling regimental histories, and other such papers. We are currently on a five-year project researching the 1855 rebellion in India and we are trying to collect as much information as we can about those men who participated. I hope we are not mistaken in assuming that the Edward Basildon who resides here is the son of Major

Edward Basildon?"

The woman was a mouse-haired, plump creature. She listened attentively.

"Why, you are referring to my grandfather!" She declared with a smile. "And yes, my father, Major Basildon's son, does reside here and I am sure he would love to talk to you. He was extremely proud of his father, you know."

The woman showed them into the narrow hallway of the house.

"And what is your name?" Clara asked as they squeezed in; there was barely room for them to stand squashed by the wall with the staircase running up the hallway.

"Mary Parkes," the woman introduced herself. "I live here and look after father. He is rather frail these days and my mother passed away just after the war."

"I'm sorry to hear that," Clara said.

Mary Parkes waved away her comment, she did not need pity.

"I don't ever feel sorry for myself, it is a bad habit. No, I live here and look after father, which suits me fine as my own husband perished in the last war," Mary Parkes pushed past them and escorted them to the back of the house, the property proved to be longer than it at first appeared, with a room at the front and a room behind, with a tiny window squashed to one side. The kitchen was built to cover part of this back room and the hallway, with a narrow passage running along the side. Edward Basildon was sitting in the small back room next to a blazing fire. The heat that came out of the room made Clara feel flushed, it was like being battered by a furnace fire. In contrast, Edward was not only wearing a cardigan, but had his legs covered by a thick blanket.

He was carefully constructing a model from matchsticks. It was too early in the process to say what the object was going to be. Edward's hands trembled madly as he lifted each matchstick, sliced off the head with its flammable tip, dotted glue on the section he was constructing and carefully applied the stick of wood. The process would at first glance seem impossible with the terrible tremors he was suffering, but despite his shaking the work was coming along smoothly and the model was an impressive work of precision.

Opposite Edward, leaning back in a second armchair and watching the old man work with a slightly bored expression, was a young man. He was in his mid-twenties, a burly individual with thick, curly black hair. Mary Parkes had shuffled into the room ahead of them, and starting making introductions.

"This is my son, Mortimer," she introduced the younger man, "and this is my father, Edward. Father, these people are researching the 1855 India rebellion and want to ask about grandfather."

Edward looked up with sudden interest.

"Really? How exciting! About time someone paid attention to that. Too many people these days are discussing Indian independence and acting as if we were monsters over there. My father would talk about the atrocities he had seen. Some of those Indians were thugs; they killed their own, along with British subjects. They tortured and killed in horrendous ways. Oh, there were some decent ones too, father always said that. People had to be there to understand what he went through," this was clearly a subject that was dear to Edward's heart. "I was always so proud of him. He was a brave and heroic man. During the rebellion he saved three Indian ladies from being drowned in a well! Hardly a monster, huh? He protected anyone who needed help, that was my father."

"I'm off, if its going to be all talk about the 'Major' again," Mortimer Parkes rose from his seat, his tone sullen and unpleasant.

"Don't be like that," Mary pleaded with her son, in a voice that suggested they had had this discussion before.

"Let him go," Edward grumbled. "He doesn't know what respect is, that's his trouble. My father would be ashamed of him, thoroughly ashamed!"

"Father! You don't help," Mary complained, she was sandwiched between the two warring parties, and she was never going to win.

"I don't need any stuffy old army major's approval," Mortimer sneered as he marched out of the room. "What good did it do him anyway? Living in a hovel all his life and barely enough money to keep him out of a pauper's grave when he died! If that's what bravery gets you, you can keep it."

Mortimer stormed out and they shortly heard the front door slamming.

"I apologise…" Mary began.

"Don't," Edward scolded her, "let them see what a pathetic excuse for a man he is. He never served in the war, you know. Supposedly the doctor at the recruiting station told him he had a bad heart, and they wouldn't take him."

"He came home with a letter, father," Mary protested.

"What twaddle!" Edward snapped. "If I had been young enough I would have done my duty, bad heart or no bad heart. He is a lazy oaf who doesn't give a damn for his country!"

"You are being harsh, father," Mary said softly. "And our guests don't need to know all that, anyway. I'll go make some tea."

Mary looked dejected as she left the room. Clara could only guess at the family rift she had managed to clumsily step into by her arrival and questions.

"Ignore them," Edward distracted her. "Take a seat, there is an extra chair in that corner."

Clara took the armchair as directed, while Tommy found a wooden chair in the corner and brought it over.

"Did you serve?" Edward asked him fiercely.

"Yes," Tommy answered politely. "All four years."

"What rank?"

"I was a captain, by the end," Tommy said.

"Good man, I could see you were officer material," Edward nodded. "As for me, my father wouldn't hear of me going into the army. Said it was not a life he wished on anyone, and so I worked all my days as a teacher."

Edward nudged his matchstick model.

"Mortimer is right about one thing, my father deserved to end his days living in luxury. He was a hero, but there was nothing here for him when he got home. And my mother contracted a sickness in India that never went away. My father was desperate for a cure, spent every penny on doctors and cures. All to no avail. By the time my mother passed there was very little left, and then father became ill and I took care of him and my own family with what money I had," Edward looked around the small back room. "I guess I can see why Mortimer is angry. But he is a fool, there is more to life than wealth. There is respect, honour and being a good man. My father was a hero and that can never be taken from him."

"I have heard about the ceremonial daggers that every officer was awarded for his part in quelling the rebellion," Clara said.

"Oh yes, that was quite a thing. A sure mark of the gratitude felt by the authorities. My father had it on a stand above the fireplace all his days. When he passed, it was left to me. I had it on display too until my daughter moved in," there was a hint of resentment in Edward's words. "She insisted it be put away. Said it made her uncomfortable to have a big dagger on display all the time. That's why Mortimer is such a namby-pamby, you know, because of her. Never did me any harm looking at that knife as a boy, reminded me of what struggles my father had been through. I used to ask if I could polish it and I would shine it until you could see your face in the blade."

"You still have it then?" Clara asked.

"Of course! I was going to leave it to Mortimer, until he turned out such a limpet," Edward snorted. "He'll only sell it the second he can, that lad thinks about money all the time. No, I am going to be buried with it, to scupper his plans and grin at him from my grave."

Edward found this very amusing.

"Would you like to see it?"

"I would," Clara assured him. "I have not seen one of the actual knives, only a drawing in a textbook."

"Oh, you can't appreciate it from a drawing," Edward rose stiffly, having to press himself up with his arms as his knees creaked in protest. Tommy started to help him, but was pushed away crossly. "You'll see what I mean when you are face-to-face with it. Beautiful thing, it truly is. I keep it in this drawer, which is such a shame, really."

Edward hobbled over to a small bureau and fumbled with a drawer handle, his shaking hands making it difficult to clutch the tiny brass clasps.

"The Indians were always big on ceremonial knives, quite a thing for them. I suppose that is where the idea came from. During the rebellion, a maharajah's palace came under attack and the British defended it. He was very grateful, I believe he was part of the ceremony to present the knifes," Edward started to ease the drawer open in jerky movements. "My father remembered that day vividly all his life. He could recall the sunlight glinting on the blades as they were handed out. He felt such pride."

Edward finished easing the drawer open and stared inside. He moved some papers about and pulled out a book of stamps and some parcel twine. Then he became very still, his spine stiffening.

"It's gone," he said, his voice twanging with fury. "Damn thing is gone!"

Chapter Twenty-Two

Clara and Tommy mulled over the mystery of the missing dagger as they headed home. Edward Basildon had been, quite naturally, furious about its absence and he had no qualms in instantly accusing his grandson. He had ranted about the acquaintances Mortimer brought home, who he called lowlifes and scum. He worked himself up into such a fit of rage that he ended up having a funny turn and being helped up to his bed by Mary.

Clara and Tommy had let themselves out.

"Mortimer looks likely for our murderer," Tommy observed as they walked.

"Hmm," Clara mused. "He may have taken the knife, or it might have been one of his cronies, as his grandfather pointed out. Either way, he is involved with the problems in that alley. Maybe not directly, but he certainly knows the people who are. That knife links him. I think the Inspector should hear of this. We now know where the murder weapon came from."

They left a message for Inspector Park-Coombs at the police station, as he happened to be out on another matter, then walked the remaining distance to their house. Annie was waiting for them.

"A gentleman by the name of Professor Montgomery sent a message asking if you could be at the Brighton Institute for Astronomy at seven o'clock. He says he shall be waiting for you at the tradesman's gate. That is all very clandestine," she said as they walked into the hallway and hung up their coats.

Clara glanced at Tommy.

"Ready for a little game of subterfuge?"

Tommy grinned.

"Always."

"Well, I am going to visit Peterson again," Annie informed them. "I think he is going to sink if he is not helped soon."

"Tell him I know where the knife came from and that it did not belong to the woman who died. Her name was Jenny, by the way," Clara explained.

"Do you think that will help him?" Annie looked troubled.

"It may give him hope we are digging into this matter. Promise him he is my priority."

"I will Clara," Annie gave a smile, but there was no real joy to it. "I'm scared for him, that's all."

~~~*~~~

At seven o'clock they were at the back of the Institute, stood by the heavy-duty tradesman's gate and awaiting Professor Montgomery. He was late.

"Who would have thought stargazing would cause such trouble," Tommy mulled, looking up at the dark sky. "I like stars, but I never had the inclination to study them."

"I recall father having a telescope," Clara replied.

"Oh, yes, someone bought it for him as a Christmas present," Tommy remembered, smiling. "I think the novelty of it lasted around a month and then it was tucked in a cupboard. It's probably still there."

"I wonder if I could use it for secretly observing

suspects?" Clara said as the thought suddenly struck her.

"I think it might be noticed, it was for quite long distance," Tommy chuckled.

It was then that Professor Montgomery appeared out of the shadows, hurrying towards them.

"Miss Fitzgerald, my apologies for being late, I was detained by a porter and it was difficult to make an excuse without appearing suspicious," Montgomery was a little breathless. "You have brought someone?"

"This is my brother Tommy," Clara explained. "He is my assistant."

"Very well," Montgomery nodded. "I am going to sneak us all in via the back stairs. We have to be careful, as the kitchen staff will still be around. However, the bursar and librarian will be safely back in their chambers at this time of night."

Montgomery opened the gate for them and showed them through. The grounds were unlit, and at this side of the Institute there were only lecture rooms and offices, meaning there were no lights on in the windows or, for that matter, people to look out of them. The professor knew his way through the grounds without a light and ran rather fast, causing Clara and Tommy to have to keep pace and do their best to avoid any obstacles they might not see in the dark.

"He is very agitated," Tommy observed as he stumbled where the edge of the path met a raised grass verge.

"It is not every day you surreptitiously enter the place you are in charge of," Clara pointed out. "He is worried about what this will look like if he is caught."

"Surely he could just demand that box be handed over to him?" Tommy suggested.

"It would cause a huge fuss, which he is endeavouring to avoid," Clara replied. "Mr McGhie, the librarian, has been in his post longer than Professor Montgomery. There is a sort of unofficial power that comes from being in your position that long. You gain respect and an authority that is not technically yours."

"A bit like Annie and the kitchen. Neither of us dare move anything in there, even though it is our kitchen," Tommy said.

"A bit like that, yes," Clara laughed.

"Please, be quiet, we are reaching the door," Professor Montgomery spun around and hushed them.

Considering the amount of noise they had made by running through the grounds, Clara thought his attitude slightly ironic, but she did not counter him, as he was her client and the client is always right.

"I am hoping the kitchen staff will be occupied and will not see us enter," Professor Montgomery said anxiously as he pushed open the door and peered inside. There was no light in the hallway either. He waved a hand at Tommy and Clara to encourage them to enter behind him. "The staircase is just there."

He pointed and was about to move when there was the sound of someone approaching and he froze. Clara glanced back at the door they had just entered, wondering if there was time for them all to slip out, but the footsteps were very close and she suspected that even if one of them could escape, the other two would not have time, the movement of the door would alert whoever was coming their way.

Professor Montgomery was pinned to the spot in mid-stride. He had one foot held out as if he was about to take a step; he dare not even put it down on the floor, but balanced precariously on one leg. Tommy was stifling a chuckle at the sight and Clara had to admit it was all very comical, even if the outcome of their being spotted could be quite serious for the director.

The footsteps kept approaching and someone could be heard humming. There was a turn in the corridor ahead and the flicker of a lamp marked the progress of the unseen person. Just as it seemed they were to come around the corner and see the intruders, the lamplight jerked to the side and the footsteps started to head away.

"Went down into the cellars," Montgomery said in a tight voice. "Quick, to the stairs!"

He darted to the staircase in an ungainly fashion and Clara could not help but wonder what a sight the trio would make to anyone seeing them. Montgomery was certainly no cat burglar, that was for sure. They made it to the stairs without delay and were soon heading upwards. The stairs were tight and built into a narrow shaft, with several twists and landings to fit them into the unaccommodating space. There was no natural light other than what could come in from a skylight far above. Clara stubbed her toe on a step and grumbled. Professor Montgomery was getting further and further ahead, still flapping like a demented scarecrow. Clearly subterfuge was not something he found easy to pull off.

Finally, the professor stopped at a landing; the stairs continued upwards to the attic space. Clara and Tommy came to a halt behind him, a little out-of-breath. Tommy's knees were protesting the sudden climb and he rubbed them, making a quiet groan. Montgomery shushed him again.

"These stairs come out close to the library," he hissed in a voice that was far louder than Tommy's groan. "I must check and see that no one is about."

The professor turned the door knob with little care and made quite a noise as he opened it. If anyone had been around, they would certainly have heard him. He appeared not to appreciate this, as he ducked his head around the door and peered up and down the corridor. From what Clara could make out from behind him, the hallway was pitch black and no one was about.

Professor Montgomery took a deep breath and stepped through the door, motioning for Clara and Tommy to follow. They stood in the passage, Clara feeling disorientated in the dark, while Montgomery swung his head left and right.

"All clear," he sighed with relief and then turned to his left.

They followed him along the corridor to another door. He grabbed the handle and turned it sharply, only to discover it was locked.

"How dare he!" Montgomery declared rather more loudly than he intended. He gasped and pressed a hand over his mouth. "No matter, I have keys in my office, wait here."

Montgomery disappeared as fast as he could. Tommy leaned back against the wall behind him and folded his arms across his chest.

"Personally, I would have brought the keys with me, considering the complication this box is causing," he said.

"Professor Montgomery is not as cynical and cunning as us," Clara smirked at him.

The professor returned with the keys jangling, which made Clara cringe. He didn't seem to notice, he was too flustered. He placed a key in the lock and turned it, the door obligingly opened.

"Mr McGhie has been told to never lock the library, in case there is ever a fire," Professor Montgomery explained to Clara and Tommy. "In the event of a fire, it is imperative we get all the books and important documents safely out of the library. A locked door would impede such an effort and potentially result in the loss of the entire contents. I must have words with McGhie."

"You do recall we are not supposed to be here," Clara reminded him. "And you must be careful what you say, else your colleagues will discover what we have been doing."

Montgomery's face fell.

"Well, yes…" he muttered, masking the fact that he had completely forgotten. "I shall say I came up early in the morning for a book and found the door locked."

Clara did not argue with him further. They entered the library and headed straight to the librarian's counter, behind which was his office and storeroom with its substantial door. This too was locked. Montgomery's face fell.

"I don't have a key for this door."

"Maybe it is kept in the library?" Tommy suggested.

They all began to search the drawers of the cabinets

nearest the counter, and then around Mr McGhie's desk. Tommy pulled out a small metal cashbox from a drawer.

"For overdue fines and such," Montgomery said, waving away the discovery.

Tommy ignored him and continued to look in the drawer for the cashbox key. He found it tucked into a box of paperclips. He unlocked the cashbox.

"Are you thinking of helping yourself?" Montgomery accosted him.

"I was thinking where I would hide a key that I didn't want anyone to find," Tommy hissed back at him, his tone angry. Montgomery was getting on his nerves. "And look what I found."

He produced an old door key. Professor Montgomery fell silent. Tommy went to the storeroom and tried the key. It turned smoothly and the door unlocked. Pushing it open, they could see only darkness within. Professor Montgomery fumbled near the door and found a chain that connected to a bare bulb in the ceiling of the cupboard. He switched it on, and the room was illuminated with a weak yellow glow.

"Where would he put it?" Montgomery muttered, stepping into the room and then turning around.

"What's on that very high shelf?" Clara pointed up to the corner of the ceiling where the glow of the bulb barely cast any light.

Professor Montgomery reached up and felt about.

"Ah!" He pulled something off with a scraping sound. "This is it!"

Montgomery took down the box, pulling away a piece of string that had apparently fallen over it. He stepped out of the room and placed it on the library counter. The box had no lock, (Professor Lynch had not been that skilled a craftsman) but was sealed with a burgundy-coloured wax. Tommy offered Montgomery his pocket knife and the academic sawed through the wax, which was thick in places and difficult to break through. Clara wondered if they would be able to fully mask the signs of their activity once they were done. It would be possible to reheat the wax and maybe smooth over the marks of the knife, but it would be awkward, and no one had thought to bring sealing wax or a candle.

Professor Montgomery was grunting as he went to his task, it seemed to be taking ages.

"Do you hear something?" Tommy asked his sister.

Clara paused to listen, though the scrape of the knife made hearing subtle sounds hard. Suddenly she glanced at Tommy.

"Running footsteps!"

At that same moment Montgomery released the lid of the box and it slid off to the floor with a dull clang.

"Aha!" He cried in delight, just as the library door burst open and a frantic Mr McGhie appeared.

"Stop right there Montgomery!" McGhie yelled, before having to cough heartily. "I knew you would try something like this!"

"You were in your rooms!" Montgomery said in alarm. "How did you know?"

"I always suspected you were a sly fiend!" McGhie said triumphantly. "I rigged the box with an alarm. I attached a string to it with sealing wax and ran that string through the walls to my room where it was tied to a bell hanging from my ceiling. The box was enough weight to keep the bell in place, but once it was detached, the bell slipped to the floor of my room and awoke me!"

"That is clever," Tommy remarked in admiration for the man's ingenuity.

"Wait," Montgomery became indignant, "you drilled holes through the walls of the Institute without permission?"

"Slightly beside the point," Tommy mumbled.

"I had to do it, to trap you!" McGhie was pointing a finger at Professor Montgomery. "As soon as you brought in that detective, I knew something like this would occur! You have no faith in old Lynch, none at all! Put that lid back on at once!"

"Before you do that," Clara said calmly, "maybe you ought to take a look inside."

Chapter Twenty-Three

Mr McGhie did not want to hear of looking in the box, but Clara had started to unpack its contents and the fraught librarian rushed over to grab them. At which point he started to become uneasy. The first paper he picked up was a bill for lemon throat sweets, on the back of which was a scrawled note that said Lynch had been overcharged for them and that anyone reading this in twenty years' time should collect the extra along with the interest on the sum for the Institute.

"He always did have a sense of humour," Montgomery remarked.

"There is a letter here," Clara pulled out a piece of paper. "Should I read it out?"

"No, no, this is not how it was meant to be," McGhie protested weakly, the throat sweet bill had thrown him. "He asked for the king and bishops."

"I think I should read the letter aloud," Clara said gently.

"Go ahead," Montgomery agreed, suddenly appearing a lot more confident.

Clara cleared her throat and started to read.

"To my colleagues reading this letter twenty years

hence, especially to those who have questioned my astrological inclinations. Over the last few years my health has been fragile, and my continuing existence has at times felt too much of a burden, yet I do not give up hope for some relief and I still wish to live, for I have so much to do.

"My studies into astrology began as a way of alleviating a bad period of depression I suffered some years ago. I felt lost, my usual comforts had abandoned me, I could not look upon the stars without feeling that for all my science, all my efforts to understand this universe, I was utterly inadequate to save my own life. I had no answers, only questions. At my lowest ebb, Mr McGhie paid me a visit and remarked on an interesting book he had just read about astrology…"

"Mr McGhie!" Professor Montgomery snapped, interrupting Clara.

The librarian blushed at being caught out.

"I was just trying to cheer him up," McGhie said. "That was when he had that bad bout of pneumonia and he lost so much weight he looked like a skeleton wrapped in skin. I hoped to revive his spirits."

"You are responsible for all this," Montgomery growled. "I should have known."

"It was only an act of kindness for a sick man. I never knew he would construct this box, did I?" McGhie protested.

"I begin to doubt that!" Professor Montgomery replied fiercely. "Maybe this was all your idea, huh?"

"No! I never knew about the box until Professor Lynch sent it to me, a few days before he died, with a note attached to it saying I should keep it safe for the next twenty years."

"We are going to have a long discussion about your continuing role at the Institute, Mr McGhie," Montgomery said darkly, and the librarian flinched.

"Shall I continue?" Clara asked.

"Go ahead, Miss Fitzgerald," Montgomery replied.

Clara picked up where she had left off.

"The volume Mr McGhie loaned me was typical of its

kind and I must remark that I have always been most sceptical of such things, though I did appreciate the lengths the author went to in an effort to explain the science behind the astrological charts he presented. I also found myself bored and desperate to distract my mind, so I began to play around with the techniques mentioned in the book and I drew up my own birth chart. To my surprise, it proved a remarkably accurate description of my personality.

"With time on my hands, I found myself returning to this game over and over. I made charts for my colleagues and was amused to see how often they proved correct in view of their personal traits and flaws. Only once I was through with this task, did I begin to wonder about charts for predictions. The main element of astrology is that the stars we are born under predict our paths through life and can enable us to take a peek into the future. A load of nonsense, as my dear colleague Professor Montgomery would surely say, and I would have agreed with him up until recently…"

"He knew you well," McGhie said solemnly to Montgomery.

"We worked together for so long," Professor Montgomery gave a sentimental sniff as he recalled his long-departed friend. "What else does it say, Miss Fitzgerald?"

"To prove something in science, appropriate tests are required," Clara continued to read. "These tests must be repeated and have consistent results. As a man of science, I was well placed to test the claims of the astrologers and determine if there was anything to this strange artform other than wishful thinking. I began by using the stars to make predictive horoscopes for my friends and then monitored the results. I found that if I informed a person of the horoscope and what it said, then there was a ninety percent chance of it coming true. However, if I did not inform a person of the horoscope and merely kept track of their lives, then the chance of success reduced to fifty percent.

"I concluded that there was a strong element of human influence in the results. A person was likely to work unconsciously to make a prediction come true if they knew of it, or at least to interpret events differently to prove the prediction accurate. I should add, I only told individuals about my predictions for them if they were interested in astrology, and this therefore further skewed my results, as a sceptic might have been less willing to allow, or perceive, a prediction to come true.

"I also noted that elements of the predictions could be vague and possible to misconstrue. I aimed to make my predictions as detailed and precise as possible, to eliminate this but, ultimately, I felt my results were being tainted by a natural tendency in my participants to encourage the predictions to come true.

"There had to be an ultimate and final test, something conclusive that would prove either the astrological charts had a value as predictors of the future, or that they were a load of hocus pocus. I hoped for the former result, I feared I would discover the latter."

"He had not lost his mind," Professor Montgomery said softly. "He was still the rational scientist I had always known."

"Please, let Miss Fitzgerald continue," Mr McGhie puttered impatiently.

Clara had finished the first page of the letter and now turned to the second.

"The only hope was a long-term test, something where there could be no influence by the individual in question. I needed a subject who could be objective. As I considered this plan, I concluded I must write charts to predict the course of the future for people who I had never met, and nor could I ever speak to. These people could therefore be relied upon to live their lives without somehow being influenced by the predictions and making decisions that would cause the prediction to come true artificially.

"However, I could not resist also developing a chart for myself. My health has been poor these last months, and I am fearful of what may be coming, yet, I have drawn predictions for myself that offer great hope. One of these charts assured me that I should still be alive in twenty years' time. Because of this joyful assurance, I decided to instruct that my box be kept sealed until twenty years hence. All of my predictions should have come true by then, and I shall be delighted if it is I who shall be opening this box.

"Unfortunately, the rational scientist in me doubts all this, and I have therefore made arrangements for the box to be handed to Mr McGhie in the event of my untimely death. This will, of course, automatically void the prediction for my own longevity, however, there may still be some value in the remaining predictions.

"So, I leave this box in the hands of friends. My only condition for this is that when this box is opened it be done so in privacy, with only the senior lecturers and the director present. I believe this shall assure for a sensible assessment of the contents. The bursar and Mr McGhie shall also be present, to see for themselves what this box contains.

"Astrology has provided a solace these last days of my…"

"Wait a minute!" Professor Montgomery said forcefully. "Read that last part again."

Clara did not need to ask him what he meant, she flicked her eyes back up the page.

"My only condition for this is that when this box is opened it be done so in privacy, with only the senior lecturers and the director present."

Montgomery shot a fierce look at Mr McGhie, who had taken a step back from the counter and was trying to look anywhere but at the Director.

"He specified privacy!" Montgomery hissed.

"There were other instructions," McGhie mumbled.

"Show me them! Show me this letter that gave these

strange instructions!" Montgomery demanded.

"I can't recall where I put it," McGhie muttered.

Tommy glanced around him and moved back into the storeroom. After a few moments of rifling through shelves he returned with a piece of paper.

"This could be the note that came with the box, it was on the shelf where the box was sitting."

Montgomery snatched the letter from him. Tommy cast Clara an offended look, she just shrugged. Professor Montgomery was rapidly losing his composure.

"This is it!" Montgomery snarled. "Dear Mr McGhie, I would like to request you hold onto this box until the year 1922, when it should be opened privately in the company of the senior lecturers, the bursar, yourself and whoever is the director at that time. It contains various astrological charts concerning future events and when you open it, you will be able to determine if there is any value in such predictions. I am only saddened that I shall not be with you to see this event, my own horoscope has proven faulty. If there is any worth in astrology, then this box may go some way towards proving it. However, it may just as easily demonstrate the fallacy of the craft. I wish to thank you again for loaning me the volume on astrology and offering me your words of comfort in my troubled days. Your friendship has been of great consolation to me and I know you shall respect my wishes in this matter."

Montgomery came to a pause. The tone of the letter, so gently conversive, had suddenly brought Professor Lynch back from the dead, albeit, temporarily. His voice spoke from twenty years past and Montgomery clearly felt emotional at the impact. Here was the friend he had known and cared about, the man of science who he had judged for stumbling into the field of astrology. A mixture of guilt and sorrow was stirred up by the letter.

"You..." Montgomery's voice was tight with emotion. "You were willing to blot his name and reputation by this ridiculous ceremony you concocted. Why?"

Mr McGhie ducked his head further.

"Professor Lynch was always very modest about his skills as an astrologer, but I believed he had a great power within him. Many of his charts had proven highly accurate. I was certain this box contained prophecies of great value and I feared if it was only opened in private, the contents would be hushed up, even if they were hugely significant. I could not allow that to happen. Astrology must be recognised as a science…"

"Poppycock!" Montgomery snapped. "Its all a load of nonsense!"

"Precisely my point!" McGhie sharply snapped back. "You would never allow the contents to be made public unless you were forced to!"

"So, you concocted this bizarre scheme involving the king and bishops?"

"I never thought that would happen," McGhie admitted. "But I hoped you would compromise to a smaller public opening. I had to try."

"And what if the contents proved laughable? Huh? You would have ruined Professor Lynch's academic name and the name of this Institute! It was precisely what the professor feared and the reason he asked for the box only to be opened in private!"

"I knew his predictions would be accurate!" McGhie countered. "I never feared otherwise!"

"Gentlemen," Clara intervened as the argument was escalating to no avail, "before you fight further, may I suggest looking at the contents of this box."

Clara had removed five astrological charts from the box. One was the chart that predicted Professor Lynch would be alive and well to open his box in the year 1922. This she showed to Mr McGhie, who flinched at the implication. The other charts had the details of their predictions written on the back.

One was for Lord Kitchener who the stars predicted would be contesting the role of Prime Minister in 1919.

Lord Kitchener had died when the ship he was on sank in 1916. A second chart indicated that the future King George V would come to the throne in 1907, he actually became king in 1910.

McGhie picked up the chart.

"This one is close," he said.

"It is three years out," Montgomery shook his head. "It might as well be ten years out. A prediction either must be truly accurate to be considered worthwhile, or else we may as well have drawn years out of a hat."

The third chart was for Alexander Graham Bell, the inventor of the telephone, who had passed away just a few weeks ago in Canada. The chart said that Bell would invent a machine that would enable men to go to the moon by 1915. Even McGhie had to fall silent when he read that one.

Lastly there was a chart for Captain Robert Falcon Scott, that said he would fulfil his ambition of being the first man to reach the South Pole and would return to England a national hero in the year 1906. Scott did, indeed, attempt to reach the South Pole. However, he was not the first there, that honour being claimed by a Norwegian rival. Scott died on the return route from the pole to his ship. He never returned to England alive, though he was celebrated as a national hero.

McGhie read this final chart with a quiet air of disappointment.

"The bits that are correct are clearly based on facts Lynch knew at the time he was making these charts," Montgomery pointed out, his tone mellowed with the defeat of his opponent. "We all knew that Kitchener was a keen politician, that George V would come to the throne at some point and that Scott was hoping to find the South Pole. His first expedition to the Antarctic was just underway when Lynch died. The rest was guesswork."

"I…" McGhie stared at the charts forlornly. "I really thought he was a master of astrology."

"It is not a science," Montgomery told the dejected man,

though his voice no longer had its fierce edge. "It never will be. Professor Lynch knew that, and he proved his point. In the end, he remained a scientist to the very last."

"I…" Mr McGhie put down the charts and stepped away. "Please, excuse me."

He disappeared out of the library and could be heard scuttling down the corridor to his room.

"You will not be too hard on him?" Clara said to Montgomery.

Montgomery snorted.

"He did no harm, in the end, and the disappointment of all this is going to eat at him for a long time. I would be a harsh man to punish him further," a smile crept onto Montgomery's lips. "I never should have doubted Lynch. He really was a wise man, right to the last."

Chapter Twenty-Four

With the business at the Institute resolved, Clara could focus all her attention on the murder of the woman called Jenny and the attack on Private Peterson. The next day she set out to find Jenny's mother and see if the woman could be of any help in determining why her daughter had been killed. Tommy accompanied her once again. He had brought with him his old service revolver, tucked into the pocket of his jacket. The revolver had not worked since the war, having been so clogged with Flanders mud that its internal mechanisms had completely seized up. A clever gunsmith could probably clean it out and repair it, but Tommy had no desire to see it working again. He brought it with them purely for show and to scare off any thugs that tried to threaten his sister.

Rose had given Clara the name of Jenny's mother – Matilda Greystone – but could offer no address for her, so they began by asking around the local pubs to see if they knew where she was. Most of the landlords knew Matilda, but they could not say where she was right at that moment. Clara was not entirely sure if they were lying to her, perhaps protecting Matilda, but there was not a lot she could do about it if they were.

She kept moving and after visiting twenty-three pubs without success, she shifted her plans to checking out women's doss houses. These were far less common than the male equivalent, and it did not take long for her to have made her enquiries at all of them, without any luck. Clara was now certain people were deliberately lying to her, there was something about the hasty way they told her they knew no one by the name of Matilda that rankled.

She was leaving the last one, with Tommy a step behind, when she bumped straight into Rose who was coming along the road hastily.

"Oh!" Rose declared, taking a moment to realise who it was she had stumbled into. "Miss Fitzgerald."

"Call me Clara," Clara said. "I did not expect to see you here."

Rose shrugged.

"After you told me about Jenny, I was awake all night thinking how I just abandoned her to her fate as soon as I had the chance to move on. I felt I had let her down."

"You had no option," Clara told her sympathetically.

"Well, it felt like I should have done more for her," Rose hunched up her shoulders and looked miserable. "I want to know what became of her and so I thought I would ask around. I know you said you were looking into it, but I just couldn't sit around doing nothing."

"I completely understand," Clara promised. "And perhaps this is a fortuitous meeting, for I am having considerable bother locating Jenny's mother. I am under the impression that even if people know where I might find her, they will not tell me."

A mischievous grin came to Rose's face.

"That's because you are clearly not one of us, not in that nice dress, hat and shoes. People ain't going to tell you where she is, not without good reason."

"I was beginning to realise that," Clara groaned. "Maybe you could help?"

"Be glad to, I want to do anything I can to help Jenny.

Let me do the asking, people will remember me and talk to me."

They retraced Clara's journey around the various pubs and doss houses in the area. After another hour, with Tommy grumbling about the ache in his knees, Rose emerged from a pub with a look of excitement on her face.

"Old Sam says he thinks Jenny's mum is sleeping in the kitchen of the Red Lion," she said. "The landlord there always had a soft spot for her and when she isn't too drunk, she can whip up some nice grub. He is letting her sleep there if she cooks for him and for customers."

"Sounds promising," Clara agreed, recalling with a touch of annoyance that the Red Lion was the second pub she had visited that morning. If Matilda was there, then she had been close to finding her.

They walked to the Red Lion with Rose leading the way. She suggested that Clara and Tommy wait outside while she talked to the landlord first. Clara was getting restless, but she agreed. Rose was gone for over ten minutes, before she returned to them.

"He needed some persuasion, but he says we can all talk to Matilda," Rose said. "I explained you were private detectives looking into the murder of Jenny. He was shocked to hear she was dead, and its plain Matilda does not know. I promised you are not the police."

"The only time the police will be involved is when they arrest the murderer," Clara assured her.

Rose didn't seem to take this possibility too seriously.

"We ought to go around the back, the landlord wants us to keep this quiet," she said.

Clara guessed her presence in the neighbourhood had drawn attention and people were wary of what she was about. They followed Rose around to the back of the pub and entered the yard. The rear door was open and there was a pleasing smell of roasting meat coming from inside. Someone was humming, rather untunefully, as they bustled about the kitchen. Rose entered first followed by Clara and then Tommy.

Matilda Greystone was a tiny woman, barely five foot in stature and with the worn and weathered appearance of the lifelong heavy drinker. She was smoking a pipe as she peeled potatoes into a large pan. Her hair was as white as snow, but her face the colour of walnuts – Clara was not sure if that was a result of being outdoors a lot, or simply dirt. She had a bottle of gin strategically placed beside her, but she did not appear at that moment to be drunk.

She stopped in her work as the new arrivals appeared and cast them a suspicious look.

"What you doing back here?"

"Matilda, don't you remember me? Rose," Rose said quickly.

Matilda shot a glance in her direction.

"Oh, yes, I do recall you. I haven't seen you in years," Matilda gave a haughty sniff. "Jenny said you had gone up in the world and weren't interested in the likes of us no more."

Rose was visibly stung.

"That was never the case. I always loved Jenny, she was like a sister to me."

"Then where did you go?" Matilda snorted. "Doesn't matter anyway, who are these posh posies? Your new friends?"

The sneer in her tone made Rose flinch.

"This is Clara and Tommy Fitzgerald; they are trying to solve a murder that happened in the alleys the other night. They are kind people, not the police."

"And what does that matter to me?" Matilda snorted. She started to peel potatoes again.

Rose cast an anxious look at Clara, who instantly took over.

"Mrs Greystone…"

"I ain't never been married," Matilda snorted. "I'll be Miss Greystone to you, as you want to be all posh, like."

"Miss Greystone," Clara continued, undeterred. "I am really here because of your daughter Jenny. I take it you have not been in contact with her for a while?"

"She ain't a child no more, she does as she pleases, just like me," Matilda snapped. "And I don't like your tone."

She wagged her knife at Clara.

"I did not realise I had a 'tone'." Clara replied calmly. "I am not here to be your enemy Miss Greystone, or to judge you. I am here because the other night your daughter was stabbed to death in an alley."

It was blunt, maybe even brutal, but Clara knew she had to attract Matilda's attention and subtlety was not going to work. Matilda froze, but aside from her lack of movement, there was no obvious indication of her feelings. Her expression had not changed and she continued to puff away on her pipe with a rhythmic suction.

"You repeat that," she said at last, with a slightly threatening tone.

"Your daughter was stabbed to death the other night. No one was sure who she was, or should I say, no one was prepared to come forward and say who she was. I discovered her identity yesterday. I am looking into the crime to find out who killed her."

"And why are you doing that and not the police?" Matilda barked.

"Because I am damn curious and I can't let things be," Clara replied, her own words sharper. "And because a woman died, and someone ought to be brought to justice for that."

"You ain't the police," Matilda snorted.

"No, I am not, and maybe that gives me an advantage. I have no one dictating to me what to do, no superiors, no Chief Constables and no paperwork. I can just dig away at things until I reveal the truth," Clara pressed home her point. "I think your daughter was either in the wrong place at the wrong time, or knew something that was not good for her, and she was murdered as a result. And I think the people who did that would very much like to remain anonymous, and I am not going to let them."

Clara's words had taken on the dogmatic determination Tommy had heard before and knew meant business. Once she was in that mood, nothing was going to hold her back; threats and lies would only stir her on to greater action. She was like a terrier going down a hole after an angry badger; she simply would not back down. Matilda seemed to sense something of that too and she became less obtrusive.

"I didn't know," she said. "Maybe I never would have known if you had not come and found me. That... that is something."

"I wish I did not have to bring you such bad news," Clara said.

"Bad news is what makes the world go around," Matilda said placidly. "One of these days it was going to be either me or Jenny winding up dead in a back street. I knew that and so did she. I had hoped I would be a goner first, but you can't have everything."

Matilda took the pipe from her mouth and picked up the gin bottle. She consumed a large swig and then placed it down again.

"Did you just come to tell me about my daughter being dead?"

"No. I hoped you could help me work out why she was killed and who by," Clara answered.

"I don't know much about my daughter's life," Matilda huffed. "Ain't that obvious?"

"But you will know something, I am sure," Clara was not sure at all, but she was desperate for any lead. "Can you tell me a little about her daily life? Where she liked to work and if she was regularly associating with any particular man?"

Matilda frowned.

"Jenny always worked out of the Green Dragon," she said. "The landlord there was sweet on her and let her hang around. She picked up men there, or in the neighbourhood. There is this little alley down the side of the pub where she took her punters."

"The Green Dragon is not far from the picture house,"

Rose pointed out.

"Why would someone kill her?" Matilda groaned, the gin bottle coming to hand again as she attempted to drown her misery.

"I shall find out," Clara told her, though such promises were easy to make and not always so easy to keep. "Is there anything else you can think of, anything about Jenny's recent life that might be useful."

Matilda stared at her gin bottle, a hopelessness developing on her face that suggested a deep gulf of despair opening inside her.

"Jenny never really told me anything," she said. "We lived our lives away from each other. She was ashamed of me, and that shame deepened when she began to succumb to the bottle like her old mum. Apple never falls far from the tree."

Matilda sniffed and wiped her nose on the back of her sleeve.

"Seemed to me she was involving herself with something other than the usual lark," she continued. "She never talked about it, but I had this impression there was more to her life than turning tricks for any Tom, Dick and Harry. Last time I saw her, she gave me some money. I was stunned by the amount. Asked her where it had come from. She said she had been saving up, and wanted me to have some. She did care about me, after all was said and done."

By now Matilda had nearly finished her gin bottle and there did not look likely to be any boiled potatoes ready for dinner at the pub. She flopped back onto a wooden chair, which creaked in protest. Matilda gazed vaguely at them.

"I think she had a steady fella," she slurred. "Not... not a regular... not like that. I mean, someone she was with."

"A boyfriend," Clara elaborated.

Matilda nodded.

"That's what I think...k...k...k," the gin bottle slipped from Matilda's hand and dropped to the floor with a nasty clunk. Luckily, it did not smash. "Y...y...you know, wha...

I mean...?"

"I think so," Clara assured her. "Thank you for your help."

Matilda began to sob to herself.

"M...m...my g...g...girl..."

Rose tapped Clara's arm and indicated they should leave. Clara wanted to offer some comfort to Matilda, but she could not think how and probably Rose was right – Matilda needed to grieve in peace.

Back on the road outside the pub Rose flicked her hair back over her shoulders and looked serious.

"You run around in this business long enough, the idea of having a protector becomes appealing," she said to Clara. "Mine came in the form of my sister and her boarding house. For Jenny, maybe she found a man who would watch over her."

"And perhaps he was part of this alley gang?" Tommy suggested.

Matilda shrugged.

"I can show you the way to the Green Dragon. It's not far."

Chapter Twenty-Five

The Green Dragon stood on a corner, sandwiched between the yard of a warehouse and a pawn shop. The alley Matilda had mentioned ran behind the pub, dividing its back wall from the shop. The pub had the look of being respectable, even if its clientele were from the lower end of society. It had been neatly painted recently and the front step was swept and washed, while the windows sparkled and showed no trace of dirt. Someone cared about this place and took pride in it.

"I wonder if the landlord knew about Jenny's male friend, considering he was sweet on her," Tommy asked quietly as they entered.

Rose frowned and pursed her lips.

"He must have done," she said. "Even if it would not have pleased him."

The landlord was stood behind his bar, polishing the brass and wood taps of the pump handles. He smiled at them as they entered.

"What can I get you?"

He seemed a friendly, welcoming soul. Not one to dabble in criminal activity; there was an air of innocence about him. Clara could imagine how he had felt sorry for

Jenny, and had turned a blind eye to her activities, perhaps thinking that the vague love he felt for her was reciprocated.

"We are not here to order anything," Clara said, coming near so she did not have to speak loudly. "We have some bad news about Jenny."

The landlord stiffened, his expression freezing on his face. He licked his lips and seemed to not know what to do, then he managed to speak.

"Bad news?"

"Jenny has been attacked," Clara said carefully, trying to break the news gently.

The landlord looked appalled.

"Where is she? Can I see her?"

"I am sorry, but the attack was fatal," Clara hated saying the words. "She was in an alley not far from here and someone stabbed her. I am trying to discover who. I am a private detective."

The landlord didn't seem to know what to say. The shock was plain on his face. He glanced around his pub, looking for something that would enable him to make sense of what he had heard. His whole world had just crumbled to pieces.

"Excuse me," he said, before disappearing through a back door that had the word 'private' etched on the glass.

Jenny shook her head.

"That didn't go well."

"It's never easy explaining to people that someone they care about has passed in a violent fashion," Clara replied. "I hope he comes back."

They waited for half-an-hour, while other customers came in, looked for the landlord and departed without a drink. Some seemed annoyed, others were curious at his absence. A couple looked at Clara's group suspiciously. Clara guessed this was not a place where strangers often came; everyone would know everyone else.

Finally, the landlord reappeared. He had been crying. His eyes were reddened and swollen. However, he acted as if nothing was the matter.

"I didn't expect you to still be here," he said.

"We need to ask you questions about Jenny," Clara explained. "That is the only way to find her killer."

The landlord gulped and looked like he was on the verge of crying again.

"I don't want to talk."

"You must," Clara insisted. "You may be the key to finding out what happened to Jenny and bringing her killer to justice."

"Justice?" The landlord looked cynical. "No one is fussed about justice for girls like Jenny."

"I am," Clara promised. "And this is Rose, an old friend of Jenny's, who wants to see her killer caught too."

"Yes," Rose picked up the thread of the conversation. "I used to know Jenny years ago, we were so close. We lost touch a little these last years, but I would still have done anything for her, and I want her killer found. I won't let them get away with this."

The landlord looked baffled, as if he was unable to comprehend what they were telling him. He turned from them and pulled himself a half-pint of stout. Then he placed it on the bar and glowered at the dark liquid, before taking a good swig.

"I honestly don't know what I can tell you," he said.

"Did Jenny have a male acquaintance she spent a lot of time with?" Clara asked. "Maybe he was acting as her protector?"

"I don't know," the landlord said moodily.

"You do," Rose snapped at him. "I can see it on your face. We need to know all about this man."

The landlord snorted.

"Look, old boy," Tommy stepped up to the bar. "It's natural to feel hurt when the woman you care for finds another fellow to be sweet on. Especially when you had been looking out for her and making sure she was all right. Feels like ingratitude, doesn't it? But you still care about her, and you wouldn't want to think her killer got away because you were jealous, would you?"

The landlord was sulking, his head down.

"Just think, maybe it was this chap she was walking out with who did her in," Tommy persisted. "Wouldn't that make you want to do something?"

The landlord took another drink of stout.

"He wasn't good enough for her," he mumbled. "I would have looked after her a lot better."

"Jenny never could tell the good 'uns, from the bad 'uns," Rose said softly. "That was half her trouble. Did you ever tell her how you felt?"

"She knew," the landlord sniffed.

"That's a no, then," Rose continued. "Jenny could be blind to what was right before her. Maybe she would be alive today if you had been a bit more forward with your feelings."

"Don't say that," the landlord grimaced. "Why would you say that?"

"Jenny made a mistake going off with that fellow, but if she did not know there was another option, well, you can't blame her," Rose continued. "Don't hold this against her. Jenny doesn't deserve that."

The landlord's face had fallen and there was a hint of tears in his eyes.

"I did care about her," he said. "I thought, given time, she would come to see that."

"People sometimes need a hint, old boy," Tommy said.

The landlord gave a weak nod.

"The man's name was Callum Little," he said. "He is a fence, and he runs errands for any of the gangs that need something done. He was quite well in with the Seashore Boys, back before their gang was crushed by the police. He was lucky to escape that mess, but he never learned his lesson. If you want to talk to him, you can find him down King's Road, flat 3C. I haven't seen him around for a few days, but that isn't unusual."

"How long have he and Jenny been walking out?" Clara

asked.

"A few months now," the landlord looked miserable. "She told me once that Callum was helping her get out of the game. I guessed that meant she was running errands alongside him. She could walk into places where Callum would be suspicious and pass along messages. I knew she was hoping this would be her way to a better life."

The landlord took another long drink of stout, his hand shaking as he raised the glass to his lips.

"I would have made her an honest woman," he said quietly. "She would never have had to do anything she didn't want to do with me. I should have said something to her, but I never had the courage."

The landlord gave a sob.

"I thought she would laugh at me."

~~~*~~~

Having removed themselves from the distraught landlord at the Green Dragon, they made their way to the nearby King's Road. Rose was getting restless and walking fast, as if she sensed the end of their journey nearing. Clara was less hasty; she did not think the end was in sight, just yet.

They reached No.3, which was divided into a trio of small flats, with 3c being on the top floor, in the attic space. They knocked on the front door and an old woman answered. She was so badly hunched over that she found it hard to look up into the faces of her visitors. She leaned on an old walking stick with hands crippled with arthritis and took a moment to catch her breath.

"Yes?"

"Hello, we are hoping to catch Mr Little at home?" Clara said.

The old woman waved a hand to a staircase that ran up the side of the hallway.

"You can find him on the top floor. Just close the front door behind you," the old woman limped back into a front room and they heard her give a hefty sigh as she sat down in an armchair.

The trio entered the hallway, closing the front door as instructed, and headed upstairs.

"I'm guessing the landlady doesn't deal with the cleaning," Tommy said as he nudged aside a discarded apple core that was lying on a step. "Smells like over-cooked liver up here."

They didn't pause on the first landing, where the door to flat 3b stood slightly ajar and a man could be heard speaking fiercely in a language that was certainly not English. As they headed further up the stairs, they could glimpse him through the gap in the door, pacing back and forth and clearly practicing a speech. The foul smell had increased and hinted at mouldering socks and urine. Clara surmised that the houseguests were not the cleanest in their habits and, with the landlady so crippled she could barely walk to answer the front door, it was plain nothing was ever going to get washed or scrubbed to remove the foul odours.

On the top landing there was a pile of old newspapers and a bucket that contained black, filthy water and a mop. It stank so badly, it must have been there for weeks.

"This is disgusting," Clara pressed a hand over her nose and mouth, not that it helped much.

"I have been in worse places," Rose said complacently.

"Smells like someone has been cooking bones and cabbage up here," Tommy gagged a little.

As he spoke, a rat startled from the pile of newspapers and scurried down the staircase as fast as its little legs could carry it. Clara was not squeamish about rats, or rodents of any kind, but the sight of the creature rushing down the stairs told her all she needed to know about the quality of this establishment and the sort of people who lived here.

The landing was cramped, made worse by the rubbish in the corner. The walls were riddled with damp and the paper was peeling off them in greasy, yellow strips. The only way to go was through a door to the right of the landing. Clara stepped over a ruck in the old carpet, alarmed that her shoes appeared to be sticking to the floor, and knocked at the door. There was no answer.

"He might not be home," Tommy observed.

"That would be inconvenient," Clara grumbled, knocking again. "Mr Little? Can we speak with you?"

"Did you hear a sound just then?" Rose asked, glancing suspiciously at the pile of newspapers. "I am pretty sure it was not a rat."

"You think he is hiding?" Tommy said.

"I am not with the police," Clara said through the door. "I just want to talk to you about Jenny. Something awful has happened to her."

There was still no replied from the flat. However, the gentleman from the floor below had come out of his room to see what was going on. He peered up the stairs at them.

"What do you want?" He asked in a heavy accent that suggested he was Russian.

"We are looking for Callum Little," Clara called down to him. "Do you know if he is at home?"

"Why you look for Callum?" The Russian asked with a surly expression. "Who are you?"

Clara had no time for all this, she was fed up with having to explain herself to everybody that day.

"I am here about Jenny, his girlfriend," Clara explained as briefly as she could. "She has been found dead."

The Russian did not seem impressed by this.

"You look like trouble," he said. "I want no trouble. I am good, honest man. I don't kill any women."

"I never suggested you did," Clara remarked in exasperation.

"You think I killed Mr Little's woman? Huh? I know what this is, you are setting me up!" The Russian was puffing himself up into a panic. "I have seen this in my country. You blame innocent man for crime! No! I am no criminal!"

The Russian turned around and darted back into his own flat with the sharp slam of his door. They could hear a chain being drawn and then what sounded like a chair being dragged across the floor and placed behind the door.

"Well, that was helpful," Clara said sarcastically. "Look, I don't think Mr Little is at home."

"I'm not leaving without answers," Rose said quickly, she stepped past Clara and peered at the door. "There is no lock."

"No one bothered to install one when these rooms were changed from being bedrooms, or whatever, to flats," Tommy suggested. "That Russian fellow appears to have installed a chain on the inside of his, though."

"That only works when you are in the flat," Clara said. "What do you say we let ourselves in and see if there is anything about Callum Little's rooms that will give us a clue as to what happened to Jenny?"

Rose needed no further encouragement. She took the handle of the door, turned it sharply and rushed into the room. The opening of the flat let a further, sharp cloud of villainous aroma slip out.

"Oh, my word, its like bad eggs," Clara coughed.

Tommy was looking worried.

"I know that smell. I've come across it before," he took a pace to the door and stepped through.

Clara was not far behind. She was trying not to gag as she stepped into the flat and found the cause of the strange odour.

"I knew that scent from the trenches," Tommy said grimly.

Rose was stood beside him, her face bleak.

Lying on an old iron bedstead, on filthy sheets, was Callum Little. Someone had stabbed him repeatedly in the chest and left him where he fell. He must have been there a few days, considering the stench in the room and the buzzing flies swarming around his body. Clara was made of stern stuff and had seen a few grim things in her time, but the discovery of the corpse turned her stomach and she had to step out of the room to try and catch her breath.

"We need to summon the police," she said.

Chapter Twenty-Six

The arrival of Brighton's finest had the landlady in a state of horror. She hobbled back and forth from the front door to the foot of the stairs, pulling at her hair and crying out that the world was cruel, and these things should not happen to old, honest ladies. Clara felt like telling her that very little had happened to her, compared to what had happened to the unfortunate Callum Little.

As for the Russian in flat 3b. The sound of the police traipsing up the stairs had him in a fit of anguish and he was spotted by a constable slipping out of a window and scurrying down the road. He was apprehended, but Inspector Park-Coombs was not convinced his hasty departure was evidence of anything more than the fellow's paranoia and dread of the authorities. He had a constable watch over the man and the old landlady in a front room, while he inspected the crime scene.

"What have you stumbled upon now Clara?" Park-Coombs asked as he arrived on the top landing.

Clara was waiting outside the flat, she had no intention of going back inside.

"The gentleman in this room had been pointed out to me as the boyfriend of the woman who was murdered in the alley the other night. Her name was Jenny, and the poor soul in this flat went by the name of Callum Little."

The inspector walked through the door and could be heard gagging as he drew nearer the corpse. It was not so much the sight of the victim as the smell, which had not quite reached the stage of pervading throughout the house, but was certainly noticeable when you went into the flat. Clara waited for the inspector to return.

"Someone didn't like our friend here," he said, dabbing at his mouth with a handkerchief. He had gone pale. "Maybe Jenny killed him?"

"And then she in turn was killed?" Clara said. "No, I think it more likely the same murderer attacked them both. Callum Little was in a line of work where he was going to upset people."

"He is known to me," the inspector nodded. "Small-time fence, and not against running errands for people he shouldn't. He didn't deserve to be stabbed to death, though."

"Someone clearly disagreed," Clara remarked.

Dr Deáth appeared on the stairs, smiling as usual.

"Hello," he greeted them. "Why, it smells like five days of decay up here. I guess there is a body."

"Your patient is awaiting you in that flat," the inspector moved out of the way to let the police surgeon through. "He doesn't seem in a hurry to go anywhere."

"The dead never are," Dr Deáth grinned. "It is much easier than dealing with the living."

Dr Deáth disappeared into the flat and they could hear him humming to himself as he began to work.

"Always happy," Inspector Park-Coombs said with a mild look of amazement. "Well, what do we make of all this then?"

"Revenge? A grudge?" Clara suggested. "Callum Little was mixed up with all the wrong sort of people, he is bound to have stepped on some toes."

"And he was connected to the woman in the alley?"

"Jenny, yes. They had been walking out for months, and

she was working with him. Odds are, whatever sparked his murder, sparked hers too."

Inspector Park-Coombs glanced down to the next landing where Tommy and Rose were standing. Rose looked uncomfortable around all the police and was close to leaving. Tommy had persuaded her to stay, but Clara suspected it would not be long before she made her exit.

"You trust her?" He asked Clara.

"She was close to Jenny, but has been out of this area for some time. Yes, I trust her. She wants the killer of her friend caught."

"Best we go talk to the landlady and this Russian, then," the inspector shrugged.

They headed downstairs to the guarded front room. The police constable stepped aside to let them in. Unlike the upper floors, someone had made the effort to keep this room clean and tidy. Every surface that could be was covered in a lace doily, from the small table stood in the window, to the arms and back of the sofa and even the mantelpiece. It appeared that the old landlady barely left this room, the sofa doubling as a bed when she needed it and she had made a hasty effort to hide an old-fashioned chamber pot behind a cupboard. She sat on the sofa at a peculiar angle, her crooked back not allowing her to sit against the cushions. She still struggled to look up to the faces of Clara and the Inspector because of her deformity, so Clara sat down on the carpet to be able to speak to the woman properly.

Beside the landlady sat the Russian; a big, burly man with an impressive moustache and a very anxious look on his face. He had one eye on the constable at the door and was trying to work out how to make another escape.

"Might I take both your names," Inspector Park-Coombs began.

"Mrs Lamb," the old woman said. "What has happened upstairs?"

"Your tenant, Callum Little, has been murdered in his bed," Inspector Park-Coombs told her.

"I didn't do it!" The Russian declared suddenly. "I had no complaint with him, except for the rats. He was a filthy man, always leaving his rubbish about, but I did not kill him over rats!"

"Your name?" Park-Coombs said in his matter-of-fact tone.

The Russian looked bleak.

"Igor Valentovsky," he said.

Park-Coombs tapped his pencil on the side of his notepad.

"You are going to have to spell that out Mr Vorsky."

"Va-len-tov-sky," the Russian repeated, some pride returning to his demeanour. "Sergeant Valentovsky. I was in the army before the Revolution."

"Nasty business that," Park-Coombs nodded. "You've been here ever since?"

"No. I was a prisoner of the Germans until the peace came. I was lucky. I lived. I was helped by English prisoners, they got me to England."

"Mr Valentovsky has been my tenant for three years and he is very reliable," Mrs Lamb told the inspector in a determined tone. "He keeps an eye out for me. I'll hear no word said against him."

"What about Mr Little?" Park-Coombs asked.

"I don't see him much," Mrs Lamb puttered. "He isn't what I would describe as respectable, but an old woman can't say no to a lodger. I need the money. I'll say this for him, he might have been a criminal, but he always paid his rent on time."

"When is the last time you saw him?" Park-Coombs continued.

Mrs Lamb sighed and gave this some thought.

"Is it Friday today? Must be because I heard the dustbin men earlier with their cart," she mumbled.

"It is Mrs Lamb, tonight is my talk at the Russian Refugees Association," Valentovsky politely interjected.

Clara saw how the big Russian tenderly spoke to the old, crippled woman, and she knew that what Mrs Lamb had said was true. Valentovsky cared about his landlady and took an interest in her wellbeing.

"Ah yes, that it is," Mrs Lamb nodded. "Then it must have been…"

She counted on her fingers.

"Saturday evening," she said at last. "Mr Little came home with his lady friend. They went upstairs a while, then I heard him come down and show her out the front door. I always have this room door open, so I can see who is coming and going. I was having one of my bad days and was lying on the sofa. I called out to Mr Little, asking if that was him. He came to the doorway and said he was just seeing Jenny out and he was going to bed."

"How did he seem?" Park-Coombs asked. "Was he relaxed? Anxious?"

Mrs Lamb hesitated, trying to prise open another corner of her memory, eventually she spoke.

"He looked wary. He asked me if he should lock the front door right then, that made me wonder as he had never asked that before. I told him that I was expecting Mr Valentovsky later and not to lock it. Mr Little seemed worried about that, started talking about how maybe everyone should have a key to let themselves in, then the door could be locked. I didn't really pay much heed. I've never bothered with giving tenants keys. Half the time I forget to lock the front door at night, anyway."

"I have said to Mrs Lamb that this is not safe," Valentovsky spoke up. "You never know who is lurking about at night."

Mrs Lamb shook her head.

"My mother never locked her front door, and no one ever set foot inside her house who was not invited. I shan't worry about such things."

"Yet, it appears Mr Little was worried about it," Clara observed from where she was sat on the carpet. She had been watching the old woman's face, considering her honesty. So far, she did not doubt a word she had said.

"Mr Little mixed with dubious people," Mrs Lamb

snorted. "Like those fellows who turned up on Sunday, just around lunchtime. They walked right in the house without knocking."

Mrs Lamb did not seem to notice that she had just demonstrated how easy it was for an intruder to walk into her house, and that she did not have her mother's record for no one uninvited stepping inside her home.

"I was on the sofa, trying to drink a cup of tea. I have trouble lifting my arms these days. I heard them enter and shouted out who was there. They never said anything, just looked at me briefly, then turned and headed up the stairs. A short time later they came back down and left. Had Mr Valentovsky been home, I would have asked him to find out who they were."

"You were absent that day?" Park-Coombs turned to Valentovsky.

"Yes," the Russian said uneasily. "I was at the Russian Refugees Association. I am secretary. We are hosting a fundraising event soon and are holding extra meetings to arrange everything."

Park-Coombs noted this. It would be easy enough to check, if it was Sunday when Mr Little had died. Clara suspected the strange men who had entered the house were the ones the fence had been worried about.

"Was it usual for people seeking Mr Little to walk into your house uninvited?" Park-Coombs asked Mrs Lamb.

"No. I don't like business being conducted on my premises and Mr Little was quite in agreement with that. No one but himself or his lady friend ever came here. He liked his privacy."

Park-Coombs glanced at Clara and she knew what he was implying with his gaze – the men who turned up on Sunday, stalked into the house without saying a word, and went to visit Mr Little were likely his killers.

"Do you think you would recognise these men if you saw them again?" Park-Coombs returned to questioning Mrs Lamb.

"I would think so," Mrs Lamb replied. "One was tall, the

other shorter. The tall one had a slight limp to his left leg and he had a broken nose, smashed across his face it was. He had nasty eyes. I remember thinking that to myself. His pal was weedier, and looked like a pickpocket, shifty and always had his hands in his pocket. He had a polka dot neck scarf, that made me stop and think. I didn't like the look of either of them."

"I shall have a constable bring along a book containing photographs of known criminals in Brighton and if you would look through it, you might recognise someone," Park-Coombs suggested.

"I'll certainly try," Mrs Lamb agreed. "I don't like to think of them killing Mr Little. He was up to no good, but he never did me wrong."

"I think he had talked to the wrong person," Valentovsky said slowly. The inspector's lack of interest in him had caused him to relax and start to open up. "I saw him late on Saturday night. He was sitting on the stairs that led up to his flat, smoking. He wanted to know if I had locked the front door. I said I had, and he looked happier. I asked if something wrong, and he shook his head. Just a misunderstanding, he said. The wrong information going to the wrong person."

"Did someone kill him because of something he said?" Mrs Lamb looked mortified.

"We'll aim to find out," Park-Coombs reassured her. "In the meantime, I suggest you start locking your front door Mrs Lamb, though I don't think either you or Mr Valentovsky are in any danger."

"When did you last see Mr Little's lady friend?" Clara asked.

Mrs Lamb tilted her head towards her for the first time, it was an awkward move, even with Clara sitting on the floor.

"Saturday," she said. "When Mr Little saw her out."

Clara said nothing, but her eyes met with Park-Coombs. Days after her lover had been slain, Jenny met her own demise. It looked like here was the motive for her murder.

"Thank you," Park-Coombs wrapped up the interview. "I'll have that book brought over at once."

He stepped out into the hallway with Clara.

"This reeks of a gang killing," he said once they were away from prying ears. "Callum Little made a mistake and he paid for it with his life."

"Or Jenny made the mistake while working with him and they both died," Clara pointed out.

"True," Park-Coombs tapped at his lips. "If only we knew what that mistake was, we could narrow down some suspects."

"What about Mortimer Parkes?" Clara asked. "Any luck with him?"

"No sign of him," Park-Coombs admitted. "Looks like he disappeared the day you spoke to his grandfather. He probably guessed that in the course of your conversation, his grandfather would want to show off the knife, and knew he would be blamed for its disappearance."

"He is a key suspect in all this. If he was not wielding the knife, he certainly brought it along that night. Unfortunately, he does not have a broken nose, nor is he small and shifty, so he cannot have been one of the men who killed Callum Little."

"I'll track him down," Park-Coombs promised her. "In the meantime, I think I need to dig into the mystery of this unused alley deeper."

"Could I borrow the book of criminal photographs later?" Clara asked.

Park-Coombs looked surprised.

"What for?"

"I have an idea, it might not work, but just maybe a photograph of the right criminal will jog Private Peterson's memory. He is currently our only real clue."

"Worth a try," Park-Coombs agreed. "I'll put it at your disposal, but I don't hold out much hope. Seems to me that man's mind is shot."

"Have a little faith, Inspector."

Chapter Twenty-Seven

Clara was accompanied by Sarah Butler that evening when they went to the hospital. Sarah had brought the book of photographs and was there on an official capacity – if Peterson picked out a face from the pictures, she was to note it down and report to Park-Coombs. However, before going to the hospital, Clara had to pay a visit to Lovall Road.

Mary Parkes opened the door of No.10, looking very tired and worried. There was a hopefulness on her face when she saw Clara, which was unsettling to see. Clara had to let her down quickly.

"I don't know where Mortimer is," she said.

"No, why would you," Mrs Parkes groaned, before a thought struck her. "How did you know he was missing?"

"Because your grandfather's knife turned up at a murder scene. It was used to stab a friend of mine."

Mary Parkes went white.

"I think you better come in," she said, and ushered them through to the back room where once again Edward Basildon was working on his matchstick model.

He had had time to build it up and it was now plain it was going to be a ship of some description. The old man glanced up as Clara and Sarah entered the room.

"Grandfather's knife has been used to kill someone," Mrs Parkes burst into tears the second she was in the room and slumped into a chair.

Edward looked shocked for a moment, then his face hardened.

"Mortimer," he said. "Have the police arrested him?"

"The police cannot find him," Clara replied. "Your grandfather's knife was used to stab a woman who perished, it was then stabbed into the back of a friend of mine. Private Peterson. He is in the hospital fighting for his life."

The last was a lie, but it would cover why Peterson had not been able to say who was behind the attack.

"I am sorry," Edward grimaced. "To think my grandfather's knife was used to stab a soldier, and a woman. After all that it stood for…"

"Mortimer is not a killer," Mary Parkes interrupted, finding her resolve again despite her despair. "He has fallen in with the wrong people, that's all."

"Mortimer was always easily led," Edward snorted. "He doesn't take after my side of the family."

"Do you know anything about Mortimer's friends? Their names? Where they worked or lived?" Clara asked. "As you may imagine, I want to track down who is responsible for hurting my friend."

"Mortimer never spoke about his friends," Mary said. "He knew neither I, nor his grandfather approved of them."

"They were criminals, I could tell that," Edward muttered. "I said that lad would get into trouble, Mary, if he didn't get a regular job and settle down."

Mary just shook her head.

"It could be that Mortimer has become involved with a gang," Clara persisted. "Did he ever mention something like that? Or maybe you overheard something you weren't meant to?"

"If I knew anything, I would tell you," Mary swore. "I know my son is not a killer, but something has to be done to get him out of the clutches of these terrible people."

"Bah! You give him too much credit!" Edward snapped. "If he killed someone, then he will hang for it, as is right and proper."

"Oh no!" Mary Parkes wept into her hands. "Don't say that!"

"Do you have a photograph of Mortimer I could borrow?" Clara asked hastily, before father and daughter descended into another argument. "I would like to show it to some people and see if they know where he is."

Mary was weeping too much to reply. Edward Basildon grumbled to himself then rose from his chair and shuffled to the bureau where he had looked for his grandfather's knife. He pulled open a drawer and produced a photograph album. Turning to the last pages, he drew out a photograph of Mortimer.

"His mother insisted on taking it the day before he had to go to the army recruitment office. When he was called up, she feared she would never see him again," Edward scowled. "More's the pity he didn't get taken on and died in France. Then he would be a hero, rather than a scoundrel, and I could have some respect for him."

Clara took the photograph and expressed her thanks. There was nothing else she could say; she and Sarah departed the house, where they had only added to the misery of Mary Parkes and her father.

"Delightful people," Sarah said drily as they headed for the hospital.

"Mortimer Parkes has a lot to answer for," Clara replied. "Though, the pressures he was under from his grandfather to be like a man he never met, probably did not help."

Sarah tutted and cast up her eyes, as if that was obvious.

They arrived at the hospital in time for the start of the visiting hour and headed upstairs. The police constable was still on guard outside Private Peterson's room and nodded as Sarah and Clara approached. They went inside and found Peterson as he had been on every occasion previous – flat on his belly, staring at the floor as there was nothing else to look at. His wound was going to take time to heal and until it did, he was not allowed to move or turn over. He looked depressed, which Clara could well understand.

"Peterson," she said softly.

The young man seemed to take a moment to register her presence then turned his head a little to look at her. Clara sat in the chair beside his bed.

"There is good news at last. We know where the knife came from and the police are no longer considering you a suspect in this case," that was pushing the truth, but Clara knew the evidence they had gathered all pointed at someone other than Peterson as the killer.

The young man's eyes brightened.

"I didn't kill her?"

"No. It appears that the woman was killed because of something she had said. Another man has been found dead, her boyfriend, and he was killed the Sunday before she died. We have a witness who can describe the men who murdered him and neither of them were you."

Peterson started to breathe fast.

"I had convinced myself I had murdered her," he said. "I thought I would deserve to hang."

"And that is ridiculous," Clara informed him. "All those who care about you and know you have said over and over that you would not do such a thing. But, the real killer is still out there and I am hoping you might be able to help find him."

Peterson frowned.

"How? I am stuck in this bed."

"I just need you to look at these pictures and see if any of them seem familiar," Clara told him, holding up the photograph album. "They might even jog your memory as to what happened that night."

"I shall try," Peterson said, his voice stronger as he filled with hope. There was at last a light in his eyes that suggested a will to go on, a will to fight this. Clara could not say aloud how relieved she was to see that look, nor did she let her emotions show in that moment. She had to focus on the task at hand.

"I'll go through the photographs and all you need to do is say if the face rings a bell. You don't have to say why, just call out if the face is familiar," Clara opened the album and began turning the pages slowly.

Peterson frowned in deep concentration, barely blinking as he scanned the photographs. For several minutes he said nothing, then he reached out his hand and touched a photograph.

"Him," he said. "I recognise him."

Clara smiled. Peterson had pointed out the photograph of Robert Hartley.

"He looks... different," Peterson said, beginning to doubt himself.

Clara hastened to explain why the face had looked familiar.

"This is the man who helped you after you collapsed in the alley. This picture was taken several years ago, but he has not changed that much."

"He is a criminal?" Peterson looked anxious.

"He was. He leads an honest life now. He saved you," Clara let this news sink in, then added. "You see, your memory is not as faulty as you feared."

Peterson had not realised this when he first touched the picture, now the information sank in and he looked even more ecstatic.

"I remembered," he said, the amazement plain on his face.

"Exactly," Clara grinned. "Let's see if any other faces are familiar."

She continued to turn the pages, but she ended up at the last page without Peterson seeing anyone else he knew.

"I'm sorry," he said sadly.

"It's not your fault. The people could not have been in this book. Maybe they have never had their photograph taken by the police," Clara reassured him. "There is one last picture I would like you to take a look at."

Sarah handed the photograph of Mortimer Parkes to Clara. Clara placed it on the open final page of the photograph album where Peterson could have a good view. She watched as Peterson took in the image and his eyes widened.

"You recognise him," Clara stated, she could see it on the young man's face.

"He…" Peterson paused to swallow. He took a moment to study the picture closer. "He was the man with the knife."

"You saw him holding the knife?" Clara asked.

"Y…yes," Peterson considered the picture. "He was angry, it made his face look… different. But this is him."

"Peterson, this is the most you have remembered of that night, do you see how important this is?"

Peterson didn't understand.

"This must prove to you that you did not stab that woman. There was this man with the knife. His name is Mortimer Parkes. Remember you said the woman shouted something? You thought she said 'monster', when really she was shouting the killer's name, Mortimer," Clara paused. "Do you recall anything else?"

Peterson gave a small sigh and kept looking at the picture.

"Nothing much," he admitted. "But…"

"But what?" Clara gently nudged him.

"There is this vague picture in my head, rather like a dream. I… I can't be sure it is correct."

"Tell me about it anyway," Clara persisted. "I want to know."

"In it… in it I see this man yelling at a woman. I can't make out the words, but they are arguing fiercely, and I see the knife in this man's right hand and this sick feeling comes over me, rather as if I know something awful is about to happen…"

"Go on," Clara said. "I want to hear it all."

"I see the man lose his temper and go to strike out with

the knife and I rush forward thinking I will stop him, but at the same time knowing I won't be in time…" Peterson shut his eyes. "Then things become… strange. There is this blank part, where there seems to be nothing, no picture to fill it and then I have this vivid recollection of the pain in my back. I don't really remember anything after that."

"You have remembered enough," Clara promised him, resting a hand on his shoulder. "You didn't kill this woman, Peterson, you were trying to save her. You are a hero; you have always been a hero."

Peterson winced at the word, as if it stung, then his eyes filled with tears.

"Do you mean that?"

"I do," Clara swore. "You put your life at risk to try to help a stranger. That you were not near enough to succeed is not your fault. You acted exactly as I would have expected of you, exactly as Captain O'Harris would expect. You are not a murderer, or a dangerous lunatic. You are a good man, a brave man, who nearly died trying to stop a thug."

Tears slipped down Peterson's face.

"You don't know what it means to me to learn I am not a killer," he said, choked with emotion. "I had lost all faith in myself."

"Never doubt yourself again," Clara told him.

The visiting hour bell rang out. Clara squeezed his shoulder.

"Captain O'Harris would like to be able to visit you, will you let him?"

Peterson nodded, then he turned his face into the pillow to hide his sobs. Clara and Sarah left him in peace, to shed tears of joy and relief over the discovery that he was not a wicked man after all.

Back in the hospital foyer, Clara contemplated what to do next.

"There is probably enough here to charge Mortimer Parkes with murder," Sarah voiced exactly what Clara was thinking. "We just don't know where to find him. He might disappear for good."

"That's what worries me," Clara agreed.

"We need to find a way to lure him out," Sarah said. "I doubt he will risk going back home, though we have a constable watching the house. He has to have a good reason to reveal himself and take the chance of being caught."

"Maybe being offered a way of avoiding murder charges?" Clara mused.

Sarah gave her a questioning look.

"Mortimer is clever enough to work out the police will connect him with his great grandfather's missing knife, he also knows his grandfather will have no qualms reporting the theft and pointing the finger at his grandson," Clara explained.

"We've already had the old man at the station telling us all about it," Sarah nodded.

"The knife alone, however, might not be enough to convict Mortimer of murder. At least, that's what we want Mortimer to think. If he were to believe that the real danger to his freedom and his neck, is an eye-witness to the murder, then he might take a chance to eradicate that threat."

"Private Peterson!" Sarah said, grasping the idea. "Use him as bait?"

"Not literally," Clara replied. "Just, place the thought in Mortimer's head that he needs to be rid of Peterson for good. Then hope he will be reckless enough to come to the hospital and try to dispatch him."

"We set a trap," Sarah fully understood. "Spread the word through the usual sources that the police have a witness to the killing and that he is at the hospital."

"I think Robert Hartley could be key to this," Clara said. "He is in the right place to spread talk and I bet his mother is a good gossip."

"Before we do anything, I shall have to run this past Inspector Park-Coombs," Sarah continued. "I think this could be the only way to catch our man."

"And then maybe we shall have a better idea of what was going on in that alley," Clara nodded. "Maybe."

"The Inspector is quite concerned about that, he thinks there is something big going on, right under his nose. You know how much he dislikes that," Sarah added. "He will be glad to catch Mortimer Parkes."

"Well, let's just hope we can create a tempting enough trap for this big rat."

Chapter Twenty-Eight

It was not difficult to convince Park-Coombs that the only way to catch Mortimer Parkes was to lure him out of hiding. He liked the idea and agreed to go ahead with the plan. Clara paid a call on Robert Hartley the next day with Sarah. The ex-gangster was fixing a shoe in his back yard when they arrived. He looked up at them sourly.

"If you have no news, I don't want to talk to you," he complained. "Most of the street won't talk to my wife or my mother now, they think we are fools and don't want to be associated with us in case it gets them into trouble."

"What if I could offer you a way to change that?" Clara said.

"What do you mean?" Robert asked suspiciously.

"Supposing you had seen the error of your ways in helping that young man the other night, and you happened to have gathered some important information about where he was and what he remembers of the incident?" Clara said. "And supposing you passed this along to those who would find this information useful, as a means of warning them."

Robert was listening keenly.

"You want me to stitch someone up," he observed.

Clara smiled; Robert Hartley had been around, and he

knew how things worked.

"Ever heard of a man called Mortimer Parkes?" She said.

Robert nodded.

"He works around here. I don't take any interest in the gang that is keeping this neighbourhood in fear, you know that, I don't want to know anything. But Mortimer is hard to miss. He is one of the gang's enforcers and likes to swagger about with a knife."

"Was it Mortimer you saw the night Peterson was hurt?" Clara asked.

Robert shook his head.

"One of the other thugs," he replied.

"Well, we are pretty certain it was Mortimer who stabbed that woman and Peterson, but he has gone into hiding. We want to lure him out."

Robert smirked.

"I know how this one works. So, what information do you want me to make sure gets back to Mortimer's ears?"

"I need you to tell him that the man he stabbed has regained consciousness in hospital and remembers everything. That he has identified Mortimer from a photograph and says he stabbed both the woman and himself. Tell him, this young man is the key to the police's case against him, without his testimony, they will have nothing substantial."

Robert nodded, still with that smile on his face.

"I dare say I can do that."

~~~*~~~

That evening the rain clouds clagged in and it was a foul night to be out. A man wrapped up in a heavy raincoat and with a trilby hat pulled down firmly on his head entered the hospital just as the bell for visiting time went. He took a moment to shake water from his coat and hat, then he headed for the staircase, seemingly certain of where he was going.

On the second floor he walked along the corridor and paused by a map on the wall, as if suddenly lost. He had one eye on the police constable stood before a private room, but it would have seemed to a casual observer that he was merely studying the layout of the hospital. After a moment he walked away from the map and back down the corridor. He turned a corner and then bent double and started to shout for help.

A nurse appeared from a ward and asked what was the matter? Pretending to gasp for breath, the man informed her that someone had just run into him and taken his wallet. The thief had run off towards the stairs. The nurse, as he had expected, darted to the end of the corridor and called to the handy police constable that they had a pickpocket wandering the hospital. The constable obediently abandoned his post to attend to the drama.

His only obstacle attended to, the man stood up and walked down the corridor. He hastened his step near the room door where the constable had been standing guard and entered before anyone could stop him.

The room was pitch black, the patient was sleeping, and the rainy night outside provided no illumination. The man reached out for the light, he wanted to be able to see what he was doing and get the job done properly this time. The bright dazzle of the bulb for a second blinded him.

"Hello."

The man had taken a step forward, before his eyes had adjusted. Now he stopped and looked at Clara Fitzgerald sitting on the hospital bed.

"Were you expecting someone else Mortimer Parkes?"

Mortimer panicked, he turned to leave, but Sarah was behind him, blocking the door. She looked fearsome in her police uniform, truncheon ready in her hand, like a real Scottish banshee. Mortimer opened his mouth to swear, then he decided not to waste time and launched himself at Clara. He didn't get very far – Sarah had been itching to use her truncheon on him.

Clara watched as he crumpled to the floor clutching at

his head. He groaned as Sarah stood over him, slapping her truncheon into the palm of her hand.

"What really annoys me," she told him. "Is I am not allowed to arrest you. Women police can't do that. But I can slap you with this truncheon until you cry for your mammy."

Mortimer Parkes glowered between the two of them.

"You think you have won? You think I'll be done for this? Hah!"

"Who is going to come to save you," Clara asked him coolly. "Your boss? Why would he get his hands dirty for you?"

Mortimer hesitated, plainly starting to question himself. Then he scowled.

"You have no idea what this is all about. None!"

"Maybe I don't," Clara said. "But I'm not the one who is going to hang for murder."

Parkes' eyes grew big as he realised the predicament he was in, he was contemplating trying to escape, but at that moment Inspector Park-Coombs arrived to make the formal arrest.

"Mortimer Parkes, what a coincidence. I've been looking for you. Your grandfather claims you stole his father's knife."

Mortimer Parkes cursed his grandfather's name as Park-Coombs slapped on handcuffs.

"Now, now," Park-Coombs said calmly. "There are ladies present."

Mortimer completed his crass demonstration by spitting at Clara's feet. Sarah thumped him hard on the head with her truncheon again.

"Constable!" Park-Coombs accosted her.

Sarah merely shrugged.

"My mother always said you have to slap the rudeness out of some people."

Park-Coombs had no reply to that, he just hauled the dazed Mortimer towards the door. Clara followed him out, turning right and going to a room further down the hall.

She opened the door a fraction and looked in to see Private Peterson talking with Captain O'Harris. They were both blissfully unaware of the drama that had occurred in Peterson's old room. Clara closed the door, smiling to herself, and headed for the police station.

~~~*~~~

Mortimer Parkes might be bruised and battered, but he was not in the mood to make a confession. He sullenly remained silent throughout his interview, until the inspector became fed up and went to have a cup of tea. Mortimer's silence was disappointing, but not unexpected. He was a tough thug who knew when to keep his mouth shut. At least he could not escape the charges brought against him. The knife and Peterson's testimony would send him to the hangman for sure. The only question that was left hanging over them was why? Why did he kill Jenny?

"He'll probably never tell us," Inspector Park-Coombs informed Clara. "My guess is that Callum Little made a mistake and Jenny was involved somehow. They both had to die. Whether Jenny knew Callum was dead we'll never know."

"Peterson said she was arguing with Mortimer," Clara remarked.

"Maybe he had accosted her with what she had done wrong and she was giving him a good tongue-lashing over it. She was feisty, she wouldn't have gone down without a fight."

Clara leaned against a desk. The kettle was beginning to whistle and the inspector moved to pour hot water in the teapot.

"You did what you set out to do," he said. "You proved Peterson innocent."

"I don't like all these unanswered questions, and we still have the problem with the gang Mortimer worked for."

"That's for me to worry about," Park-Coombs told her

firmly. "I don't say this to you often Clara, but this business is out of your league. It's too dangerous and I don't want you investigating it further, understood?"

Clara looked glum, but eventually nodded her head. She saw the inspector's logic, even if she didn't like it.

"I'll keep working at our friend, he might confess eventually. He has nothing to lose by doing so."

Behind them there was a sudden commotion. Park-Coombs stood up as several police constables darted out of the room and into the corridor.

"What is all this about?" He hurried after them and Clara was close behind. As they neared the door they could hear cries for help.

Reaching the corridor, they saw police crowded around the door of the room where Park-Coombs had been interviewing Mortimer Parkes. The inspector pushed through the constables until he was stood in the doorway. He came to a halt, staring inside. Clara hung back, her heart sinking as she sensed something awful had occurred.

"Summon the police surgeon," Park-Coombs snapped at the nearest constable. "And the rest of you get back to work!"

The little crowd dispersed as the constables went back to their duty. Clara stepped behind Park-Coombs. In the interview room stood a police constable looking white as a sheet. On the table stood a mug of tea that he had just been bringing the suspect – Inspector Park-Coombs always maintained his manners, even with criminals.

At the constable's feet, lying on his back, was Mortimer Parkes. His eyes were bulging from their sockets and he was frothing at the mouth. By his outstretched right hand was a cigarette, partially smoked. Park-Coombs bent down by the young man who was just alive.

"Looks like cyanide poisoning," Park-Coombs groaned. "Let's keep everything quiet and put the light out, if you can keep the patient as calm as possible sometimes that helps."

The police constable turned off the light and went to

fetch a lamp, while on the floor Mortimer began to twitch violently. The inspector tried to hold him still. Clara ran into the hallway, grabbed a coat off a hook and bundled it up to place under the fitting man's head. At least it would stop him bashing out his brains on the floor.

"He had nothing on him but the cigarettes," Park-Coombs said, before glancing at the partially smoked cigarette in Mortimer's hand. "Who gave you the cigarettes, Mortimer?"

Mortimer grimaced, the twitches were turning into spasms.

"They deliberately poisoned you," Park-Coombs told him. "They decided it would be better if you were out of the way."

Mortimer gave a small moan, his throat was rapidly constricting. Cyanide killed by making it impossible for the victim to breathe.

"C…Ca… lum," he said, his voice trembling. "S… sold information t… to a L… London gang."

"He sold information about your boss to his rivals and your boss found out," Park-Coombs elaborated.

"H… had to m… make example…" Mortimer mumbled.

"And Jenny?" Clara asked.

Mortimer coughed up more foam, his face was going purple and Clara did not think he had long. But the realisation his boss had betrayed him was making Mortimer talkative. It was the only revenge he had left.

"J… Jenny s… stole the in… information… first place…"

"She and Callum were working together," Park-Coombs nodded. "It was how she got all that money to give to her mother. So, you killed her?"

"Orders…" Mortimer hissed.

"Who do you work for?" Park-Coombs demanded. "Give me that before you go find out what's on the other side."

Mortimer's arms were starting to jump up and down,

his legs were violently moving too. There was no antidote for cyanide poisoning, all you could attempt to do was keep the patient as relaxed and quiet as possible until the toxin left his system. But it all depended on how much poison they had ingested and it rather looked like Mortimer had received a hefty dose.

"Mortimer, just give us a name," Park-Coombs pressed.

Mortimer ground his teeth together as the spasms became violent. Clara tried to hold his head still, but he was contorting so madly that it was difficult to contain him. The inspector was holding his legs and began calling for help. The constable returned with the lamp and grabbed Mortimer's arms, together they aimed to keep him as still as possible.

The ordeal seemed to last forever, but when Mortimer finally became still, Clara knew that they had failed. He had stopped breathing. It was not long afterwards that Dr Deáth arrived and pronounced him dead.

Clara had seen men die before, but it never was an easy thing to watch. She needed the fresh cup of tea that the inspector called for as they retreated to the main office of the station. Around them constables were typing reports, or filing complaints made by Brighton residents. The sound of business was comforting, even if Clara knew the image of Mortimer's twisted face would linger for a long time.

"If only he could have given us his boss," Park-Coombs muttered, pacing back and forth.

"We know something at least," Clara said, catching his attention. "Our gang are big enough to have a rival gang after them in London."

"You are to keep out of this Clara," Park-Coombs pointed a finger at her. "These are dangerous people."

"I have no intention of becoming involved further," Clara assured him. "As long as Peterson is safe, that is all that matters to me."

The inspector eyed her suspiciously, but Clara was telling the truth. Whatever this gang was doing, and whoever was in charge, they were too big for her to deal with. For once, she was prepared to leave the matter in the hands of the police.

"The poisoned cigarette," she said slowly. "Doesn't it remind you of another case?"

Park-Coombs gave a sigh.

"I don't like this one bit, Clara. This is going to give me a headache."

Clara could not offer him any comfort.

~~~*~~~

Peterson returned to the convalescence home a hero. He was welcomed by the staff, his comrades and O'Harris with cheers. The press had been informed of what Peterson had done and the story had been printed, making it plain that he had nearly died trying to save a woman. It was the best publicity the Home could have got.

Clara watched Peterson's return from a distance. She was still haunted by the death of Mortimer Parkes. He had been a nasty thug, but it was still a terrible way to die, and his demise had left a lot of unanswered questions.

Captain O'Harris came and stood beside her.

"You did me a great service helping Peterson," he said.

"You know I could never let him be tried for a murder he didn't commit."

O'Harris smiled at her and then quietly took her hand.

"I don't know if what has happened will help or hinder Peterson's recovery, but I am glad he is back with us."

"Maybe being that close to death will remind him what it is to be alive?" Clara suggested.

"Maybe," O'Harris replied.

He was silent a moment, then he leaned over and kissed Clara. She was surprised for an instant, then turned into him and kissed him back. O'Harris lifted his head and whispered in her ear.

"I love you, Clara Fitzgerald."

Clara hesitated for just a moment, taking in this sudden

announcement. Then she moved closer to him, squeezing his hand hard.

"I love you too," she whispered back.

O'Harris grinned.

"Well, he said, that's settled then."

Clara was amused.

"What is settled?" She asked him.

"Everything," O'Harris winked at her, adding no more.

Clara shook her head.

"Men are extremely confusing," she sighed. "And they say women are complicated."

Captain O'Harris attempted to look hurt, but was too happy to achieve the expression. Clara nudged his arm with her elbow.

"I think you best go rescue Peterson before he is overwhelmed by words of welcome," she said.

O'Harris took a step forward, reluctant to let go of her hand. He paused.

"You promise you love me?" He asked, a sudden hint of uncertainty coming into his voice.

"Are you calling me a liar?" Clara asked him.

O'Harris squeezed her hand.

"Never!"

He went off to save Peterson from handshakes and well wishes. Clara stood back and watched him, a smile creeping over her face. Then a chill wind whipped around the edge of her dress and she shivered. Clara looked over her shoulder as if expecting someone to be stood there.

She had this feeling – this unwelcome sensation – that trouble was brewing for her and those she cared about. There was no logic to the emotion, and she hoped she was wrong.

Still, there was something more than the autumnal breeze making Clara shake and wish to get indoors quickly.

Printed in Great Britain
by Amazon